A Scotsman in Love

By Karen Ranney

KAREN RANNEY

A Scotsman in Love

AVON

An Imprint of HarperCollins*Publishers*

AVON BOOKS
An Imprint of HarperCollins*Publishers*
10 East 53rd Street
New York, New York 10022-5299

Printed in the U.S.A.

To Trudy Wilson,
a truly talented artist and a fantastic mother.

Chapter 1

Glengarrow, Scotland
1852

Every morning and afternoon, Margaret Dalrousie walked the grounds of Glengarrow, daring the ghosts to accost her.

Over the last few months, it had become a game of sorts. She was determined to persevere despite her feeling the house disliked her. Or perhaps anyone disturbing Glengarrow's eerie serenity would have felt the same.

This morning, dead leaves in shades of persimmon and ochre clustered in bunches in front of the gates. A gust of wind suddenly tossed the leaves into the air, and as they tumbled across the brittle grass, they made a sound like slippered feet on a wooden floor.

No one had danced at Glengarrow for years.

Between the front parlor windows was a space where the yellow silk curtains didn't meet, revealing furniture draped in pale linen shrouds. Janet kept the dust in abeyance and her husband, Tom, armed himself with the task of ensuring that all was well in the Earl of Linnet's ancestral home. To that end, he did as much as he could with no funds. The roof leak was patched; the rotting window-sill in a third-floor maid's room was removed and replaced. Six months ago, a squirrel had ventured into the south wing and created a nest in the fire-place; a generation of birds had raised their young in the ornate carved cornice above the blue-velvet curtains of the ballroom.

At least—as Tom said—the birds and squirrels brought life and sound to the house, banishing the eternal silence.

The villagers said Glengarrow was haunted, that it had been for years, ever since the Earl of Linnet left for a trip to the Continent with his family. But if ghosts lived there, they roused only to guard the sprawling old house. They showed themselves to mortals with a flick of a curtain, a glimpse of moonlight reflected in a window, or a soughing sound as the wind careened through the trees.

If she believed in such things.

The house was deceptively small from the front. Two long wings stretched to the back from either side, and in the rear of the house was a large court-yard, its ornamental urns now draped in burlap, the yews and rosebushes likewise protected against winter.

Margaret slid her gloved hands into the slits of her cape and stared up at the front of the house through the rusted iron fence. Window frames of faded white contrasted vividly against brick the color of dried blood. Broad gray steps led to a wide front door badly in need of painting. No doubt the pitted brass fixtures had once gleamed brightly.

Glengarrow seemed to know it wasn't at its best and, consequently, wasn't the least welcoming. Four rows of windows reflected a pewter-colored sky and a long, straight lane framed by gray, skeletal trees. The old house was perched on the top of a rise, its back to an outcropping of Ben Mosub. Almost a stubborn house. Or Scot. Glengarrow was definitely Scot.

The wind pushed against her, and she wrapped her cape tighter. Despite the fact the bare branches of the trees were coated with ice, and snow was hinted at in the gray sky, the weather was still temperate compared to what she'd experienced in the last three years.

She shook her head. Now was *not* the time to think of Russia. Instead, she began to walk once more, taking the path to the gates of Glengarrow as she did every morning and every evening. Her walks were meant to take time away from her thoughts, not allow them to overwhelm her.

"Commune with nature, Miss Dalrousie," the physician had said. "Allow God in His mercy to show you what a wondrous world this truly is. Find a place rife with beauty and let it sink into your soul. You will be yourself within weeks, I venture."

She had not exactly chosen Scotland as a refuge. Instead, it had chosen her. As for beauty, there were plenty of places in this corner of the Highlands that brought a sigh to her soul. Each time she witnessed the birth of a dawn bathed in gold and pink or saw the mountain's craggy peak swathed in clouds, she wanted to weep.

What good was beauty when she couldn't replicate it?

No, she wasn't going to think about *that,* either.

Someone had cleared the walk, removing the dead branches and the worst of the leaves. Tom, again.

Tom was the one who'd advised her to begin walking Glengarrow's paths. "Oh, the earl be abroad, Miss Dalrousie," Tom had told her months ago. "Gone near three years. He'll not be caring." Tom had looked sad then, but she'd not asked the cause for his sudden expression. As she'd grown more private, she'd reciprocated by respecting the privacy of others.

She pushed open the iron gate and slid inside. Flanking the gate on either side was a red-brick pillar. Atop each was a stone lion, carved in a lion rampant pose more often found on a coat of arms, the beast seated with one paw raised.

As she did every morning, she nodded to the lions but they ignored her in favor of staring impassively down the lane. Today, instead of taking the path closest to the house, she took the lower walk, choosing the approach to the gardens along a tall brick wall.

She began to count the steps, another habit she'd acquired. Forty steps to the wall. Fifty-three additional steps to the bench in front of the embrasure. Sometimes, she'd sit on the bench and stare at the urn carved in relief on the wall, wondering whom it honored and why at that particular spot.

This morning, however, she passed the bench and continued on, down the gradual slope to the edge of the forest. From somewhere deep inside the woods came the sharp cry of a fox. Just as suddenly, a flock of birds flew swiftly up from the top of the trees, alarmed at her approach.

She veered to the right, still following the path, returning to counting again. The numbers kept her from thinking. Thinking led to remembering, and memories were not good company of late.

Yesterday afternoon she'd surprised a deer in this very spot. The two of them had stared at each other, both nervous creatures. Had the deer felt Margaret's sudden fear, or had it simply been alarmed for its own safety? It had turned and bolted into the forest, leaving her to stare after it, wondering what type of haven the deer sought.

Was there a haven anywhere?

Resolutely, she continued on the path, her gloved hands clasped together beneath the folds of her cape. Made of brilliant red wool, it was the warmest garment she owned, and still it was not warm enough. Once, she would have passed over the cape in favor of something lined in fur, an ankle-length cloak with a hood, perhaps. She'd sold that garment before leaving Russia, to a minor noble who wanted it as a gift for his mistress.

Not again. She halted once more, staring into the forest, the trunks of the trees now only a mass of sticks with a few die-hard leaves affixed to them. The winter forest bounding Glengarrow was ugly, without color, a stark representation of her mood.

Why today? Why was she determined to revisit the past today?

She began walking again, keeping her mind empty, her feet on the path and her gaze on the monochromatic landscape. A bird, braver than his compatriots, flew down and perched on the wall bordering Glengarrow as if to take a look at her. He, too, was winter-colored, with a brownish gray plumage. He tilted his head as he regarded her, then flew away, leaving her feeling as if she hadn't passed his inspection.

The air was colder now, but she was walking into the wind, heading back uphill. To her left, the base of the mountain was separated from the house by only a thin strip of forested land. She welcomed the cold, her thoughts finally diverted from the past and fixed on the effect of the wind on her exposed skin.

A fox cried again, but that was the only sound other than the sough of the wind. Margaret wrapped her arms around her waist beneath the cape. Perhaps she was not as immune to Scottish winters as she'd thought. This was a damp cold seeping into her bones and making them ache.

She'd have a cup of tea, perhaps, when she reached her snug little cottage. Later, she'd have one of Janet's jam tarts. That, and a book she'd not yet read, part of a shipment from Edinburgh. There, the afternoon was planned, as her mornings always were.

The sudden sound was oddly discordant. A deep thumping echoed from the forest and back again, as if Glengarrow had suddenly developed a heart, and it was now beating furiously. Startled, Margaret remained in place, her eyes darting from the trees to the wall between her and the house, then to the lane ahead of her. The sound was louder, but she still didn't recognize it.

A rider abruptly appeared at the end of the lane, as if he'd magically sprouted there. Then, suddenly, where there had only been one rider, now there were four of them. No, six. A carriage rumbled down the road, followed by a slower wagon piled high with trunks and cases and followed by still more outriders. The strange drumbeat now sounded like thunder.

She marked the exact moment the leader saw her. His gaze was straight ahead, directed at Glengarrow. A moment later, he glanced to the right, in her direction. In less time than it took for Margaret to realize she was in danger, he spurred his horse and began riding straight for her.

She turned and started to run, leaving the path and heading into the forest. The peace of the early morning had been shredded and in its place this terrifying cacophony. Her heart was beating so hard it was difficult to breathe. She raced through the trees, up a gentle slope, all the while seeking sanctuary. But winter had stripped the forest of any covering, and the trees were too young to provide any hiding place behind their trunks.

As she ran, she glimpsed shadows on either side of her, horses with caped riders, dark specters flying over the frozen ground. Her breath escaped her lungs in panting gusts, little clouds of terror.

Glancing over her shoulder proved that her fears were real. She was being pursued by five more horsemen.

This was Hell, revisited.

She emerged from the line of forest to face a small clearing. On the other side of it were granite boulders the size of a man, marking the base of the mountain.

One by one, the men emerged from the trees, each horse and rider ringing her until she was surrounded.

A scream caught in her throat and emerged from between her lips like a kitten's tiny cry. Last time, she'd begged for mercy. This time, she wouldn't beg. But they would have to kill her before it happened again.

One man garbed in a black greatcoat urged his horse closer. He held up his hand as if to silence the others. But none of them had spoken. Nor were there any smiles in evidence.

Her assault was to be no matter for amusement, then.

The leader still didn't speak, merely walked his horse closer. He had a handsome face, but she'd learned attractiveness was no guarantee of character. Sometimes evil was exquisitely beautiful.

His hair, thickly black, was too long, curling over his collar and falling down on his forehead. His nose was narrow, and his lips thinned by anger. He would tower over her if standing next to her. Even on a horse, he was commanding.

His face was ruddy with cold, but he wore no hat. That absence alone marked him as arrogant. Did he think himself impervious to the weather?

When she awoke this morning, she had no idea her life would end today. She had no inkling that today, of all her days, she would die trying to protect not her virtue, but her very soul.

This would *not* happen to her again.

She pulled her hands back beneath her cape,

clenching them together out of sight. With more daring than she believed possible, she straightened her shoulders and tilted her chin up so she might face him with her own show of arrogance.

"Why have you waylaid me?" she demanded.

"Why are you trespassing on Glengarrow land?"

She stared at him a moment. "You're the Earl of Linnet, then?"

He nodded. "I am. Who are you?"

Being an earl did not render him less dangerous than he appeared. Being an earl was merely a title, and she'd already been the victim of men with titles.

"Will you let me pass? Or have you other plans, you and your men?"

He didn't answer. Instead, he lifted his left hand again. Just that, and the five men on the opposite side of the clearing disappeared, fading into the winter forest as if they, too, had become black and white and gray.

Still, four men were behind him, each of them intently focused on the confrontation.

"Who are you?" he asked again, and she understood. The price of her safety was information.

"Margaret Dalrousie," she said. Would there be a reaction? Evidently the Earl of Linnet paid no attention to society.

"Why were you trespassing?" he asked.

Did he think she was a threat to Glengarrow? That she was a vagabond?

"I take my walks here," she answered. "Because the area is peaceful and private, and there was no one to bother me. Until today."

He didn't speak, only raised his left hand. This time, however, the men flanking him slowly walked their mounts to the side so he could turn.

"Find another place to walk, Miss Dalrousie," he said over his shoulder. "I have come home."

Margaret was too busy drawing a deep breath to respond. As her heart slowed its frantic beat, she stared after the Earl of Linnet.

What color were his eyes? The artist, dormant but not dead, wanted to know. Why, too, had he suffered so deeply it was etched on his face? The woman, rarely curious lately, could not help but wonder.

Chapter 2

His brother-in-law and the men who'd accompanied him from France knew how difficult this homecoming was, so they fell back, allowing him privacy as Robert McDermott, Earl of Linnet, walked his horse to the front of Glengarrow.

He dismounted, watching as the other men took the path to the stables. Some of them had been here before; for most it was their first visit.

What a shame the place didn't look the same.

The weathervane on the top of the roof had fallen. The trees were overgrown and needed pruning, especially those providing a canopy across the road approaching Glengarrow. A palpable aura of neglect hung around his home, a none-too-gentle reminder that he was at fault for all he saw.

He should have returned sooner. He'd been a fool to leave anyone else in charge of his legacy.

Robert dropped the reins of his horse, and they were immediately retrieved and his horse led away. Who watched over him so carefully? He didn't know. Nor, at this moment, did he care.

His heart felt as if it were ballooning in his chest.

He was dizzy with memories; sights and sounds and scents nearly overwhelmed him.

My darling, you've returned! I didn't expect you for a week! He closed his eyes, feeling himself enveloped in a silk-and-lace embrace. Amelia.

Papa! Papa! Penelope was there, tugging at his legs, making her presence known with no decorum at all. He'd treasured that about her—she was too young to be proper or to care what the world thought.

At this homecoming, however, there was no one to welcome him. No one to whom he should send word he might be delayed. He was simply home, accompanied by a troop of his brother-in-law's men.

He must step forward. He must step onto the path leading to the front door. He must open the door and enter the house he'd not seen for three years.

One step. There, he'd accomplished one step. Another, then, and he would soon be done with this. The wagon would have to be unloaded; the foodstuffs put away. He would have to instruct the two new maids about the house, and he must ensure there were accommodations, however temporary, for the men who'd accompanied him across France and Scotland.

He must find somewhere to sleep tonight.

Another step taken, another milestone achieved. He'd already accomplished a great deal, according to the French physician who'd treated him. If he was limping now, it was to be expected after days in the saddle.

He was at the door, his chest so tight Robert wondered if his heart was about to burst.

Delmont had pressed an object on him at the last stop, and he'd stared at it dully, not comprehending the oversized iron key in his hand was to his own home. How odd that a servant wouldn't admit him. How very strange he was here alone.

He was never alone, though, was he? Nor was he ever without his companions of the spirit.

Robert extracted the key from his jacket and inserted it in the lock, turned it, and heard it click. To the best of his knowledge, this was the first time he'd ever opened the door to Glengarrow himself. There had always been a servant there, always a majordomo, someone to whom he'd entrusted the key.

How had Delmont gotten it?

He stepped into the house, closing the door behind him. Resolutely, he turned and faced the past.

Papa? Penelope would expect a present. She always did. He'd always found something interesting to give her. A rock resembling a kitten curled up asleep. A bit of candy from a shop in Edinburgh. A piece of glass swept onto the beach by the sea.

Reaching into his pocket, he pulled out an acorn he'd found on the road. The nut was larger than most, with a cap that twisted off perfectly, revealing a hole. A house for fairies. He might have told Penelope a story about one, a tiny little girl with infinitesimal gossamer wings and gold hair trailing down her back, possessed of a smile as bright as a new morning. Penelope would have clapped her hands in glee to hear about a sprite so resembling her, and Amelia would have smiled at him with love on her face.

He closed his eyes and opened his hand, allowing the acorn to drop to the floor.

Robert climbed the stairs slowly, knowing he had as long as he needed to explore Glengarrow. His companions would not enter the house until he let them know he was ready.

If he were truly a good host, he'd make arrangements now to unload the wagon, assign one of the maids to air out the bedrooms, ready water for washing. But he wasn't interested in his companions or their comfort at the moment. He was selfishly intent on greeting his ghosts.

At the landing he stopped, his hand clenching his upper right thigh. The pain proved he was alive, the twisting of the muscle to be expected. He would not, however, allow himself to limp as he climbed the rest of the stairs. At the top, he turned and looked around.

He'd always liked this view of Glengarrow. The house was only three hundred years old, not appreciably fixed in nature's memory as some houses he knew. His ancestors had created it for comfort, not for defense, for status instead of an imposing presence, although it was impressive as well.

From here he could see the gathering area—in an earlier time it would have been called the Great Hall, and the space was large enough for it. Two couches sat across from each other, perpendicular to a fireplace large enough to roast a full-grown pig. Above the white-marble Adam mantel was a framed scrap of pennant carried into the last battle of the '45. Because his family had been one of the numerous Highland clans against the uprising, the McDermott fortunes had not been decimated like so many other families.

Memories stretched long in the Highlands, however, and it had taken a hundred years to be forgiven their decision not to support Prince Charles.

Other than the pennant, there were no weapons in his home, no reminders of the Earls of Linnet's colorful past.

"A man holds his memories inside him," his grandfather had once said, and Robert had known only too well the truth of the remark.

He was the last of the Glengarrow McDermotts in Scotland. His brother had immigrated to Australia, of all places, and his sister had married and moved to London. He thought of them often, wrote to them occasionally, but never lacked for their companionship.

There was too much quiet here, too much silence. Glengarrow had never been a quiet place. Instead, it had been filled with laughter, conversation, and life itself. Now it was empty, a shell of what had once been his home, his place of refuge, his haven.

He was delaying again, wasn't he? To the left was the wing they rarely used, and only for guests. To his right was the family wing. Penelope's room was only a few doors away. His chamber—and Amelia's—was at the end of the corridor.

His suite would look just as it had the day he'd left Glengarrow. He'd sent word to Tom it should not be altered, regardless of how long he remained in France.

The bed would be the same four-poster with its old-fashioned velvet curtains. The windows would still hold a view of the orchard. The world had gone to ice, yet the panorama would be beautiful, a winter-colored scene.

The furniture in his suite was mahogany, pieces all made in France, with lion-claw feet and gently sweeping lines. Two wardrobes sat next to each other, one for his clothing, and the other for Amelia's. Twin washbasins sat in the washroom, with porcelain fixtures above a copper bath.

The suite was a mausoleum for his memory, a container into which he could pour all the various recollections of his life, a perfect place to reflect upon his barren future.

Not a place to sleep, however.

He'd find another room to call his, something facing the long approach to Glengarrow.

Robert turned, ignoring the pain in his right leg as he descended the stairs. He wound his way through the house, deliberately dulling any recollections threatening to flood into his mind.

The rear entrance was through the kitchen, and he was startled to find both of the maids had already taken up residence there. One of them was poking at the firebox through the top of the stove, while the other was seated at the table, opening one of the crates from the wagon.

"Can you start it?" he asked, realizing he'd no training in the tending of cold stoves.

She turned, an annoyed look on her face. "Yes, sir, I can, but it will take hours before it's hot enough to cook on."

He nodded, unsurprised. "There's a good amount of wood just outside," he said, knowing Tom would have kept Glengarrow stocked in readiness for his return.

"Tea will be late, sir," the maid said. "Might not have it at all."

He left the women alone, realizing as he exited the kitchen that Janet should have been there to supervise the maids.

"Your Lordship."

Robert looked up to find Tom standing on the servant's stair, lanky and loose-boned, his angular face transformed by a pleasant and welcoming smile.

"It's good to see you, Your Lordship."

The last three years had not been kind to Tom. His hair was now white, and the lines on his face had deepened to furrows. The shoulders, once wide and strong, were stooped with age.

For the first time since they'd approached Glengarrow, Robert felt drawn outside of himself.

"Are you well, Tom?"

The older man smiled. "A bit of aches in the joints, Your Lordship. But it's you I should be asking after. Was it a good journey from France?"

Traveling from Paris to the coast had been an endless slog, and the distance from Inverness to Glengarrow had been marked by delays. Days of riding on horseback had worn him down, exhausted him in a way Robert hadn't expected. But all he said was, "It was a long one."

He placed his hand on the nearest piece of furniture, a cabinet sitting in this particular place for decades. Normally used to store linens for the dining room, it now served as a brace. He leaned against it, taking the weight from his right leg.

"Tell me about Glengarrow, Tom."

"I tried to keep it in repair, Your Lordship, even when the money stopped coming."

"Is that why the weathervane is missing? Why the cupolas haven't been painted? One of the steps is chipped and hasn't been repaired."

Tom nodded. "Yes, sir. I wrote the Dowager Countess. I never got a reply."

"You should have let me know sooner, Tom."

"I didn't want to bother you, Your Lordship."

If Tom had written him a year ago, would he have returned? Or would he have remained in France, as loath to part from Amelia's family and his last memories of her as he was to return to Glengarrow? A moot point, because the letter from Tom had reached him two months ago, a summons to return to his obligations, to his life.

He nodded and turned away, then glanced back as a thought occurred to him.

"What about your wages, Tom? Have you been paid?"

Tom stared down at the floor. "No, Your Lordship. Me and Janet, we've taken another job, just to keep a little soup in the bowl, so to speak."

"Another position?"

"It don't pay much, Your Lordship, but it's not much to do at Blackthorne Cottage. We work for Miss Dalrousie. Janet cooks for her, and I do what odd jobs are needed around the place."

"Blackthorne Cottage has always belonged to Glengarrow," Robert said, frowning. "Did my mother sell the property?"

Tom looked away, then back at Robert. "There have been a lot of changes since you've been gone, sir."

"Evidently," Robert said, straightening, and wishing the muscles in his leg weren't tightening ominously. Tonight would be pain-filled if he didn't do something now to prevent it.

"Tell me about the Dalrousie woman."

Tom smiled. "Little to tell, Your Lordship. She keeps to herself, reads a lot, and takes a lot of walks."

"Around Glengarrow," Robert said.

Tom nodded again.

"The only thing odd she does is that shooting of hers."

"Shooting?"

Tom nodded again. "She asked me to arrange several bales of hay for a target, and she practices near every day. She's not very good at it, but I've never seen anyone as stubborn as that woman."

"Why the hell is she practicing shooting?"

Tom shook his head. "I don't know, Your Lordship, but all I can say is I'm glad it's not me. She gets a look on her face that would give the Devil second thoughts. She wants to shoot someone, that's for sure."

"Well, thank God she didn't have her pistol with her an hour ago, Tom, or I'm certain I would have been her target."

"Was your stay in France not long enough, *beau-frere*?"

Robert turned to find his brother-in-law, the Compte de Guallians, standing on the other side of the kitchen.

"Surely you could have charmed the woman. Instead, you speak of guns."

A teasing smile curved the younger man's lips. Amelia always said that neither old women nor young girls had the power to deny Delmont anything. Even the maids were looking at him now with wide-eyed awe, as if they'd never seen a man with blond hair or blue eyes. The fact that Delmont had absolutely no interest in anyone other than his married lover was a secret he shared with only three people, Robert being one.

Robert straightened, walking back into the kitchen, taking each step deliberately so he didn't limp.

"The woman was trespassing," he said. "At least she will not do so anymore."

Delmont raised one eyebrow but didn't comment.

Robert turned to one of the maids. "We need to air out a dozen rooms for our guests," he said.

"My men can bed down in the stables. It's no worse than what they've experienced on this journey," Delmont said. A small smile curved his lips and robbed the words of their harshness.

Delmont's view of Scotland was that it was rugged and barbaric, inhabited by tribes of naked clansmen armed with cudgels and broadswords.

"That's not necessary," Robert said now. "Glengarrow has plenty of empty rooms. And by the look of the sky, we'll have snow by morning."

He glanced at one of the maids, and she nodded.

A good Inverness girl, hired but two days ago, she'd already impressed him with her willingness to work.

"We can't stay," Delmont said.

"A day or two to rest, surely."

Delmont nodded. "A day or two, then. What can I do now?"

"Assign some men to finish unloading the wagon. I need to see if the cistern is sound." He turned to face Tom, who still stood on the staircase. "Have you checked it lately, Tom?"

"Yes, Your Lordship. I've checked it every week."

Still, he wasn't going to abdicate his responsibility any longer. Robert would check on the cistern himself, despite the effort it would cost him. He turned and walked to the door, intent on the attics and the approach to the roof.

"Are you happy to be home, Robert?" Delmont asked before he made it to the door.

He turned at the doorway and looked at Delmont, not a challenging stare as much as one that simply acknowledged the depth and breadth of their mutual loss. Even if Tom had not been standing there, he would have been hard-pressed to answer the other man.

"I've been home less than an hour, Delmont," he said, answering his brother-in-law in French.

"I am concerned, Robert, that you will do something to damage your recuperation."

"I have just ridden horseback over two continents," Robert said, almost amused. "Stop being an old woman. I am fully healed." He held his arms away from his body and turned in a slow circle. "See? I can stand without falling, and I can walk just fine. And the only true discomfort I feel is occasionally when my scar itches, as if to remind me that I am among the living while others are not."

How quickly his humor faded.

Delmont nodded, his Gallic face revealing his thoughts only too well.

How many looks of pity was he supposed to endure? Robert turned and left Delmont and Tom standing in the kitchen with the two maids. Suddenly, the attics and the roof were more preferable places to be.

Margaret raised the heavy pistol and sighted it. She didn't have to use both hands anymore; one was adequate. However, there was hay strewn ten feet or so on either side of the fence, which meant her aim had not improved. But then, she'd only been practicing a matter of a few months. One day, and hopefully soon, she'd begin to hit the target, a bale of hay the size of a man's chest.

She closed one eye, lined up the target, and pulled the trigger. The gun recoiled, but she was prepared. The first dozen or so times she'd fired the pistol, she'd been knocked to the ground.

Lowering the gun, she squinted at the target. Drat! All she'd done was hit the hay to the right of where she wanted.

She reloaded the gun, sighted it once more, and moved the barrel slightly to the left. Instead of the target, she envisioned a face, one whose features were obscured. This time, when she pulled the trigger, her arm barely moved with the recoil.

She was cold, and her feet were wet, and the wind was rising again, but she wouldn't quit. Her aim was abysmal, but she would practice, just as she practiced for hours to get just the right shading on the pearls around the Grand Duchess Alessandra's throat.

The pistol was one of a set of dueling pistols, a gift from an ardent admirer in Russia. He'd bowed low before extending the velvet-lined box to her.

"I make this for you, Mademoiselle. You see the pretty engraving on the ivory handles? It is nowhere near the talent in your fingers, Mademoiselle Dalrousie. It is but an approximation. You honor me with its acceptance."

"Dueling pistols?"

"My only claim to fame, Mademoiselle. I earnestly hope, however, there is no occasion for you to have need of them." He smiled shyly. "Despite the fact that any number of men would relish the notion of championing your honor."

Under normal conditions, she would have refused the gift. But the man had been so earnest, and her monogram had been inscribed in the ivory handles. Now, she was grateful she hadn't refused the pistols. No one had ever even hinted at fighting a duel for her, but she had plans for the guns herself.

Today, of all days, when it had come rushing back at her, she must never forget. First, she must protect herself, then she must prepare.

*   *   *

Robert retraced his steps up the grand stairs to the second floor. At the end of the corridor, he took the smaller set of stairs to the attic. Here, generations of Glengarrow's inhabitants had stored furniture or other detritus of well-lived lives.

The attic was a dull and dusty place, surprisingly well lit by porthole windows. He drew his greatcoat around him as he ascended a short ladder leading to a trapdoor in the roof.

Luck, never one of his allies, was with him as he pushed the trapdoor upward, easily breaking through a thin layer of ice. He climbed out onto the roof of Glengarrow, a task he'd not set for himself for many years.

The cistern was made of wood, constructed of planks of wood tightly banded together like a barrel. For a hundred years, it had rested on top of Glengarrow, collecting rainwater and sending it down through well-maintained pipes to the sinks and baths throughout the house. In winter, the snow and ice melted and served a similar function.

The cistern looked the same. No doubt the wood had darkened since his great-great-grandfather had it built. His ancestor had reasoned that to make it any taller than three feet would put too great a strain on the roof, and had made up for the lack of depth by extending the cistern until it stretched over most of Glengarrow.

As it was, the cistern supplied more than enough water for their use, eliminating the need to use the two wells in the courtyard.

He continued his inspection of the cistern, walking slowly around the structure. There were no signs of leaks, no damage to the roof itself. He pulled on one or two of the planks to make sure the seal was strong and there was no movement. Everything looked as sturdy as it had when he'd last inspected the cistern, a dozen years ago.

There, one chore done. Endless hours stretched out in front of him. How did he fill those?

In France, he'd had a goal. He'd driven himself to prove he could survive, not because he wanted it—there were days when he'd prayed for death. Then, he'd begun to walk again, learning to mask the pain with a smile on his face. Not one person in Amelia's close-knit family had realized how difficult becoming ambulatory had been for him and how much he was willing to do to be able to cross a room without crutches or a cane.

His third goal, never expressed or verbalized, had been to simply endure.

In France, he'd always been surrounded by people, well-meaning relatives by marriage who always wanted to know how he fared. He'd been grateful for their caring, but for their sake he'd always pretended an equanimity he didn't truly feel. He didn't want to cause more pain to Amelia's mother, who was enduring her own grief.

But they'd acted as a buffer, hadn't they? Alone on Glengarrow's roof, he had a premonition about his future. There would be nothing to stop him from feeling the full measure of his grief, no occupation to engage his mind.

What the hell was he to do with his life?

The wind was fierce, and he gathered his coat closer around his body. From here, he could see all his land, save the section on the other side of Ben Mosub. To the east, he could view the beginning of North Linden Village. To the west, the small cottage that had belonged to Glengarrow for generations. Why had his mother sold it?

He stood where he was, unconcerned about being buffeted by sleet and wind.

The gunshot so startled him that he grabbed the edge of the cistern to keep from falling.

He strode to the other side of the roof and stared in the direction of Blackthorne Cottage. The Dalrousie woman stood on the icy ground in her crimson cape. As he watched, she raised her arm and the sound came again, followed by a puff of smoke. The trees blocked the view of her target.

Practicing with him in mind? Perhaps he should warn Delmont's men to be watchful for a black-haired termagant with murder on her mind.

A solitary figure, she stood immobile, an ice sculpture dressed in red. She was the brightest spot in the scenery, and perhaps the most confusing.

He'd cornered her, and her response, besides her obvious fear? Rage. Anger nearly matching his. Any woman would have been frightened by being surrounded by so many men on horseback. But would they have been angry?

What was her name? Margaret. Her accent had a foreign note to it, and he realized he was curious about her in a way he hadn't been curious about anyone or anything in a long while.

There, some occupation for his endless hours—the investigation of his neighbor. Who was she, and how did she come to be here?

Chapter 3

"**I** do not like leaving you here alone," Delmont said, mounting.

His troop of men clustered around him, protecting the Compte de Guallians even here. After all, they were still in a barbaric country. Robert hoped nothing occurred on Delmont's journey home that would validate his opinion of Scotland.

"I'll be fine," Robert said, stepping back. They'd had this discussion before, and Robert had no intention of repeating it yet again. "You worry too much, Delmont."

He'd be fine at Glengarrow by himself, armed with his small staff. If he needed extra help, he'd hire them from the local village, or import them from Inverness. But he didn't need a nursemaid. Or a keeper, for that matter, a role Delmont had assigned himself for the last three years.

Delmont turned in the saddle and stared at Robert for several long minutes. The look was filled with concern, but there was nothing Robert could do to dispel it. Delmont had been witness to one of the worst moments of Robert's life, and the memory would forever affect how the other man viewed him.

Delmont had been the one to find the overturned carriage on the road leading to his estate. All Robert could remember was that the horses had become frightened by something—a noise, a rabbit, the scent of some other animal. The driver hadn't been able to control them, and the carriage had tumbled off the road and down a steep embankment. Delmont and his men had righted the carriage, and found Amelia and Penelope. The only clear memory Robert had was Amelia calling to him, and the awful silence that followed.

There would always be the Robert before the accident, and the Robert afterward. The Robert of afterward would never be as carefree or as quick to laughter or as interested in the world around him. This Robert had become more insular, less caring, more introverted. To Delmont, the world, and certainly to himself, his life would be forever demarcated into those two sections.

Delmont had been responsible for his excellent care, and the fact Robert had survived his initial injuries. Delmont had sat with him that horrible day of Amelia and Penelope's funeral, when he'd been too injured to attend. Delmont had relayed details of the entire service for his sister and niece in a soft voice.

Penelope, ever-curious child that she was, would have been fascinated by the French service. French was the language of princesses, she'd announced the day before she died. With her five-year-old wisdom, she'd decreed that being half-French was better than being wholly Scot. He and Amelia had exchanged a smiling look over her head.

Delmont finally turned, facing forward.

Robert watched until Delmont and his men were out of sight, then walked slowly up the steps and let himself in the front door of Glengarrow. He was limping, but there was no one to see him.

Slowly, he took the staircase up to the second floor. At the top, he hesitated, staring at the double doors at the end of the corridor.

He wished, fervently, that ghosts did exist. He would do whatever necessary to welcome them to Glengarrow, as long as one of them was a fair-haired woman with an enchanting smile and a child with a twinkle in her eye.

He heard the sound of muted laughter and his heart stilled for a moment, until he realized it was one of the maids. Should he issue a moratorium on amusement or banish speech and conversation, the better to encourage spirits to linger at Glengarrow? Perhaps they roamed at night with more freedom than day. Was sunlight too brilliant a backdrop? Was night kinder and softer to the departed?

He did not fear ghosts, but he could not yet visit the suite he'd shared with Amelia.

Margaret stormed down the gravel path to Glengarrow, circled the baroque fountain, and took the broad stone steps up to the double doors. Holding on to the stone balustrade, she was ever mindful of her trailing skirts and the fact the steps were coated with ice.

Anger would not rob her of sense.

She knocked on the door, but it was not readily answered. Nor was her patience rewarded after five minutes. Was the Earl of Linnet hiding? Did he suspect she was here for a confrontation?

She turned and began making her way gingerly down the steps. As her foot hit the last step, she heard the door open.

Sighing heavily, she turned and looked up, expecting to see a servant at the door. Instead, the Earl of Linnet himself greeted her.

"Did you do that on purpose?" she asked. "Wait until I was at the bottom of the steps to open the door? Did you hope I might slip and fall?"

He didn't respond, only stared at her as if he'd never before seen her.

"Margaret Dalrousie," she reminded him.

"I know who you are, Miss Dalrousie."

Once more she began to ascend the steps. At the top, she fixed her sternest look at him, clasped her hands together, and proceeded to upbraid the Earl of Linnet.

"You can't do it. I will not let you. You can't take Tom and Janet from me. I depend on their services, if not their companionship. I will not allow it."

"Tom and Janet have always been on retainer to Glengarrow. If you can convince them to remain in your cottage, by all means they're free to do so."

She frowned at him. "Retainer? You didn't pay them. There is a word for that, you know. Serf."

He stepped back and regarded her as he might a rodent that had somehow burrowed itself into his chamber. She fully expected him to flick his wrist and somehow summon a waiting retainer to "deal with her, posthaste."

Instead, he simply moved his head, a negligible shake, really. A thoroughly dismissive gesture, for all it wasn't a gesture at all.

She frowned at him. "You know quite well they have a certain loyalty to you." She took a deep breath, biting back all those unflattering comments she'd dearly love to make. "But is that a reason to steal them out from under my employ?"

"Was I stealing them?" he asked calmly. Too calmly for this impassioned discussion.

According to the Russians, who were emotional in their own right, artists were supposed to be volatile. She'd never believed in the stereotype, but she wished she were possessed of a more histrionic nature at the moment. She might even screech.

"You surely do not need their assistance," she said, forcing herself to modulate her voice. For good measure, she curved her lips into the semblance of a smile, wondering how sincere it appeared. "I expect you have filled Glengarrow to the brim with servants. What are two more?"

"I haven't filled Glengarrow to the brim with servants, and if I had, I'd still single out Tom and Janet. Tom looks after Glengarrow, and Janet is my cook."

"I've hired them myself for those very reasons," she said, annoyed at the reasonableness of his tone and striving to match it. "They've lived at my cottage for the past six months," she added. "Many times they've mentioned how much cozier it was than living in . . ." Her words trailed away. In actuality, Janet and Tom had both commented on how haunted Glengarrow had felt, but those weren't words she'd repeat to its owner.

"Regardless," she said, "I hired them. I have diligently *paid* them as agreed. But at your insistence, they'll move back to Glengarrow, and I will be left without a staff at all."

"I haven't insisted they move back," he said, leaning his weight against the doorframe.

She wondered, suddenly, if he were ill, then remembered Tom's words. "He was in a carriage accident, miss. Nearly died he did. Busted up something awful. A metal bit from the roof went right through his stomach, and another nearly sliced off his leg."

"You should sit down," she said, annoyed that his coloring was a little gray.

"I should finish this conversation," he said, his stare pointed and unfriendly. If she knew him better—if she knew him at all, she'd ask why he disliked other people so earnestly. Or was it only her?

"Then they can stay with me?"

He looked up at the doorframe in a decidedly insulting gesture.

What a very irritating creature he was.

"No," he said, after a long moment of silence. "They cannot stay with you. I've asked them to come back to Glengarrow, and they were both enthusiastic about the prospect."

When she would have spoken, he held up a hand, another insulting gesture and one capable of truly, truly annoying her.

"You can have Tom," she interjected before he could speak. "And I'll have Janet."

He looked startled. "No," he said. "Janet's my cook. Do you intend I starve?"

"Are you helpless? Do you even *know* where the kitchen is?"

He frowned. "Of course I know where the kitchen is. But I'm not as good a cook as Janet," he said. "Nor am I willing to spare Tom."

"Then let me have them at night," she said, her mood suddenly lightened.

He studied her for several moments. "I've brought two maids with me from Inverness. You're welcome to hire either if you wish. I would be more than happy to arrange for some time for you to meet with either or both."

There was nothing wrong with his suggestion. In fact, it was very charitable, all in all. She had it in her mind to retain Tom and Janet, however, a bit of obstinacy that wasn't at all charitable or reasonable, perhaps.

"Is there any reason why Tom and Janet must be at Glengarrow both day and night? Do you command your servants to remain within earshot at all hours, in case you require something? I am more than willing to fend for myself during the day. I'm not that messy a creature, after all." In truth, even though she counseled herself not to leave a trinket or a book or a cup merely lying about, she was constantly surrounded by clutter.

His face stiffened.

She was not handling this at all well. In fact, her behavior was oddly reminiscent of some of the young Russian nobles who'd so annoyed her.

"The fact is, I do not want to remain alone at night."

That was a bit more information than she wanted to share and probably more than the situation warranted.

"I'm not a fearful creature," she added, feeling a need to explain herself to this frozen-faced man. "I would just feel more comfortable if someone was with me."

"Have you considered hiring a companion?"

"Never mind," she said, biting back a rude comment. "I should have known you'd be incapable of reason."

He was still standing beside the door, attired informally in white shirt and black trousers. He was tall, his hair too long, and his expression too unfriendly.

Still, she might have painted him once. Women would have certainly called him handsome, but she wasn't interested in the symmetry of his features. She'd have been careful to capture the look of suffering around his eyes, the lines radiating outward, signs normal on a much older man. His bottom lip was full, the upper lip thinner, and neither looked as if they'd had much experience smiling of late. The line of his jaw was too sharp, set into prominence either by the thinness of his face or the severity of his expression. His forehead was wide with dark brows. Long black eyelashes shadowed eyes the color of sapphires.

But it wasn't the surprising color of his eyes that made her mourn for the ability to paint the Earl of Linnet. She wanted to test herself, to see if she could replicate his expression, the utter dreadfulness of his pain.

The question intriguing her was very simple—
why did the Earl of Linnet, a handsome man, and
one reputed to be wealthy, have such a look of anguish in his eyes?

She turned and began to descend the steps.

"They are not my serfs," he said.

She flattened her right hand on the stone balustrade, and glanced over her shoulder at him.

"Where they spend their nights is not up to me.
If they have no objection to drawing two salaries,
why should I?"

She would have thanked him then, but he stepped
back and abruptly closed the door in her face.

Idiotic man.

Idiotic woman.

Robert stood with his back to the door and
closed his eyes. He could still see her there, tendrils
of black hair escaping the hood of her outlandish
crimson cape.

She was an irritating creature, Miss Margaret
Dalrousie.

He really should hire a majordomo, but whom
would he supervise? Tom? Not likely. Janet? He
could just imagine what Janet's reaction might be
to his importing a majordomo from Inverness. A
housekeeper, then, if he couldn't convince Janet to
take on the task. That way, he'd be prevented from
having to have anything further to do with Miss
Margaret Dalrousie.

She'd taken him by surprise. If he'd been prepared for her appearance, he would have given her
a more schooled answer. He was good at the polite
response, wasn't he? He was adept at diplomacy.

Amelia had always been proud of him. She'd always wanted to know what occurred in the halls of Parliament. She'd been disappointed to learn it was mostly mundane conversation interspersed with one or two moments of high drama. Still, he'd liked talking to her about his day. And occasionally, if the topic was one that interested her, he'd solicited her opinion.

He looked up at the ceiling and bit back a sigh. He had absolutely no idea if this pain would ever subside. Coming home had been like pulling a bandage off a newly healed wound.

The house was in as good a shape as Tom could keep it, without funds or manpower. He'd asked for an accounting from the shopkeepers in the village and been pleased to find he didn't owe all that much to them. His mother was a different matter, and he would have to address the issue as quickly as possible.

He'd given the care of Glengarrow to his mother. She'd never before acted a flighty woman with the focus of a gnat. Why now? Why had she allowed the estate to go without money? Thank God his fortune was still intact, but not for her lack of trying to decimate it. He still had to go through the mountains of bills his solicitor had handed him in Inverness. In addition, he'd sent a request to the man for copies of the Bill of Sale for Blackthorne Cottage. That transaction needed a little more investigation—not to mention explanation.

He would have to ensure that the houses in Inverness, Edinburgh, and London had not been as financially neglected as Glengarrow. He doubted, though, that he owed money to any of

the servants. Londoners were notoriously stiff-
necked and would simply have found employment
elsewhere. Nor would most Scots have tolerated
being unpaid.

Bless Tom and Janet for their loyalty.

His steward had ensured him the home farms
were prosperous. There were sheep grazing on the
other side of the mountain, and he was told, the
numbers would double come spring if the birthrate
was the same as it had been the past two years.

Life was touched with a little bit of magic at
Glengarrow, as if this glen with a mountain at its
back was an enchanted place. He could almost close
his eyes and believe nothing had truly changed. At
any moment Amelia would descend the stairs with
her radiant smile, and somewhere from above he'd
hear Penelope's excited laughter.

Robert walked into the foyer and stood there
with his eyes closed, willing to hear the sounds
that would label him a madman. But there was
nothing but silence, and so he was sane after all.
Sane and bereft.

He'd forgotten to ask the Dalrousie woman why
she was shooting. He could have told her the noise
was disruptive to his mood. But she would probably have curled that very large mouth of hers into
a sneer and told him what he might do with his
mood. He'd never thought to have someone like
Miss Margaret Dalrousie as a neighbor.

She wanted Tom and Janet. Very well, he would
consult with them himself to ensure they were
not being asked to do too much. After all, they
had been loyal to Glengarrow; it was up to him to
ensure the loyalty was not one-sided.

If they decided it would be too much for their advancing years to work at Glengarrow during the day and work for Miss Margaret Dalrousie in the evening, he would deliver the news to her himself.

No, he would send her a note. A note on the stationery he'd used at Parliament. That should give her some inkling of whom she addressed so rudely. Not once had she made any concession to his rank. Not that he normally required it. He was considered egalitarian in most circles. However, something about her irritated him and made him want to impress upon her the exact nature of his status.

Who did she think she was?

Chapter 4

Margaret heard laughter and looked around the edge of the high-backed armchair to see Janet and Tom entering the parlor.

"Will you look, Miss Margaret, at what the earl gave me?"

The voice was not young; it held a slight tremor. Janet's face was furrowed like newly turned earth. The hand directing Margaret's eyes to the cameo brooch pinned at her throat was riddled with veins and marked with a pattern of small brown spots. Her frame was slightly bent, as if Janet were forever intent upon a pot cooking on the stove, or coaxing a fire to become hotter. Her diminutive stature would no doubt become even smaller as the years passed.

Only her eyes were young, bright blue, clear, and accepting, they measured others with interest and intelligence—the eyes of a woman well pleased with life and deeply happy.

Janet's husband, Tom, stood behind her, his hands on her shoulders, support even in this innocuous conversation. Tom was often there, to offer comfort to Janet or wise counsel should she require it, an ever-present vigilance borne not from duty but from affection.

Janet bent down so Margaret could look closely at the newly acquired piece of jewelry. Margaret surrendered her embroidery, a mundane rendition of pale pink roses whose bloom seemed already to have faded, and prepared herself to be suitably impressed by not only the earl's generosity but the object itself.

She'd grown fond of this sweet and generous couple, had learned Janet's graciousness was more than surface deep, but bred in the bone. Tom's infatuation with his wife of sixteen years continued unabated, as if he were in the first flush of youth.

They genuinely loved each other, a fact obvious even to strangers.

Margaret reached out her fingers to touch the coral of the cameo. The brooch was old, the edges of the carving had softened as the features of a face is aged by life itself. The setting was gold; it too was mellow, less bright although no less beautiful for its rich patina.

She sighed. "Does this mean you're going back to Glengarrow?" As an inducement, it was a lovely one.

"We wouldn't do that to you, Miss Margaret." Janet glanced over her shoulder at her husband. "The earl needs us, though. That's what we think. So, we'll stay here at night and work at Glengarrow during the day, if it's all right with you.

"Perfectly all right, Janet," she said, picking up her embroidery again. "Do you think the earl will agree?"

Janet nodded. "It was his idea, Miss Margaret."

Not quite his idea, but Margaret didn't comment. She'd won this skirmish with the earl; she should be content. Still, it wasn't fair of him to pass her idea off as his.

Tom kissed his wife's cheek and murmured something as he left the room.

Janet glanced after him, as if she was afraid they wouldn't see each other for a while.

"You love Tom very much, don't you?"

At Janet's look of surprise, she realized how rude she'd sounded.

"Forgive me, Janet. The question was intrusive."

Janet didn't respond, and in the silence, Margaret found herself explaining far more than the occasion warranted. "It's just that I've never felt that way for anyone."

"Never?"

She was familiar with Janet's look.

Margaret shook her head.

The desire for love had simply faded beneath all of those other wishes and wants she'd had.

"You've never wished to marry, Miss Margaret?"

"Never. I never met a man who was as worthy of my attention as my painting."

"And children?"

"Is being a mother the true goal of every woman? It seems a great deal of bother."

She'd had a friend in Russia to whom she'd confessed that very thought, and Therese had been appalled at her honesty.

"Motherhood is the highest calling to which a woman can aspire," Therese had said.

Margaret didn't bother to point out Therese had a nanny and a score of servants to care for her children, both of whom were more familiar with their servants than their mother. Therese saw her son and daughter for a scant hour per day, just long enough to check on their growth, perhaps, and remark upon their attractiveness.

"You haven't painted since you've been here, Miss Margaret."

Was that a condemnation? She glanced up from her needlework. No, the other woman's expression was kind, not censorious. Janet simply stated a fact.

"No, I haven't."

She concentrated on the needlework in her lap, waiting for the question. What would she say when Janet asked her why the trunks in the storage room went unopened? Why there were leather cases gathering dust and not attention?

Janet, however, declined to pursue the subject, in favor of another one.

"You are too young, Miss Margaret, to be a spinster."

Margaret stared straight ahead, wondering how many times in her life she'd been called that. A hundred? A thousand?

She'd never allowed herself to compromise for anyone. Not once had she succumbed to tears over a man. On no occasion had she ever considered giving up her vocation because a man wished it of her. And so, when people spoke of love, she saw the word sacrifice, and it didn't interest her at all.

Tom and Janet, however, might be considered exceptions to the rule. When Tom looked at Janet, he couldn't help but smile, and when Janet responded, there was a warmth in her eyes not there for anyone else.

Still, this discussion had proven to Margaret that it wasn't wise to comment about personal matters. The arrow always came full circle to aim for her.

"I am perfectly happy the way I am."

A look of speculation came into Janet's eyes then, and it wasn't difficult to figure out what the older woman was thinking.

Margaret decided to end this conversation about her private matters once and for all.

"But other than giving you the brooch, Janet, the earl made no other comment?" Margaret asked.

"He just wanted to know if the arrangement would be too much for Tom and me. But then, he's always cared for those who worked for him." Janet fingered the brooch and smiled brightly.

Except for paying them. Janet and Tom had been visibly grateful when Margaret had hired them.

How could he have forgotten? How could he have neglected to care for those in his employ? Was it because he was an earl and such details were beneath him?

Margaret wasn't overwhelmed by the fact that the man living at Glengarrow was an earl. She'd been surrounded by titles in Russia. The Grand Duchess of this and the Grand Duke of that, the Prince of this palace and the Princess of that hovel.

The Russian court was glutted with royalty. And at one time, perhaps, she had been as fascinated with them as Janet expected her to be with the earl.

Being a noble was an accident of birth, nothing else, and a great many men who held a title deserved to be addressed more as "Bastard" than "Your Lordship" or "Your Grace."

"I think, just between you and me, that it was a present to make up for forgetting about us," Janet said.

"It's the least of what he should do," Margaret said, annoyed at the older woman's demonstration of faith in the earl. She didn't think she could tolerate this conversation about the Earl of all Saints one more moment. She put down her embroidery and picked up a book on the table in front of her.

"You don't know what happened to the earl in France, do you, Miss Margaret?"

"A carriage accident, wasn't it?" Margaret said. "People become injured, Janet. It doesn't make him a better person. It's difficult, true, but he will eventually heal."

Janet placed both hands against her midriff and stared at Margaret as if she'd suddenly turned blue. After a moment, she sighed deeply and shook her head.

"It was more than that, Miss Margaret. He lost his family in the accident. His wife, Amelia, sweet Amelia, was killed. And so was little Penelope. Only five years old, she was."

Margaret stared at the page in front of her, wondering what she was reading. Poetry. How very odd. She disliked poetry, thought it too maudlin or too romantic. Russians loved it, but then they were given to extreme bouts of emotionality.

> *Give me heaven and I'll ask no more of you.*
> *Give me heaven and I'll not protest*
> *When twilight greets me anon.*
> *Give me heaven and I will die of bliss.*

How utterly nauseating.

Yet staring at the page was preferable to looking up at Janet again.

She didn't like pain, actively avoided it, in fact, and she especially didn't like the ache in her chest Janet's words incited. No wonder the Earl of Linnet was such a dour Scot. He had reason to be, did he not?

She didn't want to recall the look in his eyes, the measure of pain visible to anyone. If that much pain was evident, what did he hold back?

"When did it happen?" Margaret asked, for want of anything else to say.

"Three years ago," Janet said. "It's beyond time for him to come home, I'm thinking. He'd be better at home than in France."

If she'd wanted to discuss her past, Margaret might have told her France was a lovely country, that she'd spent several years there herself. Her greatest career boost had come in France. Instead, she remained silent, understanding that while Janet was fiercely loyal to the Earl of Linnet, she was just as fiercely Scot.

No country could be as wonderful to a Scot as Scotland.

"Still, it can't be easy for him, Miss Margaret, three years or no. To come home and be faced with all those memories."

Now she understood the look in his eyes, his impatience—even anger—with the world. The Earl of Linnet was not so much aristocrat as he was torn apart by circumstance, what other people called Fate, or even God.

Did the Earl of Linnet loathe Fate as much as she?

Chapter 5

The next morning, Janet and Tom were both gone when Margaret awakened after a night filled with troubling dreams. She made herself breakfast, and then, despite her fatigue, dressed for her morning walk.

For a long moment she stood in front of the armoire before selecting one of her three good day dresses. This one was of blue silk, embroidered with a delicate climbing red rose pattern down the front of the bodice and replicated on the full sleeves. She wore two petticoats beneath her full skirts, one of them of wool.

Slipping on her cape, she tightened it securely at the collar and buttoned the front. Her hat came next, a puffy thing made of feathers from the belly of a swan. She pulled it on her head and tucked her ears beneath the brim. The snowy white hat with its red band had been a present from a duchess, a member of the royal house who'd been grateful because Margaret had rendered her quite handsome in her portrait.

True, she'd made the duchess's cheekbones a little sharper, and her teeth a little whiter and more even. In addition, she'd slimmed a sagging jowl and eliminated the flesh on her throat. The woman deserved to be rendered a little more attractive. In fact, the duchess deserved to be made a saint for putting up with the duke's philandering, but she hadn't made that comment aloud. Nonetheless, she quite liked the hat. She pulled on her gloves and left the cottage, securing the door behind her.

The path to Glengarrow was a well-trod one, long before she'd come to the Highlands. She gave a thought to all those people who must have come this way over the years, wondering who they were. Servants employed but not sleeping at Glengarrow? Merchants from the nearby village? Or lovers creeping through the forest?

She dared herself to take the path around Glengarrow instead of continuing to walk down the tree-flanked lane once again. She told herself she was simply tired of walking in a straight line up and down like a child being exercised by her nanny.

Let the earl chastise her. Let him yell at her. Let him look down his aristocratic nose at her. She might even ball up her fist and hit him in the stomach. No, that wouldn't be fair, would it? The man had been injured. Perhaps she wouldn't hit him after all, but she would certainly let him know by her own officious look that he'd not found favor with her.

She would walk through the grounds of Glengarrow this morning, and perhaps she would even stop and sit upon the bench and stare at the urn recessed in the wall. She would look to her left and to her right, where the poor rosebushes were buried in the snow and dream of spring. Spring only lasted a matter of weeks in the Highlands. Summer was as quickly done, then autumn arrived, filled with its gorgeous colors and scent of winter.

First, however, she would have to endure the snow and the ice. She'd done so for years, though, hadn't she? Yes, but she'd had her own troika and well-paid servants to ensure that she was warm even when the snowdrifts were higher than her sleigh.

She walked through the gates, nodding first to the lion on her right, then to the lion on her left, feeling as if she'd neglected them in the past week. Had it only been a week since the earl had returned home? She gripped her hands on the outside of her cape and looked to the right, where a dozen windows faced her. The curtains had not been opened. No one was watching her.

The wind was blustery, as if it wished to toss her around like a leaf. Snow was coming again, and the air seemed to welcome it, chilling until it was almost brittle. Her eyes began to water, and she pulled the scarf close around her neck, trying not to think of how cold she was. These morning and afternoon constitutionals were for her health, but they were even more salubrious for her character. Truly, the very last thing she wanted to do was to go for a trek in the snow, but doing so demonstrated her discipline.

She continued on her way, walking steadily on the path curving left into the forest, feeling grateful she'd taken the chance to walk here today. It was a lovely vista even with all the snow that had fallen last night. Another reason for taking the path around Glengarrow—the lane was nearly a foot deep in snow.

She hesitated at the bench before the urn and, as if daring herself again, brushed off the bench and sat. The silence of the morning enveloped her, bringing her a sense of calm she hadn't felt since the night before when she'd been awakened from another nightmare. She took several deep breaths, unclenched her hands, and stared down at the tips of her serviceable shoes.

In Russia, she found it difficult to carve any time for herself. She was either in demand at a sitting or an audience with a member of the royal family or returning home to change clothes at midday, only to attend an audience with another member of the Russian royal family. Every single hour had been occupied with either painting or the inevitable social obligations needed to acquire another commission.

Over the last nine months, she'd gradually become accustomed to solitude. Still, if she had to paint a portrait of herself, the canvas would be blank, left white and untouched. Granted, she was a fully grown woman with experiences and a past. But who she had become was so entwined with her art, it was difficult to separate the woman from the painter. Without her talent, she didn't know who Margaret Dalrousie was.

She glanced up at Glengarrow. The house should not have been there, especially perched as it was beneath a mountain, approached like a sedate country manse. Glengarrow was strangely out of place in this rugged landscape, and yet in another sense, it was perfectly positioned.

"Are you feeling courageous, Miss Dalrousie?"

She glanced to her left, and there he was, standing in front of a magnificent-looking horse, holding the reins loosely in his left hand.

"I came to thank you," she said, knowing it was true the moment she said it. She'd wanted to encounter him, unwise as it might be. "For allowing Janet and Tom to stay with me."

"You were kind to them when I was not. It was only fair."

"A unique attitude to take. It's been my experience that few people care about fairness."

"Then you have been associating with the wrong people, Miss Dalrousie."

"I would agree wholeheartedly," she said.

His expression changed, became less rigid, softer somehow. He was more adept than she at hiding his emotions, however, because she couldn't tell what he was thinking.

"I spoke with Tom and Janet," he said. "They expressed no reluctance about the arrangement."

"They have not," she said, wishing she knew what he had said to them. She certainly didn't want him to have elicited pity for her. She didn't want pity, she wanted companionship. And if she had to pay for it, then very well. She'd not yet acquired the ability to stay alone at night. Her nightmares came too furiously. How much worse would they be if she were alone in the cottage.

"Why do you walk every day? Especially in inclement weather?"

"All in all, I'd rather dance than walk," she said brightly, "but I have no music and no partner."

He frowned at her but didn't comment. How very autocratic he was. Not unlike a Russian prince.

"Are you French?" he asked.

She smiled. "I speak French fluently," she said, not adding she also spoke Italian and Russian as well. For some reason, languages had always come easily to her. "But I was born in Fife."

He looked surprised, as everyone did when she divulged that fact.

"But you've not lived in Scotland all your life."

"No," she said. "I haven't." She waited for another question, but it didn't come.

She wished she didn't have the urge to shiver. If she gave in to her chills, however, she'd be miserable by the time she made it back to the cottage.

His voice didn't sound as if the cold mattered to him. But then, he was bundled up in a heavy greatcoat, hat, and gloves. There was even a muffler around his neck. Nor did the horse look discommoded by the weather. Perhaps it was the weight of the heavy saddle blanket. Or were Scottish horses as arrogant as their owners?

The Earl of Linnet's features were stiff, his eyes guarded, and she wondered if it was the cold creating such a mask of his face. Or was it something else? Emotion, perhaps?

"I had no idea Tom and Janet had not been paid all the time I was in France."

What a very odd comment. Did he care about what she thought? Of course he didn't. He was simply being the Earl of Linnet, a little stiff, certainly haughty. Still, the mention of France brought back Janet's story.

She was not given to overt acts of empathy. Most of the time she studied people simply with an eye to composition, the curve of a cheek, the highlights in the hair, the exact shade of their skin. She was an observer, and rarely moved to involve herself with the subject of her intense scrutiny.

Once, a princess in St. Petersburg had started sobbing so much during her sitting Margaret had no choice but to put down her brush and engage the girl in conversation. Her story was not unexpected—the princess had fallen in love with a man not her equal, and, of course, her parents objected. Margaret had uttered what comforting words she could, given the order for tea, and an hour later the girl was consoled enough to keep her pose.

Ever since then, she'd imposed strict requirements on her subjects—they were to be accompanied by one other individual, a guardian or friend. That way, if the subject became overwhelmed by emotion, there was either a friend to commiserate or a guardian to chastise. Either way, Margaret was not pulled into the role of confessor. Instead, she could be free to concentrate on her work.

Now, however, she was uncomfortably aware no one could act as her proxy. She could not summon a maid. Nor could she send a note.

She looked up at him, wanting to say something, but being unable to push the words from her mouth. Finally, all she could manage was to fix her gaze on the Earl of Linnet, and say, "I am so very sorry."

He looked down at her, a disdainful look, if she were given to ascribing emotions to gestures. She might have painted him, perhaps as Caesar.

But instead of commenting, he simply directed his attention back to the neck of his horse, patting it absently as if caring more for the animal than for her effort at sympathy.

His was an arresting face, but it wasn't simply his looks fueling her curiosity. She wanted to see his eyes more clearly. She wanted to look into them and decipher the emotion she'd only caught a glimpse of a second ago. Perhaps the Earl of Linnet was not as arrogant as she'd originally believed. Or perhaps his arrogance was like hers, a shield to protect her. She wanted no one to come closer, and to that end, she was polite but distant.

One thing was evident—neither one of them was adept in the giving of comfort or the receiving of it.

She stood, brushing her skirt surreptitiously in case snow clung to it.

He turned and faced her. "Why have you come to Blackthorne Cottage, Miss Dalrousie?"

She stared at him, startled. "Why?"

"Why not some other city in Scotland?"

"Is there any reason I should answer that question? Why is it so important you know?"

"Can I not evince some curiosity about my only neighbor? Why should I not?"

"I came here for the bracing air. For the conviviality," she said. "For the amity of the neighborhood."

She had no intention of telling him she'd nearly been destitute in Edinburgh, despairing of any way of earning her keep when she'd been contacted by a solicitor. From him she'd learned of her bene-factor, a man who wished to remain anonymous, but who'd evidently admired her work enough to bequeath Blackthorne Cottage to her. If she were frugal, there was enough money as well to maintain herself for the rest of her life.

"You're out riding," she said, ignoring his question. "Isn't it a bit cold for a canter?"

"I'm going to Inverness."

"On horseback?"

He didn't say anything. Nor did he even nod in response. Instead, he simply mounted, then turned his horse and rode away.

As she watched him, it occurred to her she'd been tactless. Was she simply rusty in the art of conversation, or was it her reaction to him?

He wouldn't want to ride in a carriage, would he?

She wished she hadn't had that insight into the Earl of Linnet. She'd much rather feel irritation for the man than this unwelcome sympathy.

Annoying man.

Chapter 6

Margaret returned to Blackthorne Cottage and made herself a cup of tea. Her next task was to write her solicitor, a chore she'd been avoiding for the past week. In all actuality, it seemed a very dubious exercise of her time and energy. She wrote him, and he always answered in the negative.

> No, Miss Dalrousie, I have not been able to secure any of your funds from Russia. No, Miss Dalrousie, I have not yet been able to discover the origin of the crest you gave me.

Still, she needed to keep some communication between them. Perhaps one day he'd have different answers.

Resolutely, Margaret put her cup down on the table and stood, sighing audibly. There was no one in the cottage to hear her, but the dramatic gesture felt good nonetheless.

She would need to retrieve her writing desk. Every week, Tom rode into the village to purchase supplies and collect the post. Tomorrow was his normally scheduled day, and the letter would have to be ready.

She took the narrow staircase to the second floor and turned left. Hesitating on the landing, she looked toward the room where she'd had her trunks stored. Without giving herself time to think, she crossed the landing and opened the door.

Here there was no bedstead, no dresser, no armoire, only three trunks, a small upholstered chair, and an easel set up beside the window.

She went to the largest trunk and flipped the catch. Slowly, she pushed the trunk lid up and back, letting it rest against the wall. The trunk was not as beautifully packed as when she'd left St. Petersburg. She'd not packed it then, leaving her pigment powders and brushes to be stored away by the apprentice she'd hired.

Peter, that was his name. How odd she could recall him so clearly, as if he were standing here now. He'd only been with her for a matter of months, and rarely in her company. She'd relied upon him to prepare the canvases for paint, to blend some of the pigments in the proportions she'd requested. He was responsible for building the canvases as well, in the size she required for the next commission.

When she'd left Edinburgh, she'd not packed as carefully as Peter, but she'd been careful with her brushes. Her sable brushes, made in Italy, the mahogany handles bearing her initials in gold, were individually wrapped in leather and lay side by side, graduated by size. The special fan brush, so very necessary in creating lace, was wrapped with gauze so as to not damage the shape of the bristles.

Now she simply yearned to hold a brush again, to stand in the same position as she'd once stood easily for hours.

For those moments in time she could feel the emotions of her subjects, experience their joy or their sorrow and somehow use those feelings to translate their form, their substance to canvas. Sometimes, when the painting was complete, she felt as if it were more tangible than the human being in front of her. She knew that for as long as this painting existed, a moment had been captured. Perhaps if she had been very fortunate, and very skilled, the image could evoke emotion. What more could a painting be?

Her subjects had always complained about the silence she imposed during a sitting, of the sheer boredom of sitting or standing for hours. Not once had anyone asked if she were tired, if she were bored, if her back pained her from her pose or if her arm was stiff from holding the brush.

When it was done, when they all relaxed or stretched indolently, not one of them had ever asked her if she wanted to sit, if she wished tea, if she felt as drained as they.

With every painting, she gained little more insight, a little more experience. But with every painting she felt as if part of herself were left on the canvas. A confession she'd never made to another living soul, save Peter. He'd only looked at her with wide brown eyes and nodded, and she couldn't help but wonder if he were a painter as well, and not simply an apprentice to one.

She'd never asked.

Instead, she'd been focused on herself in those days, enamored with her own status as painter to the Imperial Court of Russia. She'd been so enmeshed in her work, and so thrilled with her own stature, she'd probably treated people around her with the same disdain the Russians treated everyone not in their circle.

Perhaps she should have been as temperamental as the Russians, but she'd never known any circumstance deserving of such excess of emotion. A ruined gown was an expense, not a tragedy. A burned curl, a badly laundered chemise, both of these could be supreme annoyances, but not cause to shriek at a maid.

She preferred a more balanced approach to life, a less emotional outlook.

That was before. Now? She wasn't certain exactly how she would react to any circumstance. In a way, she was still learning herself, the woman and not the painter.

She went to another trunk and opened it as well. From it she withdrew two of her most utilitarian brushes, before closing the trunk and moving to the opposite side of the room.

When she'd left Edinburgh, she'd destroyed those paintings she'd been trying to finish. The work had been abysmal, sloppy, and unworthy of her. But she'd taken the prepared canvases on the off chance that one day she'd be able to paint again. Now she retrieved her easel and placed a small canvas on it.

The canvas was dry, pristine, and naked, awaiting the first tentative touches. Sometimes, she sketched in the scene, particularly if it was a difficult composition. She liked the feel of charcoal in her hands, smudging her fingers. Perhaps the weightlessness of the burned wood reminded her that even the idea of art was an ephemeral one.

The moment when her painting was first viewed by the world always seemed to her to be the same sensation a new mother would feel upon revealing her child. *I have created this. Not solely or completely, but this creation lived beneath my heart, and I brought it into the world in suffering and in joy.*

When a portrait was finished, she often stood on the other side of the room and watched as a subject viewed his likeness for the very first time. Her attention was not on her work but on the face of the person she'd painted. She wanted to see that first spark of recognition, that look of surprised delight or perhaps even awe.

Would God now show pity on her and grant her the talent she needed? Could she push herself out of the way enough to allow the talent to show through? Could she banish her fear, summon her courage to the degree she could devote herself entirely to the task at hand?

If so, she would succeed. If she could not, then even the effort of painting would be a disaster.

Wasn't that what had happened to her since Russia? The person had occupied too much of her mind. Margaret had become fully fleshed, no longer a painter but a woman, wounded, hurt, and afraid.

There was no pigment on the brush, but her fingers knew how to hold it regardless. Her mind could almost see the portrait she needed to paint.

She stretched out her arm, touching the tip of the brush to the prepared canvas. She was trembling so badly the end of the brush was shaking. Still, she held her pose, biting her lip to fight back the emotion.

Every day, every week, every month since Russia, it had been the same.

If, for some reason, she could never paint again, she'd have to come to terms with that fact. Some people lost their sight, others their hearing. Then there were those true unfortunates who became bedridden and ill. She was none of those things. She had seen and done what most people could only dream about accomplishing in their lives.

Why, then, did she feel as if her very heart had been carved out of her chest? Ever since she'd been given her first canvas, she'd only come alive when she was standing right here in this position. Her soul was engaged, soaring so far above her that the feeling was magical.

When her talent had left her, when the ability to paint had disappeared, a portion of her soul had shriveled and turned black like charcoal.

A tear slipped from her eye, and she angrily flicked it away. She tossed the brush into the tray in front of the easel, treating her brush roughly, something she'd never before done, and left the room, pulling the door shut firmly.

*   *   *

The journey to Inverness took two endless hours. Bundled up in his greatcoat as he was, Robert didn't feel the worst of the weather, but there was nothing he could do about the sheer tedium of the journey.

He occupied himself with memorizing all those retorts he would deliver to Miss Dalrousie on the occasion of their next meeting. First of all, he would ask her why she practiced her shooting with such assiduousness. Secondly, he would ensure she understood what the word *trespass* meant. She was not welcome at Glengarrow. Let her walk somewhere else.

It had snowed earlier in the day. The air was cold, but the sheer volume of Inverness's people and traffic warmed it.

Inverness was a city with a rhythm to it, sometimes frenetic, but never placid. He'd always liked the city for its modernity, for the feeling that as Inverness went, so went Scotland. He enjoyed the bustle of it, the politics. Enjoyed, too, being in the middle of it.

When he was a boy, and there was a fight, he'd wanted to be one of the two participants and not simply an observer. It there was a debate, he'd argue his place to the death. To him, life had always been a giant tug-of-war. He on one side, and whoever he aligned himself against on the other.

Sometimes he won, and sometimes he lost, but the outcome was never as important as the fact he'd engaged in the battle.

When had he lost his passion? And could he ever regain it?

Once at his mother's home, he allowed the majordomo to remove his greatcoat, take his hat and gloves, and guide him to the sunny parlor where his mother took afternoon callers.

The house in Inverness was not as grand as the one in Edinburgh or the town house in London, but it served his mother's needs well. She flitted back and forth among the three of them like a social butterfly, more than willing to be the Dowager Countess of Linnet, hostess extraordinaire, gossip, matchmaker, and social doyenne, renowned for her ability to dictate fashion and spend money.

Now, as he waited for her, he eyed the parlor with the practiced eye of a man who'd spent the last few days poring over endless bills from shopkeepers. The porcelain statue on the corner credenza was from Italy. He'd seen the bill for it, and had approved payment for the new carpet beneath his feet purchased in London.

"My dearest Robert," Lauren McDermott said, sweeping into the room.

Her figure had become a little fuller in the last decade, and her face bore some additional lines. But other than that, and the occasional gray hair, she looked remarkably young. Too young to be his mother, of course, a remark he'd made four years ago. She'd laughed gaily, hugged him swiftly, and planted a kiss on both of his cheeks. "Now I know why you were a natural to go into politics, my dearest son. You've a touch of the Irish in your speech."

Today she was dressed simply—for her—in a dress reminding him of the bilious-colored drapes in Glengarrow's ballroom—mainly red, but with a touch of blue. An enormous ruby pin glittered at her throat, the jewels repeated in her earrings. He wondered if they were new, and where the bill was.

"Mother," he said cautiously.

She rushed forward and gripped him in a hug so tight it was almost painful. She was a foot shorter than he, and he bent down to hold her close.

"Oh my dearest Robert. You look so very tired."

And what did he say to that? He was tired, but it wasn't the kind of fatigue sleep could cure. He was tired in his soul, and he hadn't a clue how to fix it.

His mother embraced life, seemed to shake it and demand it disgorge its contents as if life were no more than a burlap sack holding an assortment of valuables.

Other than his father's death, however, his mother had had no challenges, nothing to dampen her eternal and youthful optimism.

He always felt so much older in her presence, which was, no doubt, the reason he avoided it when he could. Occasionally, he couldn't help but wonder if that was the singular reason his brother and sister had found homes away from Scotland.

Placing both palms on either side of his face, she pulled his head down so that she could stare into his eyes. She assessed quietly, and no doubt so adequately that any prevarication was useless.

"Has it been so very awful?"

"Yes," he answered simply.

She closed her eyes, took a deep breath and for a moment didn't speak. When she did, it was not to address Amelia and Penelope's loss, but a complaint he might have heard at any time in his life.

"You have not been sleeping well," she said sternly.

She was correct, but agreeing to her diagnosis wouldn't solve the dilemma of his sleeplessness.

"And you have been spending too much money."

She looked at him with narrowed eyes, but sat on the sofa facing him, and waved to an adjoining chair. He remained standing in front of the fireplace.

"Is that why you've come? To berate me for my spending? To upbraid me for my audacity? Dearest Robert, I simply don't care if I've angered you. It got you out of France, which was my aim."

He frowned at her, an expression that just made her smile grow brighter.

"You didn't answer my letters, dearest, and you wouldn't have taken kindly to my arriving in France to kidnap you and bring you home. What else was I to do? I knew coming back to Glengarrow would be difficult. Has it been?"

"It's just a house, Mother. Nothing more."

Thankfully, his mother didn't call him on that statement. She only slanted an intense look in his direction and swallowed whatever comment she was about to make in favor of a motherly smile.

Memories happened anywhere. They simply were, a part of him so real and so deep they might be his skin or his heart or his soul. He didn't need to be somewhere in particular to hear Amelia's voice, or the soft, lilting laughter of his daughter.

"I gave instructions to my solicitor to pay all necessary bills," Robert said. "There was no reason to return."

"Except you're a Scot, and the Earl of Linnet." She frowned at him. "Your solicitor has been an old and dear friend for years. He knows how desperately I worried for you. It was time you came home. Time to face life again. I told him to stop paying everything."

Right at the moment, Robert felt as if he were in the middle of a play, the sole performer in a huge amphitheater, the patrons of which expected a tale of tragedy and pathos.

He wasn't about to be an object of pity.

"There was no need to allow Glengarrow to fall into rack or ruin."

She shook her head. "Is Glengarrow truly so damaged? Tom would never allow it."

"We're fortunate Tom is still with us since he went unpaid for a year."

A shadow flitted over her face. "Oh dear, that was not well-done of me," she admitted. "May I claim ignorance on that part, at least? But I knew you would never come home for less than Glengarrow. Never mind there are people starving in the Highlands. Never mind a man can purchase a farm in Canada for what he pays in rent here. Never mind you have ignored your birthright for three years."

He was so startled by the attack he couldn't think for a moment.

"What do I have to do with starving Highland-ers, Mother?" he finally said, "Or the fact a man can choose to emigrate to Canada?"

"Nothing," she said triumphantly. "Absolutely nothing, Robert. And you should. We're losing our countrymen, Robert, every day. By death or departure. We need men like you in Parliament again. Men who could at least vocalize what's happening."

"And you made sure I came back to Scotland for that?"

She made a face. "Dear heavens, no. But as long as you're here, you might as well find a purpose for your life." She frowned at him. "Or are you going to tell me you've found one? I daresay you're flail-ing, Robert, but you needn't."

"Since when have you become political, Mother?"

"Since you spent three years in France. With very *infrequent* letters, I might add." She frowned at him again. "And never answering mine."

"I have enough to do at Glengarrow."

"Nonsense," she said. "You have nothing but ghosts there. No friends, no acquaintances. No neighbors."

"I have a neighbor," he said, unwilling to con-tinue with the subject of his future. "A very annoy-ing neighbor."

At her sudden look of interest, he realized he should have remained silent.

"Who?"

"A woman by the name of Margaret Dalrousie."

To his utter amazement, his mother looked delighted.

"Do you know her?"

"Of course I know her, Robert. Anyone with an interest in art knows Margaret Dalrousie."

He removed his foot from the fireplace fender and turned and stared at his mother. "Who is she?"

"A very famous painter, of course. She spent some years with the Russians, I understand. A court darling, evidently. But you say she's back in Scotland? I suspect a mystery there. Does she appear brokenhearted? Perhaps she fell in love with a prince."

His mother looked entirely too happy about the prospect of unrequited love.

"I haven't the slightest idea if she's broken-hearted. Nor do I have any interest in her romantic entanglements."

She sighed. "What a pity. Her paintings are phenomenal. I, myself, am enamored of more than one." Her mouth twisted into a moue of discontent. "I should have had her paint my portrait. The cost alone would have summoned you from France." She looked up at him. "She's been exhibited in Edinburgh, at the Royal Society of the Arts, you know."

"No," he said "I didn't know."

"I can invite two or three members of the Society for dinner if you like. I'm certain they have additional information about Miss Dalrousie. But surely you do as well, Robert, being such a close neighbor of hers."

"I can assure you, Mother, I know nothing about Margaret Dalrousie." *Save for the fact she is an irritating woman.*

"Her portraits are beautiful. I understand she's an attractive woman herself." Was it his imagination, or was his mother eyeing him speculatively?

"Your information is incorrect. The Dalrousie woman is not the least attractive." Which was a bit of a prevarication, perhaps. "Her mouth is entirely too large." That, certainly was *not* a falsehood.

His mother didn't say anything in response. She had a habit of remaining silent and allowing him to trip himself in his own words. He'd learned the tactic at a very young age and used it with some success on his political opponents.

"I shall have to arrange a visit to Glengarrow, Robert, if only for the chance of meeting her. She has a way with fabrics. I've wanted to reach out and touch a painting, so perfectly did she depict the silk of a dress. I know that more than once I've had to peer very closely to see if those weren't real pearls on the painting. She's a very talented woman, Robert."

"I don't care about Margaret Dalrousie, Mother. I find I don't care about very many things."

There was the look again.

"Why did you sell the cottage?" he asked abruptly.

She looked startled at the question.

"Why?" she asked. "There was no reason not to, was there? I was not under the impression you had some sort of attachment to the place."

"It was part of Glengarrow."

"Glengarrow is not entailed, Robert," she said. "But you know that quite well. Are you simply annoyed that Miss Dalrousie has moved so close? The offer I got for the cottage was quite generous."

He decided that he didn't want to discuss the cottage any more than he did Amelia, or grieving, or Margaret Dalrousie, for that matter. He wanted to be left alone, and in France he'd had his privacy. He had a feeling Scotland was going to pull him inexorably back into life, and he wasn't certain he was ready.

Was he expected to feel charitable about his fellowman? He didn't want to care about his starving countrymen, or about those who emigrated, or even mundane matters such as the state of Glengarrow's roof.

How did he possibly explain that to his mother? Lauren McDermott was a great believer in getting on with life. Barely a year after his father had died, she'd begun attending dinners and other entertainments with a series of men. She no doubt thought that the same behavior would benefit him.

"I truly wish you had an opportunity to see some of her work, Robert. Perhaps you would have more charity for your neighbor if you knew how tremendously blessed in talent she is. I understand artistic types are not easy to live with."

He didn't want to live with her—he wanted to coexist in a neighborly fashion, distant but polite. Beyond that, he wanted nothing to do with Margaret Dalrousie.

The majordomo appeared in the doorway, and Robert nodded at him before the man could intone a summons to lunch. He bent down to the sofa and offered his arm, and even though his mother shook her head at him, she took it nonetheless. As they walked into the dining room, Robert couldn't dispel the feeling his mother wasn't done with Miss Dalrousie. Or meddling in his life, for that matter.

Chapter 7

"You might as well come inside, Miss Margaret," Janet said, peering from the door. "Otherwise, I'll be treating you for the next month for a cold in your chest. The Scottish winter is not to be taken lightly." She fixed a stern look on Margaret, but there was a twinkle in her eyes.

It had been so long since anyone had cared for her that Margaret was momentarily speechless. Nevertheless, she felt a spurt of warmth for the older woman. Perhaps if her mother had not had so many children, and been so tired when Margaret was born, she might have been the same.

Why was it women who were nurturing didn't have children while women who thought children a nuisance bore too many? One of a series of questions she could never ask anyone.

"I'll be fine," she protested, but the words sounded unconvincing even to her own ears. In actuality, she felt a little guilty roaming through the grounds of Glengarrow and a little ashamed at being caught. Since the earl had been in Inverness for over a week, she felt free to walk where she wanted, and she didn't lose the opportunity to do just that. Never mind that her conscience troubled her even so.

"We've a pot brewing for tea," Janet said, holding the door open. "Come on, then."

Margaret shrugged and allowed Janet to lead her into the kitchen.

She unwrapped the scarf from around her neck and unbuttoned her cape with fingers that felt frozen beneath her leather gloves. She made a mental note to purchase some heavier ones as soon as practical. Perhaps some with fur inside, if she could afford those.

She'd simply have to resign herself to the fact that every single one of her purchases would have to be accompanied by a great deal of thought beforehand. There would be none of the extravagant, impromptu purchases she'd once made in Russia.

That time was gone, three years of being cosseted and privileged. Three years of choosing whom she wanted to paint among the leaders of Russian society. She spoke to those who entertained her, and attended events she wished or didn't, according to her whim.

Margaret stared at Janet as a memory occurred to her. Of course, how could she have forgotten? She'd seen the Earl of Linnet at a ball given in honor of the British Ambassador. And his wife? Margaret strained to remember, but couldn't recall a woman with him. He'd been standing by himself, slightly apart from the rest of the crowd, a handsome man with his face lit, surprisingly enough, by laughter. He'd not been so dour then, but that was before he'd lost his wife and child.

Had she spoken to him? Or had she avoided the British delegation on purpose as she so often did with visitors? Their questions about the nature of her stay in Russia were intrusive. Her career dictated the length of her visit, a fact none of the men were able to understand.

"Is the Earl of Linnet in the diplomatic service?" she asked Janet now.

To her surprise, Janet shook her head. "Oh no, Miss Margaret, he was with the House of Lords. That's Parliament, in London. A very great honor it was. But, get out of your wet things, and I'll put them near the stove to warm. Why would you be walking about on a day like this?" Janet asked, her face twisted into a knot of wrinkles. "I think you should find something a bit more healthy," Janet said. "I can teach you to crochet. I've noticed at night you act as though you don't know what to do with your fingers. A crochet hook, that's the trick. Or knitting. My grandma would always sit there in the corner and knit until the day she died."

"I have my embroidery," Margaret said, hoping Janet wouldn't comment on the ineptitude of her work.

All Janet did was nod, however, tactful in her silence.

The warmth from the stove was a singularly wonderful sensation. Margaret moved to stand as close as her full skirts would allow, smiling at the two maids as she did so. The radiant heat felt warmer than standing before a fire, although that would not be amiss either. Perhaps she had been out in the weather too long.

Winter in Scotland was colder, more bone-chilling. Or perhaps it was simply that when she lived in Russia, she'd been whisked from salon to palace to troika so quickly she really didn't have time to become chilled.

There was also the fact of her wardrobe. All she'd been able to afford was this thin wool cape. She'd been able to sell fifteen of her dresses, but she'd had to leave most of her wardrobe—over thirty dresses—hanging in her Russian apartment.

"I'll fix you something to eat, Miss Margaret. It's near lunchtime anyway. If you don't mind sharing what we're having."

She looked at the maids, at the scarred kitchen table, then over at Janet.

"I would be very pleased to share your lunch," she said, smiling. "Is there something I can do to help?"

The two maids looked surprised at the offer, but Janet only smiled. "No. There's a fire in the family parlor, Miss Margaret. Come along with you."

Since she'd been curious about Glengarrow from the moment she'd seen the house, Margaret didn't hesitate. She followed Janet down a long hallway, past the servants' stairs, to a carved white door with a brass handle.

Janet reached out with her left hand and pulled the handle inward.

"This is Glengarrow," she said softly, almost as if she were introducing the house to Margaret. She stepped to the left and allowed Margaret to precede her.

Here the wainscoting changed from painted white to polished mahogany. The smell of beeswax was in the air, as well as a strange acrid odor emanating from the oil lamps.

She walked a dozen more feet and found herself in a large open area.

The foyer was tiled in golden brown and white squares. Soaring high above her was a domed roof, a sight she'd not expected to see. Snow accumulated in spots, creating a lacy pattern of sunlight filtering down through the three floors of Glengarrow.

The staircase curved like the shell of a snail winding upward gracefully. The banister was wide polished mahogany. Each of the balusters was turned wood, adorned with a shiny band of gold at both the bottom and top. The treads of the stairs were carpeted with a crimson runner, caught at the base of each stair with gold clips.

To her right was an open doorway and after a questioning look at Janet, she entered the room.

A wood fire blazed profligately in the fireplace on the far wall, offering comfort to anyone who passed by or came to sit for a while. The pale yellow curtains were open, allowing sunlight to stream into the room. Outside, the cold day with its snow and ice seemed so very far away, the only hint of the difference in temperature the fog at the bottom of the windowpanes.

Two overstuffed divans sat facing each other

perpendicular to the fireplace. On the other side of the room, in front of the window, sat two large straight-backed armchairs and a footstool, evidently designed to be shared by the occupants of the chairs. All of the furniture was upholstered in the same fabric, a small blue-and-yellow-flowered pattern. The walls were covered in a soft yellow silk matching the draperies. The arms of the divans and the chairs were heavily carved mahogany, as was the table between the chairs and in front of the divans. All of the wood was so brightly polished, Margaret didn't doubt she could see her reflection in it.

If the rest of Glengarrow was like this room, then Janet and her helpers had been extraordinarily busy.

"It's lovely," she said, meaning it. It was a family room, a room where a couple and their children might gather in the evening, where they might sit and discuss their day. A mother would encourage her child to sit beside her while she read him a story. This was a room crafted for laughter and joy, for the small daily matter of living.

Obvious, too, was the wealth of the Earls of Linnet, evident in the French silk on the walls, and the quality of the furniture. There was nothing threadbare in this room, and there were other touches indicating wealth, such as the coat of arms inscribed on the brass fireplace tools, and the golden frames for the miniatures on the mantel. Nothing was ostentatious or out of place, but everything in the room revealed the extent of Robert McDermott's financial security.

She walked closer to the coat of arms mounted in a frame near the fireplace.

"McDermott? That's the family name?"

"Aye," Janet said. "A proud name it is. There's been a McDermott at Glengarrow since the place was built."

She, herself, had no such antecedents. She doubted her family could trace their heritage back more than a generation or two. The poor didn't care about the past. They lived in the day, in the *now*, and sometimes—barely—in the future. Where was the next meal to come from, or the money to pay the rent?

She'd been wealthy beyond her wildest dreams, and near destitution. All in all, she'd had more enjoyment from wealth, from the sheer freedom from fear, an experience allowing her to concentrate on her work.

Because of some anonymous benefactor, she had the freedom to paint again, only she couldn't. What was that? Irony? Or the simple humor of malicious Fate?

"Take a chair by the fire, Miss Margaret. Lunch will be ready soon."

She turned and looked around the room, almost afraid to choose a place to sit. This room was so different from her, from her life. Did it reflect the Earl of Linnet? Or had it been a creation of his wife?

"Are you certain the earl won't mind?"

"He's a generous soul," Janet said, but then she didn't know the earl had accused Margaret of trespassing.

Margaret chose the end of one sofa, half-turning toward the fire.

Why had he gone to Inverness? And was he going to be gone for weeks at a time often? If so, she needn't worry about where her walks took her. After all, she couldn't be trespassing if he weren't here to see her.

As if she'd heard the unspoken question, Janet said, "He's gone to visit his mother. It'll be the first time he's seen her since she went to France after the accident."

A shadow flitted over her face, the sudden expression of sadness so profound Margaret knew she was thinking of the earl's wife and child.

"There was no grandmother like that woman. She bought the child everything and came to visit her every few weeks, just to make sure, she said, that Penelope was healthy and happy. As if the earl would ever let her be anything else."

She sighed heavily, seemed to lose herself in thought, then stared at Margaret. "Listen to me, going on and on when there's lunch to make."

A scream erupted, and the two of them looked at each other, then raced back down the hall and to the kitchen. Flames were shooting out from the top of each of the cast-iron burners.

"What did you do, you foolish girl?" Janet screamed, rushing to the front of the stove.

"I just added a little more wood!" one of the maids said, staring at the flames. The other girl was backed up against the door, both fists pressed to her mouth. The walls were scorched; the flames looked as if they were racing up to the ceiling.

"There was enough wood in the stove," Janet said angrily.

She reached into the flames, at least that was what it looked like to Margaret, and pulled the kettle from the back burner. Shooting an angry look at the younger girl, Janet poured the water from the kettle onto the top of the stove at the same time she reached in and closed the lid on the largest of the burners. Steam hissed, rising high above the surface of the stove.

Janet turned and handed the kettle to the older girl, who filled it again from the spigot at the sink.

The fire was soon out, the crisis averted, but the young maid would not stop crying. At first, Janet addressed her sternly, and when her commands could not halt the girl's tears, she looked at Margaret, rolled her eyes, and enfolded the girl in a motherly hug. All the while, she patted the girl on the back, and murmured, "It'll be all right, Helen. It's all right, girl."

Helen, however, refused to be comforted, and wept against Janet's shoulder. She grabbed her apron and pressed it against her face, the cloth not muting the girl's tears as much as enhancing the sound of her sobs.

"Will you be all right on your own for a bit, Miss Margaret?" Janet asked, talking around the girl's head. "I'll just go and settle her down a bit."

"Of course," Margaret said. "And, please, you don't have to worry about lunch."

Janet would have enough trouble trying to get the stove dried out and lit again without having to worry about fixing a meal.

The older woman smiled in gratitude and turned and led both girls to the servants' stairs.

She really should leave now. There was nothing to keep her here. Nothing but curiosity and a little temptation. Would there be anything wrong with just taking another look at the interior of Glengarrow? In a strange way, she felt as if she'd been Glengarrow's custodian all these months. True, Tom came and checked on the house every day, to ensure the roof was sound, and there were no openings around the doors or windows to allow the cold or the rain to seep inside. Janet, too, came through once a week, and did a light bit of cleaning.

Glengarrow wasn't hers, and she'd no right to remain here. Yet she walked down the hall again to the door, opening it slowly, grateful the hinges had recently been oiled and were silent.

There was no sound from the third floor, no noise anywhere in the large house. Glengarrow felt as if it needed to come alive, as if it were waiting, somehow.

Slowly, she rounded the stairs, placing her hand on the banister as she looked upward. There was nothing to gain by going to the second floor unless it was to satisfy her errant curiosity. What right did she have, however, to breach the earl's privacy? Not only would she gain his enmity, but Janet's as well.

Despite those very fine reasons for prudence, Margaret took one step, then another, arguing with herself as she ascended the staircase. It felt as if Glengarrow was calling her, summoning her deeper into the house. A bit of nonsense, really. She did not believe in such things as ghosts or spirits or houses that magically became sentient. At the second-floor landing, however, wonder overcame her conscience.

Two corridors branched out from the landing, both of them wide and graced with crimson carpet lined with a design of green and gold. At the top, the wainscoting was heavily carved, as were the doors leading off the hall. But what was truly magnificent was the sight of the chandeliers hanging twenty feet apart from the landing to the end of each of the corridors. Of crystal and gold, they sparkled even in the muted light. She could only imagine the sight in the evening, when they were lit.

At the end of the corridor was a set of double doors. The earl's suite? No doubt. None of her concern, truly. There was no reason for her to wander there. Instead, she opened the first door on her right.

The draperies were closed, the room shrouded, but she could see the richness of the carpet on the wood floor, and the pale rose of the counterpane. Someone moved in the shadows, and she started, only to realize a second later that it was a mirror mounted on the far wall, and the person she saw was her own reflection.

She closed the door and turned toward the staircase.

What was she doing?

She needed to return to the cottage before she was found. She needed to leave Glengarrow before Janet returned to the kitchen. She simply needed to go home.

She took a step toward the stairs and hesitated, glancing over her shoulder at the end of the corridor. Even as she turned toward the double doors, her conscience shuddered in protest. Curiosity was one thing, but this was intrusion.

Slowly, as if to give herself time to reconsider, she began to walk toward the earl's suite. In front of the double doors, she hesitated. What excuse could she give if she were found? What words could possibly explain her actions? There were none, but she still turned the handle of the door on the right, pushed it inward, and closed it behind her.

She half expected the room to be draped in spiderwebs, the furniture coated with dust. Instead, everything was pristine, as if the maids had just been there. Of course it would look this way—Janet would see to it.

The room was stunning, decorated in cream and gold. To her immediate left was a bed covered in a pale ivory satin coverlet The massive mahogany four-poster was heavily carved in a pattern of thistles and roses and evidently dated back generations.

Immediately opposite the bed on the other side of the room was a vanity adorned with crystal flacons. To the left of the vanity was a large window with a pillow-strewn cushion below it. A door to the right led to an anteroom, one that looked as if it served as a bathing chamber. Across the small hall was the lavatory. On the far side of the room was another door, and this one led to an intimate, sunny parlor.

Margaret turned back to the bedchamber. She could almost imagine a woman standing there, looking like a princess, dressed in something white with touches of gold. She'd have the appearance of an angel, a beauty. Her eyes would be luminescent and her smile infinitely charming. The Countess of Linnet could be no less.

All the drapes had been left open, sunlight streaming through the windows, coloring the space too brightly for a gray and somber winter's day. Or did the light emanate from an otherworldly source? Heaven? Was the Countess of Linnet an angel, then, visiting her earthly home? Did she grieve for her husband still? Or for those pleasures hers in life? Or did the soul, once transformed by death, have no such yearnings? Did the departed only think and dream of a higher purpose? Did the Countess of Linnet want to bestow peace upon living? Or was she here to wipe memories clean, or ease her husband's grief?

If she had been an angel—had she attained that lofty goal—Margaret doubted that she would have been as ethereal. Instead, she would probably have been angry.

She hesitated in the middle of the room, so quiet that the beat of her heart was the only sound. If the Countess of Linnet was an angry, vengeful ghost, there was no trace of her here.

Margaret didn't belong here. She was so much a trespasser her own conscience started screaming at her. Go, it yelled. And her feet wanted to obey, they truly did.

She crossed the room to the countess's vanity. Approaching it slowly, she stretched out her hand and allowed her fingers to trail over the cut crystal flacons of perfume.

"You were French, weren't you? I know France quite well, you see."

Silence answered her. With trembling fingers, Margaret picked up a bottle of perfume, removing the stopper. Immediately, lilies and roses filled the air. What a glorious scent.

"He loved you very much, didn't he?"

She really shouldn't be so close to tears. There was nothing in this room that was remotely hers or had any chance of belonging to her. This was not her sorrow or her grief, but it suddenly felt as if it was.

It was not right that the Countess of Linnet should be dead. It was not right there was such sorrow at Glengarrow as if the house itself waited in vain, believing its mistress would soon return home.

She turned, half-expecting the earl to be there. He would demand to know why she was here. No words could possibly explain, especially since she didn't understand her own curiosity.

She should leave him alone with his grief. She should never walk Glengarrow's paths again. Nor impinge upon his privacy.

But he wasn't there, thank God, so she didn't have to answer for her actions.

She walked toward the door, wishing she'd never seen the room, wishing, too, she wasn't suffused with shame and her own sorrow.

Margaret pulled open the door and found herself face-to-face with the Earl of Linnet.

Chapter 8

Not one word came to Margaret's mind. She could only stare at him, her eyes widening. Her breath came in fits and starts, and her blood felt like ice.

The Earl of Linnet was not so cursed with silence.

"It was not enough you had to trespass upon my property, Miss Dalrousie? Now you've invaded my home as well?"

She couldn't think of anything to say in her own defense. Everything he thought of her, she'd done. Yes, she'd invaded his privacy, in the worst way imaginable. Shame pierced her like the tip of a spear.

His face darkened, his expression leaving no doubt as to his feelings about her.

He entered the room, raising his hand and flattening it against her bodice, pressing against her. She had no choice but to stumble backward as he moved forward.

He was too close. She could feel the heat from his body beneath his greatcoat. Only inches separated them. He bent his head, just a little, so close she could feel his heated breath.

"I thought you were a ghost, Miss Dalrousie," he said softly. "I heard you speak, and for a second I thought Glengarrow haunted."

"I'm sorry," she breathed.

"You're sorry?" He straightened, and smiled down at her. A strange smile, with a touch of madness to it, perhaps. "Of course you're sorry, Miss Dalrousie. You were caught."

"I'm sorry," she said again, raising her hand and lifting his from her chest. She pushed against him, but he didn't move, as fixed as a mountain.

"I'm sorry, too, Miss Dalrousie. Sorry you weren't a ghost. But you're not, are you? You're not my wife. You're simply an intrusive woman with no sense of decency."

He frightened her. But the fear was mixed with her own shame, and it had less impact on her than it might have if she'd felt virtuous and innocent.

Dear God, she'd never be innocent again.

He put his hand on her shoulder and then her arm, and before she realized it, before she knew what he was about to do, he'd grabbed her hand and began pulling her with him, uncaring if she stumbled as she followed him across the room.

"You want to see all of it, Miss Dalrousie? Have you tried on my wife's clothes?"

Barely an inch separated them. The pain in his eyes had burned away, and in its place was a stark and fiery rage.

Two armoires sat side by side, exactly the same. He pulled her to the one on the right and opened it. Only three dresses remained, but the scent wafting out was a combination of cedar and the perfume she'd smelled earlier.

"She packed most of her dresses for our trip to France. What a pity that more weren't left behind. You might have had a greater selection."

She knew better than to speak.

He jerked one free and tossed it at her with one hand. She didn't try to catch it with her free hand, simply let it slip to the floor.

"You don't want to try it on, Miss Dalrousie? To see if it flatters you more than Amelia?"

At her silence, he smiled. "It wouldn't have. You're too tall."

He pulled her back to the bed.

"This is the room I shared with my wife, Miss Dalrousie."

He dropped her arm abruptly, and strode to the vanity. With unerring precision, he returned the bottle of perfume she'd opened to its rightful spot and turned to face her.

"This wasn't your place," he said softly. "Not your ghosts to disturb." He took a step toward her, and this time, she cringed.

But he only grabbed her hand again, and pulled her from the room, down the corridor, opening all the doors along the way. He intoned the names of the rooms to her as he went.

"Stop, please," she said, when he reached the last door. "I'm sorry. I know it was wrong."

He turned to her. "And yet, you did it anyway. How very fortunate you are, Miss Dalrousie, not to be subject to any limitations. Are you the Queen? God in female form? What makes you so very special?"

"Forgive me." Nothing else seemed right to say. She couldn't justify her actions. There was nothing that made sense.

He looked at her as if he'd like to throw her down the staircase, but instead, he pulled her with him down the steps, reaching the bottom and waiting only a second for her to regain her footing. He turned left, in a direction she'd not gone, down a shadowed corridor.

"Here's my library," he said, opening the door to another room. "You'll note all the books. I've read them myself. Most are treatises on politics, you will find, or books on strategy. I have a great collection of guns as well. But I'm not in the mind to show them to you right now, Miss Dalrousie. I'm very much afraid I might use one on you."

The next room was a greenhouse of sorts, and he commented on the plants as he led her in a circular pattern through the conservatory and back out again. She recalled the dizzying blur of green and yellowish plants, none of which she recognized.

"My wife was a great gardener, you see."

One door after another was opened and revealed, with comments on each. She didn't know whether to be entranced by Glengarrow or appalled at her own behavior and his growing rage, evident from the punishing grip on her hand, and the glittering hate-filled look in his eyes.

Fear made her cold and light-headed, almost as if she were floating out of her body.

"Your Lordship!"

She glanced behind him to where Janet stood clutching an armful of sheets fresh from the airing line belowstairs.

"Miss Margaret? I thought you had gone on home."

"No, Janet, Miss Dalrousie wanted to see a bit more of Glengarrow. I've been showing her the house. Go along now, we won't be long." He smiled, but the expression had a feral look to it.

Janet nodded, but she glanced back several times as she walked down the hall.

Margaret wanted to call Janet back, but one glance from the earl was enough to render her silent.

He was enraged, and rightfully so, and her fear was growing in relation to his anger. A cavern opened up in the middle of her stomach, filled with ice and shivers. Her heart, the steadiest of organs, grew heavy and ponderous until it felt like a stone in her chest.

She took a step backward and realized she'd backed up to a wall.

"Are you afraid, Miss Dalrousie?" he asked, almost pleasantly.

"Yes," she said softly.

She closed her eyes, unable to look at his face, unwilling to let him know how terrified she was.

"Are you very afraid?"

"Yes."

"I doubt your fear can equal the depth of my anger, Miss Dalrousie."

"I'm sorry," she said again, knowing the words would probably only inflame him further. She crossed her arms over her chest and pressed her fingers against her mouth, not unlike the hapless maid who'd been terrified at the sight of the stove fire.

"Don't hurt me." The words were uttered in a voice she barely recognized as her own. "Please," she said, then wanted to recall the word the minute it was spoken. If he wanted to strike her, then let him do so. She would endure it.

In the silence, and in the darkness behind her closed lids, she was safe. As long as she didn't have to witness his rage, she could compose herself. She took a deep breath, forcing herself to calm. She'd borne so much more than this. Her trembling was gradually fading. In a moment, she would be strong enough to face him.

When she finally opened her eyes, she was alone.

Robert stood over his desk, arms braced, elbows locked, and his hands flat on the mahogany surface. Staring down at the blotter, he could only see the Dalrousie woman's face, her white, pinched features, and her green eyes wide and filled with fear.

She'd been terrified, and he'd been the one to terrify her. The fact that anyone had invaded his privacy infuriated him, so much so that he hadn't been sane for those few moments. In some far-off corner of his mind, he'd been appalled at his own behavior.

But she'd entered Amelia's room. She'd violated Amelia's privacy.

He stood and walked away from his desk to stand in front of the fire. Absently, he held his hands out as if to warm himself. He doubted he would rid himself of the cold filling his body so easily.

She had no right. She had no right to enter Amelia's room, to sample her scent, to look on those belongings that had been his wife's. Had she sat on the bed, testing the mattress's resiliency?

Stiff-legged, Robert walked up the back stairs and into his suite, to find he'd left the door ajar. Solemnly, he pushed it open all the way and entered the room again.

Slowly, he bent and picked up the dress he'd tossed to the floor, returning it to the armoire. Placing both hands on the doors, he closed his eyes for a moment. In the two drawers below, he knew what he would find—four nightgowns, and in the very bottom drawer, the comfortable slippers Amelia liked to put beside the bed. Tattered and worn, they'd not been fine enough for the visit to her family.

He was surrounded by the scent of her perfume, something light and flowery—roses or lilies? He'd never been good at discerning flowers.

What had happened to the clothes she'd taken with her? He realized he didn't know, any more than he knew what had happened to Penelope's belongings. Or to Teresa, that silly little doll she carried everywhere. Where did Teresa go? Dear God, he didn't know.

He closed the doors, too hard perhaps, before turning and walking from the room.

The essence of Amelia was no longer in this chamber despite her perfume and her dresses. She was not at Glengarrow. Neither was she at her grave, a realization coming to him after hours of standing there and praying not so much to God as his wife.

No, Miss Dalrousie should not have trespassed,

but she had not invaded a sanctuary. Nor had she violated Amelia's privacy. Amelia was not there.

He shouldn't have terrified her. He should not have allowed rage to overwhelm him. *Please don't hurt me.* As he took the grand stairs back down to his office, he could see her face too easily. Terror had rooted her to the spot, the kind of terror that turns the limbs to jelly. And he'd done it to her.

Damnation!

At the moment, he wasn't certain exactly who he was angrier at—himself or Margaret Dalrousie.

Chapter 9

The trees were stripped of their leaves, the naked branches scratching and clawing at the sky. Nature had compensated for their starkness by gifting the trees with a mantle of sparkling ice, but after witnessing three years of Russian ice storms, Margaret was no longer awed by the sight of crystal stalactites glittering in the morning light.

The day was gray, the air even colder than the day before. If she were in Russia, she would have anticipated a blizzard by evening. But she was still too uncertain about Scotland's weather to gauge it with any certainty.

Tom and Janet had been gone when she awakened this morning. Every morning just past dawn they left for Glengarrow and every evening at five they returned to Blackthorne Cottage. Janet would go about making dinner, while Tom sat in the parlor and lit his pipe, staring at the fire and otherwise ruminating on his day. Margaret would join him, a book in hand, and together they would spend an hour or so in quiet companionship.

Occasionally, they spoke of commonsense things like weather or foxes or the colors of the sunset streaking across the sky. But they never spoke of anything more, certainly not her painting or her past. Nor did they ever mention, either one of them, the Earl of Linnet.

He might have been a ghost himself this last week. She never saw him riding or encountered him on her walks, for which she was eternally thankful.

Curiosity, however, forever a bane of her character, was surfacing again. Unwise though it might be, she couldn't help but wonder if he were ill or had taken himself off to Inverness again.

"Oh no, miss," Janet said when she finally broached the question. "I doubt the earl could stand a visit again this soon." She looked stricken at her own words and hurried to explain.

"It's just his mother can be a little trying," she said. "Always patting his cheek or straightening his coat. You can tell it annoys him even though he doesn't say anything."

She smiled. "Tom always said that he thought the Dowager Countess liked the earl the best of her three children."

"Did the two of you work together?"

Janet dusted off the corner of the table with her apron and looked at Margaret. "Oh no, Miss. Tom worked for the Dowager Countess. He was her coachman. I was in service to a dear friend of hers. That's how we met." She smiled. "And courted. The two women were great friends, always at one another's homes. It was nothing to see Tom five times a week. Then, when we married, I left my employer and came to work at Glengarrow with Tom."

If he wasn't in Inverness, then where was he? What could be occupying his time? She was surprised to find herself so curious about a man she barely knew. Perhaps it was because small gestures of kindness were sometimes the most memorable, and in his agreement to share Tom's and Janet's services, the Earl of Linnet had proved very amenable indeed.

She'd repaid him in the worst way possible.

"You'll be wrapping up snugly," Janet said now, glancing out at the falling snow highlighted against the darkening sky.

"I will. I won't be gone long," Margaret said. The days were short, and she'd been intrigued with a book she was reading. She had just enough time to walk down the lane and back again before full night was upon them.

She left the warm cottage with a wave and a smile.

This snowfall was gentle, covering up the signs of human visitation on the land. Footfalls, wagon tracks, horseshoe prints were blanketed like a light dusting of castor sugar.

Glengarrow and its environs felt as if it had been carved out of the rugged Highland scenery, lined with velvet and tucked into a small wooden box. Here they felt protected from the worst of the winter weather, shielded by the mountain towering behind them. Glengarrow was a burrow to hide in when the outside world became too much. Almost enchanted, if she believed in such things.

How very strange that she was a Scot, and yet she'd traveled more outside her country than within it. She'd never seen the Lowlands, and she'd never thought to live in the Highlands. Until she'd come to this place, she'd never truly felt like Scotland was home. Perhaps because she'd never truly belonged to anything other than her painting.

Over the last ten years, she'd become a person without a country, without relatives or close friends. And in the last nine months, she'd become even more insular, with nothing more substantial than these two walks a day to measure the passing of time.

While it was true that in Russia she'd often risen early in the morning to paint, she'd occasionally danced until dawn. She'd played as hard as she had worked. But she'd worked damnably hard, which is why she felt such betrayal when, one by one, the members of the royal family had turned their backs on her.

Penniless and emotionally drained, she'd returned to Edinburgh in order to solicit a commission or two. She hadn't realized, then, that she'd never be able to paint again. And so, she'd no choice but to come to Blackthorne Cottage, to live out the rest of her days, immersed in books she'd never had a chance to read, and the study of nature, in the hopes that one day, perhaps, she might be able to paint a tree, or a leaf, or a snow-encrusted landscape.

She was nothing without those she painted. She did not truly exist without a brush in her hand, which meant she had been barely alive lately.

Or perhaps she'd never be able to paint again. The more she had that thought, the less she was able to tolerate it.

She pushed thoughts of Russia and painting from her mind, determined to focus on one thing at a time. What mattered was the present moment. If she were too immersed in thoughts of the past, today would slip away entirely.

The only sound on her walk was the occasional crack of an icicle falling to the ground. Winter had encapsulated her in a frozen scene. Nothing moved, and the cries of the fox and the owl would be silent as the night chilled to bitter cold. Was the earl cozy in his snug house?

She'd never thought to wonder if he was lonely at night.

As she walked slowly past Glengarrow, she looked up at the windows, not yet lit against the darkness. She wished he was looking out from the window above. She would wave and smile politely, and the greeting would confuse him. Or perhaps he would simply close the draperies in her face, giving her fair warning his mood had not warmed toward her.

This walk with its double line of sentinel trees on either side of the lane was not as scenic as the one around Glengarrow. She missed the wall with its little niche and urn, and the bench where she might sit and reflect if she wished.

Her feet were cold; her nose was cold. The tips of her ears were cold beneath her hat. The Scots seemed to endure winter with no complaints at all, as if it were simply part of their lives and nothing important to be remarked upon. Sleet and ice? Why, this is the Highlands! What else would you expect?

She was going to walk all the way to the road, and once there, she'd turn around and walk all the way back. At least the Earl of Linnet could not say she was trespassing.

The gravel of the drive was barely visible through the snow. She began to count her steps, her arms wrapped around her waist below her cape. She spent a moment longing for all those warm, rich, fur-lined coats sold to pay her creditors.

She'd had offers from more than one titled gentleman to be installed in a home with an annual stipend, with a promise of a carriage and carte blanche whenever she wished to order clothing. Each and every one of these titled gentlemen had appeared remarkably surprised when she'd answered in the same manner to each invitation: "Why should I allow you to care for me, Your Lordship, when I can care very well for myself?"

What a proud, arrogant fool she'd been. But she'd never believed she would remain unpaid for her work, that her commissions would suddenly stop, or that each member of the Imperial Court would turn his back on her.

She'd barely survived those three months in Edinburgh when her talent had abruptly left her. She'd not been able to stand in front of a canvas, let alone put a brush to it without trembling.

Would her solicitor ever be able to get payment

for the last of her court paintings? Either that, or the paintings themselves returned. If not, she'd have to spend the rest of her life grateful to a stranger for the gift of Blackthorne Cottage.

Who was her benefactor? She'd spent hours speculating on the answer, only to narrow the possibilities down to three likely candidates, all titled, all men she'd met in Russia. Yet none of them were capable of being beneficent and anonymous. No, each would want credit for his good deed.

A twig snapped, and she stopped suddenly, a sensation that she was being watched sending a wave of cold rushing through her.

She forced herself to turn, to see the Earl of Linnet sitting there on his horse. For a long moment, they simply stared at each other.

If she could paint, she'd paint him standing beside an open window, his gaze fixed on a point on the horizon. Only then would his expression be tolerable for her to endure. She would paint him not with anguish in his glance but wanderlust, as if he could not wait until the moment he could escape. The seas were calling him, or the mountains with their rugged peaks and impossible angles. He was feeling the lure of faraway lands, the hint of far-off treasure.

His face was stern, his gaze steady on hers. He was wearing his black greatcoat, muffled and protected against the weather, once again hatless against the cold. His head was dusted with snow, as were his shoulders, but he appeared impervious to winter itself.

His mount moved forward, but she stood her ground. She'd wanted to encounter him, and here he was.

What did she say? How did she apologize?

"If it's your intention to walk a trench around Glengarrow, then may I say that it appears you are well on your way to achieving that aim."

"I am nowhere near Glengarrow property unless, of course, you count this lane yours as well."

"Actually," he said, "it is. Glengarrow land extends to where the trees end. Each morning and each night you've trespassed."

"Next, you will be telling me that my cottage is on your land as well."

"It used to be," he said.

For a long moment, she stood there with her arms at her sides, regarding him as dispassionately as he stared back at her.

Did he not have other, more pressing duties to assume? What about all the work he'd neglected in the last three years? Surely there were estates to look over—factors to meet, stewards to address, books to examine? If nothing else, perhaps he could occupy himself in good works.

"I'll buy the cottage from you," he said abruptly. "Give you enough money to go anywhere you wish."

"I'm not going anywhere."

"Well, you bloody well can't stay here."

"Why, because you decree it so?"

He slowly walked his horse closer. "Take the money, Miss Dalrousie. Live your life somewhere far from here."

"Leave you to your ghosts?"

"Yes, damn it."

He glanced toward Glengarrow, breaking their gaze. Then, without a word, he turned and rode in the other direction.

Robert had discounted the feeling on their first meeting, and he'd been too incensed during their second encounter to care, but he couldn't ignore it this time. Margaret Dalrousie reminded him of someone, and the fact he couldn't remember who niggled at him. He was good with faces, and good with names—any politician had to be. But he was also good at dates and extraneous facts, a talent that had made him a good speaker in Parliament.

Instead of leaving his horse in the stables, Robert cared for the animal himself. There were still only four people at Glengarrow, a house where two dozen servants used to be employed. Tom and Janet still returned to Blackthorne Cottage in the evenings. The two maids from Inverness were giggling chits, but he was grateful to see they'd struck up a friendship between them. At least they wouldn't be lonely here.

What about his loneliness? It could strike at any time and have nothing to do with the number of people surrounding him. He fought it back as adeptly as he could, and surrendered when he could no longer combat it.

The Dalrousie woman appeared wholly autonomous, alone, carrying herself like a queen as she regally paraded down the approach to Glengarrow.

The Dalrousie woman was an annoyance. Her mouth was too large for her face.

He finished his chore and settled the horse down for the night. As he left the stable, he studied the sky. The snow looked as if it would last for days. He'd been overly cautious in purchasing supplies, ensuring he had everything he needed at Glengarrow. He hadn't wanted to have to leave his home or have the intrusion of tradesme. Consequently, they had enough supplies to withstand a siege.

Snow would simply ensure he was cut off from the world, and that state of affairs didn't disturb him one whit.

Was Miss Dalrousie similarly supplied? He'd have to ask Tom. What did a woman like Miss Dalrousie require? Bath salts? Perfume? Swan's down powder puffs from Paris? Or was she more inclined to read, perhaps? Perhaps he should offer her the contents of Glengarrow's library.

If he wanted to apologize for the brutality of his behavior.

If he wanted to behave as befitted his station and his heritage.

He didn't like irritating women, a fact Amelia had teased him about on more than one occasion. The Tory party leader's wife had been a grating sort, with a high, whiny voice and the laugh of a braying donkey. On those occasions when he'd been forced to be around her, Amelia's soft look and gently chiding smile was enough to keep him polite when he'd just as soon have escaped.

There was no one to stop him from explaining

to Miss Dalrousie that her mouth was grotesque and that she was annoying him with her constant parading around his property.

All in all, I'd rather dance than walk, but I have no music and no partner.

She was too tall. She would look odd twirling around a ballroom performing a waltz. Amelia had been diminutive and delicate. Amelia had been a pony to Miss Dalrousie's draft horse. A bark of laughter escaped him at the thought of such an equine comparison.

He'd laughed. Dear God, he'd laughed. Not at one of Delmont's crafted jests, or bawdy attempts at humor. No, he'd created this laughter himself, out of nothing more than a thought. He'd laughed, and somehow Amelia had been involved.

His hand shook as he opened the door to the kitchen and stepped inside, feeling the heat from the room instantly. He unwrapped his scarf and hung it on the peg beside the door, took off his greatcoat and hung it in the adjoining room. It felt good to be doing things for himself. When he was a guest in Delmont's home, an ever-present valet had been there to assist him. He thought the man would have breathed for him if given those orders. Here at Glengarrow, though, he'd not thought to employ a valet.

Maybe he should suggest the post to Tom, just to see how the older man would react. His lips curved in a smile, the expression evidently startling the maid sitting at the kitchen table, because she suddenly jumped up and curtsied. It was such an unlikely combination of gestures he almost asked her to repeat it so he could study it more carefully.

How odd she hadn't tipped over the chair, or scattered onions all over the floor.

He waved her back in place, wishing he could remember her name. Something pleasing, as he recalled. A flower? Petunia? Gladiola? Rose.

"What are you cooking, Rose?" he asked, almost surprised to find he was hungry.

"Mulligatawny stew," the girl answered, thankfully taking her place at the table again.

He nodded, resigning himself to the fact that food was one of the many things he would always miss from France.

He left the kitchen, intent on his office. There were still a great many files and documents needing to be sent back to Parliament. Going through all those files was a cumbersome task, but there was no one better suited to it than he. The young man who'd been his secretary had left his employ prior to Robert's traveling to France. The parting had been amicable, because Malcolm had received another offer of employment and didn't want to be away from the hub of political activities. Traveling to France with Robert and his family hadn't intrigued him, and Robert couldn't blame him. Politics was better suited to single men, those who had no difficulties with the hours or the demands on their time.

Still, his journey to France had only been planned to take a month, not the three years it had been. Plans, however, were sometimes changed because life got in the way.

Halfway to his office, he turned instead and walked toward the main staircase, then upward to the attic.

He should have brought his coat, but he had no intention of standing on the roof more than a moment. Long enough to see if Miss Dalrousie had returned home. Was she shooting again?

Robert circled the cistern and stood fighting the blustery wind with more willpower than warmth. After a moment of staring in the direction of the Blackthorne Cottage, he was rewarded not by the sight of her, crimson-caped, with a pistol in her hand, but by the sudden realization he was acting the fool. A gust of freezing wind called him back to himself and to the idiocy of his actions.

He descended the steps, a little confused as to his curiosity.

"She's a mighty sight better at it now than she was at the beginning," Tom had said when Robert had questioned the man the other day. "I can't say she's good yet, but she has the will to get better. I've never seen anyone like her, Your Lordship. Day after day, and it don't matter none what the weather be like or whether it's raining or snowing, but she's out there shooting at that target as if she's defending her virtue."

"Why is she so intent on it?" Robert had asked, but Tom hadn't an answer, only shook his head as if the vagaries of that particular woman were beyond him. Robert could only agree.

What was Margaret Dalrousie doing?

Chapter 10

G lengarrow had always seemed a friendly place, an enchanted spot in the Highlands, at the edge of ruggedness, tamed into civilization. Now, however, the sound of shots rang out again, not only disturbing his peace but changing the very environment around his home.

Even though the sound surrounded him, he knew where it was coming from—Blackthorne Cottage. Miss Dalrousie was shooting at her target.

Miss Dalrousie was being an irritant again.

In his professional life, he'd been tactful for the most part, restrained. He had watched his words and his actions with a view to the end results. He'd been eternally careful.

Yet God or Fate or simply timing had wielded a scythe through his life. Why the hell should he continue to be cautious?

He hadn't been careful around Miss Dalrousie. She had an annoying ability to push him out of his politeness. He'd actually wanted to shout at her during more than one encounter. No, come to think of it, on every occasion. There wasn't anything she did he found acceptable. She was neither pleasing to look at nor pleasant to talk with. She was like a burr beneath his saddle— a potential irritant, more than that if he didn't remove it.

Glengarrow was his home, not hers, and she'd no right to disturb his tranquility.

Still, he was on the way to apologize, another irritant in his dealings with her. He was the one who'd been improvident, barbaric. He'd frightened her, and despite how annoying she might be, she'd not deserved his cruelty.

The sound of the shooting was even louder from here. He veered from the path and took the shortcut to the rear of Blackthorne Cottage. The weather was abysmal, sleet covering the path to the grass where she stood. Although it was two hours after dawn, the sky was as gray as gloaming. The sun was bashful at this time of year, but that, evidently, didn't change Miss Dalrousie's plans.

He saw her, took a deep breath, and strode forward, pulling his gloves over his wrists. He could feel his heart begin a staccato beat as if he braced himself for battle.

She stood, impervious to the sleet, her arm extended and her gaze fixed on the hay in front of her. He could only see her from a three-quarter view, but he imagined one eye was clenched shut as she narrowed her gaze down the site of the barrel. Whoever she saw in her mind's eye was as good as dead. Not because her aim was any good but because she appeared deadly serious.

Anyone with such intensity would achieve his goal one way or another. He recognized the look— he'd had it himself. He, too, had felt the drive to achieve, the need to do so. He hadn't wanted to prove anything to the world but only to himself.

"Who are you aiming at, Miss Dalrousie?"

She jerked, the pistol going off, the shot wide. She turned and glared at him.

"What are you doing here?"

She had the singular irritating habit of never addressing him properly. She never said Your Lordship; she never even said sir. She talked to him as if he were a servant, one she employed. Was it all those years of living in Russia? Did she see people as serfs?

"I can only hope whoever you're aiming at deserves his punishment," he said, instead of answering her.

"I am not trespassing. You are."

Her directness was another irritant. She always cut right through his efforts at diplomacy.

"You can follow the path back to Glengarrow," she said, pointing with her right hand, the one still holding the gun.

He cautiously stepped back, his gaze fixed on the weapon.

"I am here for two reasons, Miss Dalrousie," he said, determined not to be sent packing by the woman. Determined, also, not to allow her to irritate him. She had the ability to stir him from his appointed task, and he would not be dissuaded.

"The first is to apologize. I did not act correctly."

She turned and faced him fully, the weapon down at her side. She didn't look away, her gaze direct.

"What I did was wrong," she said. "I freely

admit it. I had no business being curious about your wife. Nor about you, if the truth be told."

He didn't know what to say to that, so he chose to remain silent.

"It is my behavior that should generate an apology, not yours. You acted as any person, any grieving person, might."

"I didn't mean to frighten you, Miss Dalrousie," he said, unable to forget the stricken look on her face or the fact she'd trembled in fear.

She shook her head as if to negate his memory. "If I was frightened, that is my fault. Not yours. If I allowed myself to become frightened, then that is a flaw in my character."

He stared at her incredulously. "Are you saying you don't allow yourself to be afraid? What about the other emotions? Do you forbid them for yourself as well? Irritation? Anger? Hopelessness? Sadness? Love?"

"How very odd you would place love at the very end of that litany of emotions. How very odd it's adjacent to sadness. I would have thought your memories gave love a little more luster than that."

"I said there were two things I wish to talk to you about," he said, not allowing himself to respond to her words. There was no reason to become angry at her. She was simply who she was, a rather strange artist.

"I would like to commission you to paint a portrait."

She turned and stared at the target, raised her right arm, and squinted down the barrel. "No."

"Don't you wish to know any more about the proposition?"

"No."

"I want you to paint my wife. Amelia."

She turned her head and regarded him, much in the same way she'd faced the target. "My subjects are alive. I paint life. Although, I do admit there was one occasion when I did a drawing of an older gentleman in his coffin, so the Grand Duchess's family in Germany could have a rendition. Most of the time, however, my subjects have been alive."

"Nevertheless, I would pay you handsomely to execute a portrait of my wife."

"No."

She turned back to the target.

He should leave this moment, before he grew any angrier.

"Is this your way of apologizing? How did you even know I was an artist?"

She didn't look at him when addressing him, her attention back on the target and not his face. He preferred it that way.

The Dalrousie woman had a rather striking face, and intense green eyes. Her mouth was too large, and her chin too sharp, and her nose was rather aristocratic. That striking black hair of hers would no doubt fade with age.

How old was she? His age? He'd never before wondered at a woman's age. Why was he so damnably curious about her?

"No, I believe I've already apologized."

"And what likeness would I use? Someone else's work? No."

"I can tell you anything you wish to know about Amelia," he said.

"No."

Today she was dressed in her ubiquitous red-wool cape, sturdy boots, and a dark blue dress, the details of which were hidden by the cape. The silly white hat covered most of her black hair, but she'd allowed the braid of it to come loose and coil over her shoulder.

"I visited Russia once," he said.

His comments elicited a nod. That was all, no more interest than that.

Irritated, he folded his arms in front of him and regarded her with some disfavor.

She began to reload the pistol as if he weren't standing there attempting to converse with her.

Could she not hold a conversation like a normal person? Of course she couldn't. Nothing she'd done since the moment he'd encountered her had been usual or normal. He shouldn't be annoyed by that fact; he should simply accept the fact Miss Dalrousie was her own person.

"Yes, I know," she said.

"How was that?"

At her look of mild inquiry, he forced himself to smile. "How do you know I was in Russia?"

"I saw you."

The reloading done, she began to study him again.

He rocked back on his heels, looked away, then looked back at her. She hadn't ceased in her examination of him, her look studious and intent. He wanted to ask what she found so fascinating about his face, about his person, but that would be to admit it bothered him. In actuality, he'd never been subjected to such intense scrutiny from anyone.

Even the prime minister stared off into the distance from time to time when addressing him.

"You saw me?"

Was all of their conversation to be like this? She was evidently not interested in talking with him as much as examining him as if he were something scientific and interesting.

He had never sat for a portrait, even though he and Amelia had planned to do so more than once. He doubted if the experience would have been a pleasant one if it was anything like the scrutiny Miss Dalrousie was giving him at this moment.

His appearance was not something over which he had any control. He simply was who he was, what he was: Robert McDermott, Earl of Linnet.

"I bid you good day, Miss Dalrousie," he said, turning on his heel, as irritated with her as he'd ever been with anyone in his entire life. He was not a man given to overt demonstrations of anger, but he wanted to shake her. Anything to shatter that mildly interested mask she wore. But that would negate one of his reasons for being here in the first place, to apologize for his anger.

What was there about this woman that irritated him so much?

"St. Petersburg," she said.

He stopped, but he didn't turn.

"You were attending a ball for the British Ambassador. A glittering affair given by Princess Naporav," she said. "Even though you seemed amused, it was not difficult to determine that you very much wanted to be somewhere else."

"I was wanting to be home," he said. "We'd planned to travel to France as soon as I returned."

He glanced at her as she faced the target once again. Darkness was almost upon them. Did she even practice at night?

"That's where it was," he said, turning. "You were there, on the balcony, watching everyone. I wondered why you didn't join in the merriment."

"I wanted to be painting," she said.

He took a deep breath and relaxed his clenched hands. How long could she stand out here in the cold?

"Is your refusal to paint Amelia's portrait your way of reciprocating for my poor behavior?"

She shook her head. "I no longer paint," she said.

"According to what my mother says, you're very talented."

"Is that who told you about me?"

He nodded.

"Were you a good politician?"

"Why do you ask?"

She smiled slightly. "You've lost the ability to placate," she said. "If you ever had it. You don't use sophistry. You've become too blunt for a politician. If you truly wished for me to paint your wife's portrait, you would have said something like: 'What a pity, Miss Dalrousie, that an artist of your supreme talent no longer paints.' As it was, you said nothing about my work."

"I haven't seen any of your work, Miss Dalrousie. I don't know if that's being a politician as much as it is an honest man. I would like to think I could be both."

"Perhaps you could," she said. "But that does not negate the fact I do not paint any longer."

"Is it too blunt to ask why?"

She turned again and before he could prepare himself, shot at the target again. This time she actually hit it, not in the middle but somewhere near the edge, enough that a puff of hay was dislodged from the overall structure.

"You may ask, but I have no intention of answering you."

She turned and smiled at him again, slipping the pistol in a pocket in her skirt, then turning and walking away, leaving him standing there in the sleet staring after her.

Chapter 11

Margaret awoke in the middle of the night, suddenly alert. She lay flat on her back, arms out at her sides, wondering what had roused her. Normally, she didn't wake easily, as if she preferred her dreamlike state to one of being awake.

She lay silent, listening for any noise, any sound. But there was nothing other than the wind whistling around the corners of the house. Blackthorne Cottage was a snug place to spend the winter. Other than a few places near the window or beneath the door, there were no drafts. She couldn't say the same for the palaces of Russia. Their enormous ceilings and huge expanses of open space meant she could never truly get warm. Even though many of the fireplaces could have held a dozen men standing upright, they didn't give off much heat.

When she worked, she couldn't be that close to the fire, both because the heat might damage her paintings and because her pigments were mixed with ingredients that could easily catch fire. Consequently, she always had to be in the coldest part of the room.

She was fortunate she'd not contracted pneumonia while in Russia.

Perhaps that's why she'd awakened. The night had grown colder, and even beneath her two blankets, she could feel the chill.

She slid her foot out first, the air touching the tips of her toes. She drew her foot back and contemplated simply turning over and trying to go back to sleep. But if she were cold, she wouldn't be able to fall asleep again.

Where were the blankets?

A more decadent part of her wished she could simply, reach for the bellpull and summon the maid. "Chocolate," she'd order, muffled beneath the sheets and comforter. The poor maid would have to do her bidding, bringing her blankets and chocolate within a matter of moments.

The eternal slavish obedience of the servants was not the only thing about Russia that had taken her some time to accept. But she had, to her discredit, begun ignoring the servants with the alacrity of the noble class. For the life of her, she couldn't remember the name of the girl she'd hired as her personal maid. Nor was her face anywhere in Margaret's memory.

Decadence, however, was a two-edged sword. If one became accustomed to it, one also paid the price. The price for the Russians was to ignore the poverty beneath their feet, such deplorable living conditions that Margaret had been shocked every time she ventured beyond St. Petersburg.

She fussed about the cold now, but compared to the peasants of Russia, she was living a prosperous life in Blackthorne Cottage.

Life was a series of gradients. She was, perhaps, unfortunate in that she had passed from the lowest echelon to the highest and been bounced back somewhere around the middle. She'd experienced life filled with wishes for betterment, and experienced it bored and filled with ennui. Of the two, she would rather have the life filled with purpose, with a goal in mind.

Even now, relegated to the Scottish Highlands, she had a purpose, a goal. The world would not think it an admirable goal, but did it matter what the world thought? According to public thought, beliefs, mores, and rules created primarily by men, she was a fallen woman. A woman who should be shunned, avoided at all costs. Not because of anything she had done but simply because she'd been a victim.

And yet, when the victim ceased to be a victim anymore, and sought justice, the world would probably not gauge her with any more sympathy. Therefore, it was up to her to decide who she was and what she was, not the world and not a society governed by men.

Once again, she slid her foot from beneath the covers, then, resolutely, sat up, pushing the blankets away. Sliding on her slippers, she grabbed her wrapper at the end of the bed, donned it, and lit the small candle on the bedside table. The flame flickered, as if it, too, reluctantly faced the chill.

She left her bedroom, intent on the trunk room. Once there, she placed the candle on one of the shelves and turned to face the room.

Most of her belongings had been sold in Russia

in order to finance the trip back to Scotland. Only one of her Russian gowns remained, a pale blue bejeweled masterpiece she couldn't bear to sell. She'd only worn it once, for an audience with the Emperor, and it was the most magnificent gown she'd ever worn in her life. Now it occupied a trunk all on its own, packed with layers of linen so as not to crush the delicate embroidery and silk.

She'd probably never wear it again in her lifetime, but she'd always have it to remember.

No one had wanted to purchase the more mundane items of her household, such as dishes, kitchenware, blankets, and towels. She had ended up giving most of those items away, but being perpetually cold as she was, she'd kept some of her blankets, lovely crocheted creations lined and filled with batting. She found the items in the second trunk and withdrew two of them.

Before she left the room, she halted in front of the blank canvas in the corner. Sometimes in the morning, she'd slide from her bed and wrap a blanket around her shoulders, standing and staring at the half-formed creation. Sometimes, she'd be unable to remember a single brushstroke she'd done, as if she were asleep when her talent took over, and she was left with no conscious knowledge of the creative process. She felt a part of it, and yet so removed from it she occasionally felt ashamed for taking credit for something larger and grander than she was.

She dropped one of the blankets at her feet, wrapped the other one around her shoulders. She stared at the blankness, at the emptiness of the canvas, and felt almost an empty cavern matching it in her soul. Since the moment she'd been conscious of who she was, she'd had a piece of charcoal or a brush in her hand. So many times she'd thought her sole reason for living was to document what she saw, to make it permanent so others could see it and remark, "Oh, yes, I know her. What a remarkable likeness."

Without that ability, without the skill, without that talent, who was she? Dead.

She reached out and grabbed a brush she'd left on the tray below the easel. In her mind's eye, she could see the Earl of Linnet. He'd offered her a commission. A portrait. Not of a live person, but his dead wife.

Amelia. The ghost of Glengarrow.

She didn't try to paint, she merely held the brush with both hands, warming the wood in the grip of her chilled fingers. A light flickered on the landscape capturing her attention, and she stared toward Glengarrow.

As if he had been sent to her, she could see the Earl of Linnet in her mind, a stern face and intensely blue eyes. She held out one hand, and the brush trembled, but not as much as before. She saw him as he might be in her painting, standing straight, his shoulders back, one arm crooked, hand flat against his hip. The other hand would be at his side, thumb aligned with the outer seam of his trousers as if he was possessed of a military bearing. He wouldn't be dressed in his ubiquitous black but in a pale blue waistcoat, perhaps, a light touch of color, to enliven the shade of his eyes. His mouth would be unsmiling, his lips firm but not thinned. His expression would be direct, somber, but in the depths of his eyes there would be a hint of a smile, as if his amusement was retained for the most propitious moment.

Perhaps in the background, she'd have book-cases, or he would be standing in the family parlor. Rooms had always been unimportant to her, because they functioned only as backdrops for her subjects. She'd painted the Grand Duke Fedorov's daughters sitting around their father's chair on the floor, petting a puppy. Their mother had been seated slightly behind the Grand Duke. Margaret was careful not to give preference to a wife's placement.

Russian males were very conscious of their status.

She wanted to paint the Earl of Linnet seated in a large burgundy armchair, one foot up on a foot-stool. Both hands would be resting on the arms of the chair, an arrogant, perhaps regal, position. No, he needed to be standing, as if surveying all he owned. A commanding stance, one suitable for the Earl of Linnet. Or, perhaps, he was better posed on horseback. She had seen him more often astride than she had in the drawing room.

Could she even paint Amelia?

She'd been curious about the Countess of Linnet or she wouldn't have entered her room. Perhaps she'd even felt a touch of envy for the woman who seemed to have effortlessly attained everything she'd wanted in life. Or had Amelia wanted to be more than the Earl of Linnet's wife and the mother of his child?

She'd been curious about few women. True, there was her interest in the Empress of Russia. Margaret had truly wished she had the freedom to ask her one or two questions. *How do you feel to be the wife of such a powerful ruler? How do you feel to have such power at your fingertips that if anyone displeases you, he is either banished or killed?*

Amelia hadn't the power of life and death, but she'd wielded a great deal of power, regardless. So much so that, three years later, there was still a look of pain in the Earl of Linnet's eyes.

If she were a different type of woman, one with more nurturing ability, or the gift of compassion, she would enfold him in her arms, perhaps even coax him to lay his head on her shoulder. The image, however faint and out of character for her, would never be realized in actuality. The Earl of Linnet would never allow himself to be comforted in such a way, and she was not given to such acts.

Amelia had been, no doubt, exquisitely beautiful. Amelia had probably been the epitome of all the womanly graces, capable of great charm and infinite tact.

Margaret had never been schooled in such things, but she had learned to keep silent rather than embarrass herself with ignorance. People saw that as tact, and the ability to keep a confidence, and consequently told her secrets when she would much rather they didn't.

She was skilled at other things, however. She could paint flowers so realistically they appeared fresh from a garden. She was also adept at discerning a subject's best feature.

She knew the Duchess Feodorovna looked much lovelier in the evening hours with the mellow glow of candlelight, the better to soften her angular features. The Grand Duke George Mikhailovich appeared almost handsome, but only if she had him looking outward, his chin tilted slightly up, so his jowls did not appear so prominent.

Despite the fact she sought out beauty and reveled in the interpretation of it, Margaret wasn't under any delusions about her own appearance. She was tall, and if she were feeling charitable, she might say willowy instead of thin. Her hips curved as most women's did. Her waist was narrow. Her breasts were overly full.

Her face was not the most artfully arranged. Her nose was too long, her chin almost squared. Her eyes were her best feature, and she hoped they took most of the attention from her mouth. Her lips were full, and too wide. Her smile was so startling in the mirror that, the first time she saw herself, Margaret swore she'd never smile again in public. For years she'd place her hand over her mouth when she laughed until one day she simply grew weary of being foolish about her own appearance.

She was not important. The painting was.

She'd believed that until almost a year ago, when she'd been treated not as a painter, not as a renowned artist, but only as a woman, weaker, defenseless, an unwitting vessel, an object.

A year ago, she'd been a different woman. Not wanton, but certainly less afraid. Not decadent, but reveling in life. She loved to dance, and to sing, even tunelessly. Color was her elixir, producing euphoric emotions. Yellow was joy, red was adoration, and blue was sorrow, strong and urgent. Black was passion, combining all of the other colors in it, subtle hues and bright tones. Black was the color of night and mystery, as if it contained every single emotion and human frailty. Was that why some of her most successful work was deeply shadowed?

Could she even paint again? The fact that the brush had stopped trembling was no indication. The fact she saw the Earl of Linnet's stern face, the lines around his eyes hinting at past humor, was confusing.

Why him?

She went to her trunk of painting supplies and rummaged in the bottom until she found what she needed. Unwrapping the paper from the charcoal, she returned to her canvas. Without giving herself time to think, she began to draw. A moment later, she stepped back, startled.

She'd had in mind an apple, perhaps. A flower, freshly plucked from the garden. But a face appeared instead, as if it had been almost magically done, the result of an image she'd formed in her mind. She'd sketched the Earl of Linnet in three-quarter profile, an amused smile curving his lips and a hint of laughter in his eyes.

She put down the charcoal and turned away from the canvas.

He wanted her to paint Amelia. Could she paint someone she'd never seen?

Returning to the trunk, she found a container of gesso. Opening it, she wrinkled her nose at the smell. She'd prepared the mixture nearly a year ago. She stirred it with her finger, then, taking one of her utility brushes, slathered some of the gesso on the canvas and evened it out with long, practiced strokes. Because the gesso was so thick, it easily covered the drawing. She'd destroyed more than one work with such a method. Although she wasn't a perfectionist, she recognized she'd not yet finished one painting that met her standards completely. Perhaps that was part of being an artist— never being satisfied, always pushing to be better.

He would have to sit with her, of course. He would have to be there constantly, to answer questions. How tall was his wife? What was the shade of her hair near her temple? Did it catch the light? Were her eyes a pale blue like a dawn sky or more intense like a summer day?

I can tell you anything you wish to know about Amelia.

What would he reveal about himself?

"Very well, I'll do it," she said.

He halted his horse and stared down at her.

She'd stood at the end of the lane as if daring him to run her down and now fixed a look on him as if she were a schoolmaster and he a recalcitrant pupil.

He couldn't help but wonder if Miss Dalrousie's arrogance had served her well in the Russian Imperial Court in St. Petersburg. Although the Russians were fascinated with all things English—and to the Russians, Scotland was very much an English country—they couldn't have been pleased to be ordered around by such a woman.

"Have you always been so forceful in your speech?"

She blinked at him. "Are you calling me tactless?"

The irritation he usually felt in her presence bubbled free again, accompanied this time by another rather surprising element—amusement.

Margaret Dalrousie did as she pleased, and he should be celebrating the fact it pleased her to paint Amelia.

"No, I'm not," he said, annoyed that he must be the peacemaker. Again. "You will do it?" he asked, retreating to her earlier comment.

The last thing he wanted was to allow her to change her mind. Time was not his ally.

His mind tiptoed around that thought for a moment before he could admit it again to himself. He could not allow more time to pass, lest he forget what Amelia looked like. Even now, there were times when he could only catch a glimpse of her in his memory, a turn of her head, or the way she smiled, or the way she'd held Penelope when his daughter was a baby.

"You will do it, then?"

She turned and faced him and nodded once.

"Would you prefer I have my solicitor contact you, or can we come to an agreement in price?"

She named a figure that had him widening his eyes. A family of four could have survived ably for a year on that amount.

"Do you charge everyone the same, Miss Dalrousie, or only those individuals you dislike?"

"I don't dislike you," she said. "I don't know you." She regarded him somberly for a moment, and he could almost have guessed the words she'd say next. *But once I cultivated your acquaintance, I'm certain I wouldn't like you.* But she didn't say that.

"It's because I've never painted a ghost before. I haven't the slightest idea how to do it."

For a long moment he simply stared at her, uncertain how to respond to that remark.

But before he could say anything, she held up a hand. "There are several other conditions. You will attend each sitting. You will speak when I give you leave and not otherwise. You will never look at the portrait until it is finished." She fixed a stern look on him. "If I find you have done so, the work immediately ceases, and you will not receive any of your money in return. You will never question the time it takes, either for a sitting or for the portrait. Can you agree to these points?"

"Were you so dictatorial to Nicholas I?"

"Are you an emperor? Do you command a country?" She looked around her, but the look seemed not to be one of disdain but fondness. "Glengarrow is a lovely bit of Scotland, true, but it cannot measure up in sheer size with Russia."

With a dismissive wave she left him. He turned in the saddle and watched her, wondering if he'd made the right decision after all.

How much did he want to recall Amelia?

With his whole heart.

The memories were growing blurry around the

edges, and he was afraid one day he might awake to have no ability to recall her to mind. She would simply be Amelia, a name, no longer an image. No longer someone he could point to and say: that was my wife. I loved her.

Had Margaret Dalrousie ever been in love?

And why the hell did he care?

Chapter 12

In Russia, when she was about to embark upon a new commission for a very important personage, Margaret would agree to travel to their home. She had Peter carry her trunks of paints, pigments, and brushes, along with a selection of canvases already prepared for her use. They made quite a procession, she and Peter, Margaret holding the pouch of her brushes, and Peter hauling the rest of her miscellany in a covered three-wheeled carriage.

A child had once asked her if she had a baby in the carriage, and she'd been amused by the thought.

"Yes, indeed, I do," she'd said. "Her name is Creation. Or Inspiration. Perhaps even Benediction." She and Peter had exchanged a smile as the poor child had gone running to his mother for an explanation.

The Earl of Linnet wasn't all that important, but there was no space at Blackthorne Cottage to accommodate both a place for him to sit and for her easel to be arranged.

She spared a wistful moment for her studio in

Russia, then clamped her mind shut over those thoughts. She would be better served by living in the present and not the disturbing past.

Today, there was only herself as a beast of burden, and she made the trek to Glengarrow accompanied by her already prepared canvas, her easel, and satchel.

She never knew exactly what kind of composition she was going to choose until the day the sitting began. Only then could she decide how she would have the subjects sit or stand, what colors flattered them, what background would aid to complement them. The Emperor had so loved her informal portraits of his two daughters, that now it was all the rage for the Russian nobility to be painted *en famille*. At least here, at Glengarrow, she wouldn't have to choose from a selection of puppies to feature in the painting.

The day was a blustery one, which didn't make Margaret's journey to Glengarrow any easier. But she persevered. Her discomfort was a small price to pay for the ability to paint again. Or perhaps what she'd experienced the other night was only an accident, and the surge of anticipation she felt now was based on a wish more than a reality. Perhaps when it came to actually sketching in Amelia's likeness and painting the Countess of Linnet, her fingers would begin to tremble violently again, and she'd be unable to complete the portrait.

She wouldn't think of that right now. Instead, she would simply focus on the moment. Getting her satchel with her jars and bottles to Glengarrow, managing to secure the canvas and easel beneath her arm despite the wind.

In Russia, in her studio, she actually had canvases that had matured for long stretches of time. She didn't have that luxury now. Tom could always fashion stretchers for her, but she wasn't entirely certain she could afford the linen. Better to make this canvas do. Taller than it was wide, it would make for quite a commanding portrait.

If she could finish it. If she had any talent left.

Janet was in the kitchen when she knocked on the door.

"His Lordship said you would be by this morning, Miss Margaret," Janet said, opening the door wide. Instead of a welcoming look, however, her eyes were troubled.

Margaret handed Janet the satchel so she could enter the door with the canvas lengthwise and still balance the easel.

"You don't approve?" Margaret asked, propping the easel against the kitchen table.

Janet glanced toward the door and made a great show of closing it firmly. Only then did she turn to Margaret again.

"It's not my place to approve or disapprove, Miss Margaret," she said, appearing the perfect servant, the most amenable retainer. Except the description didn't match the look on Janet's face.

"Pretend it was," Margaret said. "I'll tell no one what you've said."

Janet glanced down the corridor, to the door leading to the family parlor. Perhaps she saw the earl there in her mind's eye. Or perhaps she simply envisioned what had transpired there years ago, a happy family, laughter, the drone of earnest conversation.

Finally, she turned back to Margaret. "The past sometimes needs to be left in the past, Miss Margaret. We can't relive it. We can't make it come back. Sometimes, we just have to let it go."

"Sometimes you can't let it go, Janet," Margaret said. "Sometimes it lives with you."

Janet nodded. "When that happens, Miss Margaret, you just have to wait it out. Understand it's feelings you need to feel, it's pain you have to go through. Pushing it away will only make it worse in the end."

"And you think the Earl of Linnet is living in the past."

For a while, she didn't think Janet would answer her. When the older woman did speak, however, it was not to Margaret, but to the door leading to the interior of Glengarrow. "I think that's what the earl is doing, Miss Margaret. But I don't think he knows any other way. Somehow, he needs to give up his old life, let it go, and find a new way to live."

Since she'd attempted to do the very same thing, Margaret knew it wasn't as easily said as done. "And if he can't?"

Janet didn't answer her.

Margaret reached for the satchel again, hefted the canvas under her right arm, and grabbed the easel.

"Where does he want me?"

Again, Janet looked troubled. "In the earl's suite."

Margaret didn't explain she knew the way well. Nor did she comment to Janet she didn't want to paint in the earl's suite of rooms. She didn't want the presence of Amelia around her so vibrantly. She didn't believe in ghosts, but she did believe people leave imprints on their personal rooms. The way a room was decorated, the color of the walls, a choice of the blankets, the bed hangings—all of these were indicative of a person's tastes and wishes and wants. And although she hadn't asked Janet to verify her suspicions, Margaret guessed the Earl of Linnet kept his suite of rooms exactly the same as when Amelia had last been in them.

So, although her body wasn't there, her spirit certainly was.

In moments, they stood in front of the double doors, neither of them in a hurry to enter. Finally, Janet took a deep sigh, grabbing one of the handles. A dozen paces later, Margaret was standing in the middle of the room Amelia had used as a parlor.

Although the day was a blustery one, the sun was shining brightly, and the room was flooded with light. If she were in Russia, Margaret would be overjoyed to spend hours in this one spot. No draft chilled the room. No echo magnified sounds. Once, in the summer palace of Peterhof, she'd nearly been driven mad by the sound of dripping water coming from somewhere. She'd begun to hum to herself in order to distract from the noise. That, in turn, had elicited conversation from her subject, something normally forbidden. The fact the painting had been completed and the commission a success had been a miracle.

There was no reason to object to the conditions in this cozy room.

There was a fire blazing in the fireplace on the far wall, and an area in the corner had been cleared of furniture except for a small chair and a matching footstool. A perfect place for her to sit when she needed some respite from standing. There was the scent of perfume in the air, so faint she might have missed it, except she was very familiar with that particular scent.

She knew, without being told, exactly what kind of painting the Earl of Linnet wanted of his wife. Amelia would be standing by the open window, the tree just outside naked and unadorned with leaves. Her gaze would be wistful, her arm would be stretched outward, her fingers almost touching the pane of glass. She would be a will-o'-the-wisp herself, a ghost turned corporeal for a matter of moments or hours, or however long he wished to imagine her that way.

She had never in her entire career painted a maudlin portrait, and she certainly wouldn't do so now. If she was going to paint Amelia, she would do so with her daughter on her lap. Perhaps the little girl would tug mischievously on a curl or simply be tired and resting against her mother's bosom. Amelia would be facing the watcher, a soft smile indicating the joy of her daughter's existence.

That was the legacy she'd create for Amelia.

How utterly ridiculous to want to weep. She would not feel sad about a woman she didn't know and could never know. Margaret brushed angrily at her face, defying a tear to fall.

Slowly, she began assembling her easel. Once she had it braced correctly, she placed the canvas on top of it and turned it slightly so the window was in front of her, to her right. Now all she had to do was to figure out exactly where she wanted the Earl of Linnet to sit.

"Shall I tell the earl you're ready, Miss Margaret?" Janet asked.

"No," Margaret said. "I want to gather my thoughts for a moment."

Janet left, her smile a benediction, and Margaret sat in the small chair behind the easel.

This would be a difficult room for him to be in, day after day. Why had he decided to do this to himself? Talking about Amelia would certainly not mitigate the pain of her loss. Instead discussing her, describing her would only emphasize the fact that she was dead.

As long as he grieved, he could not move beyond the loss. And as long as the loss remained real and the wound bloody, Amelia was still near.

She didn't like the tenor of her thoughts. She wasn't used to knowing people, to understanding their pain. She was more comfortable with dissecting them feature by feature. This duke had a long nose, this duchess had stooped shoulders. A princess had an overbite rendering her regrettably similar in appearance to a horse.

She'd always looked at people in such a way in order to paint them. She didn't want to know their hearts, or their wishes, or whether they were intelligent or stupid. She only wanted to know what light would be favorable to them and how to mitigate their flaws.

Even if she'd never spoken to the Earl of Linnet, or known his past, Margaret would have known this was an unusual commission simply from McDermott's eyes. In his direct gaze was the soul of a man who'd seen death and returned, the look of someone whose endurance had been tested, who knew his own limitations and strengths.

Could she match him in resolve? Could she be as strong and resolute? Could she stand here day after day and listen to his words about his wife? Could she hear and not care?

What if her rendition of Amelia was not as pure as his recollections? What if his memory made her perfect, and Margaret's talent could only make her beautiful?

She'd told more than one subject, before beginning to paint them: sometimes people do not like to see themselves revealed as others see them. Do you understand this portrait may not be as flattering to you as you think it should be?

That one question always invoked a great deal of fear. Once, she'd overheard a duchess exclaim to a friend, "Why, the woman is terrifying. She had me worried I'd be pictured as a troll. Do you really think that is how I look?" Of course, the painting revealed a woman only slightly past her prime, dressed exquisitely in blue silk, her lovely smile flattered by the candlelight.

Perhaps she told her subjects not to expect too much to excuse the fact that her emotions occasionally surfaced in a painting. If the prince was an obnoxious glutton, forever complaining of missing a meal or demanding that a footman bring him a plate of food to compensate for his irritation, his corpulent figure became even more so, buttons straining and trousers too tight when she could have just as easily rendered him more slender. If the grand duke was an ancient and unbearable roué, then a tiny brushstroke converted his smile to a self-satisfied smirk when viewed from a certain angle.

Without much difficulty, anyone looking at one of her paintings could tell how she felt about the subject. If he annoyed her, or angered her, or she thought he was an insufferable braying ass, unfortunately her thoughts and feelings were revealed in the details of the portrait.

But she'd never before been expected to paint from another person's image, or memory. Nor had she ever worried that her painting might reveal her own envy.

Every morning before she began painting, Margaret performed a ritual. Before the subject arrived, before she picked up a piece of charcoal or a brush, she'd stand in front of the easel with its cured and prepared blank canvas and stare into the white abyss. Then she'd close her eyes, her breath coming deep and even, those moments almost prayerful, certainly tranquil.

She was a supplicant before God and her talent, both equally demanding.

God decreed she recognize she was mortal, that she could not paint for hours at a time without dropping, that she must eat, sleep, and fulfill her body's needs. The easel was her altar, and she was only as good as God allowed her to be.

Her talent demanded she submit to it, that she work until a composition felt complete. Until that moment came, the painting was master, and she was simply its vassal.

She never faced an empty canvas without saying a little prayer. The words didn't matter as much as the emotion behind them. Please, God. As simple as that, and as profound.

Margaret opened her eyes to find McDermott standing there, watching her.

Chapter 13

"**I** wish you would stop making a habit of coming up on me unawares," she said, annoyed. To give herself time to regain her composure, she bent and rearranged the contents of her satchel.

Somewhere in the last few minutes, he'd entered the room, and she'd not heard him. Normally, she was attuned to noise, especially when she was becoming immersed in her painting. The first few moments before a subject arrived were the most intense of her day. It was when she questioned herself, her ability, and when every single fear or doubt she'd ever felt surfaced.

"Pardon me," he said in his low voice. "I didn't mean to startle you."

Of course he had. If he hadn't, he would have spoken out the moment he entered the room. Instead, he'd stood there, almost indolently leaning against the wall in order to watch her.

"Are you ready to begin?" he asked.

At that moment, she almost declined. She almost gathered up her belongings and made her way back to Blackthorne Cottage, the entire idea of painting Amelia suddenly foolish and beyond her capabilities.

Heat suffused her face, and she told herself it was irritation, not embarrassment.

"I'm ready. Are you?" she asked, returning to the corner. Instead of standing in front of the canvas, she sat on the small chair, peering around the easel to watch him.

He sat at the end of a yellow chaise, looking too large for the furniture. He was dressed in dark trousers and a white shirt, a casual ensemble for the earl at home. Not dressed as she would have painted him, however.

"I was told you were a politician," she said. "Elected to the House of Lords."

He inclined his head, but didn't speak.

"Isn't that unusual for a Scottish peer?"

"There are sixteen of us. Hardly unusual. I've always thought the numbers a bit sparse. I'm not in Parliament now. The election is only for one term, until Parliament retires for the session."

She could almost envision him in such a setting. He would be standing at the forefront, the Palace of Westminster only a backdrop, its only purpose to make him appear more real and more lifelike.

He moved from the chaise to the chair beside the window and looked directly at her.

Suddenly, she realized she'd been wrong. She'd paint him attired in exactly what he was wearing right at the moment. Despite the fact his clothing was casual, there was a sense of barely restrained energy in his posture. He looked as if he might jump up and leave the room at any moment, impatient with inactivity. Could the Earl of Linnet be so easily characterized by one word—*forceful?* Somehow, it seemed too simplistic a word to use with him.

"Shall we begin?" he asked.

For a moment, she debated whether or not she would accede to his request. If she began a book, she finished it, regardless of how posturing the hero or how maudlin the plot. If she began an embroidery project, she always finished it, even if it was smudged and sad-looking at the end. If she began this painting, she was duty-bound by that strange character trait of hers to finish it.

It might well be the most difficult task she had ever set for herself. But it would not be the first time she'd demanded more of herself than she'd thought she could give.

She nodded and moved to stand behind the easel in the corner. She eased her head to the right to see him sitting there, his gaze intent on her. From her satchel, she grabbed a piece of charcoal wrapped in a leather holder, and unwound the holder slowly, giving her fingers time to become reaccustomed to the tasks.

Her hands were stiff, and she was cold with fear.

"You're to dictate the pace, are you?"

"I am," she said.

"I'm not allowed to ask questions? To be curious as to your progress?"

"No," she said.

Should she warn the Earl of Linnet she was not considered a fast painter? If anything, she tended to linger on the details. The pearls at the throat, the exact fall of silk in the skirt of a dress, the gleam of light on an array of medals on an old soldier's chest were all important to her. A portrait should be as exact a replication of life as possible.

She slowly unwound the strips of leather from the holder.

"Is the chair comfortable enough for you? I've noticed you limping."

Well, that announcement didn't please him if the look on his face was any indication.

"I watch people," she explained. "I notice what a great many people miss. You have a scar on your chest, for example."

"How the hell do you know that?"

"You place your hand flat on your chest from time to time, as if to support yourself, or guard the wound."

"A stage of healing, I've been told. The physician who cared for me delineated all the steps in my recovery. Being conscious of my scars is but one of those that will fade in time."

"And your limp?"

"I don't limp," he said, and his look defied her to argue. "Very well, when I'm tired or I've exerted myself, perhaps. But only then."

"But you concentrate on not limping," she said, guessing he would hate a sign of weakness in himself. "And I think you touch your scar when it bothers you, not because you're conscious of it."

He didn't speak, didn't comment, so she was left with nothing to do but finish unwrapping the charcoal. At the exact moment she stepped toward the canvas, her hands began to tremble. After placing the charcoal in the easel's tray, she pressed her hands together tightly.

What if the other night couldn't be replicated? What if she couldn't paint at all?

Before she had a chance to fear it, she picked up the charcoal again and drew a sloping line on the canvas. Darker than most of her sketches, it nonetheless had the effect of mobilizing her. Her fingers flew over the canvas, rendering a sketch in enough detail she had an idea of the composition of the painting.

"Tell me about your wife," she said.

"What is it you want to know? Her appearance?"

"Among other things," she said. "I want to know as much about her as you can tell me. A person's character as well as his appearance is revealed in his portrait."

"Why do you never call me Your Lordship?"

She placed the charcoal on the tray and wiped her hands clean with a rag from her satchel. Doing so took a moment or two, more than the task required, perhaps, but it gave her time to frame her answer.

"I lived in Russia for some time," she said finally. "The Russian court is awash in titles. Grand Duchess, Grand Duke. Prince, Princess, an assortment of honorary peerages. I am not overly fond of obsequiousness."

"You find it obsequious to be polite?"

"I find it obsequious to address you as Your Lordship every time I utter a sentence." She stepped out from behind the easel to address him directly.

"The upper classes are no different than the lower classes. Each wants the same things from life. Each person I've ever met, whether chimney sweep or grand duchess, wants to be happy. Each wants to matter in the world, to be safe. Each wants someone to care for them."

She looked past him to the window. The icicles clinging to the roof were beginning to melt, turning clear and glistening in the morning light.

"I actually believed, once, that the upper class was somehow infused with higher ideals, that to be a duke or earl was to be somehow superior in nature."

"You evidently do not believe that to be the case now," he said.

"No, you're right. In fact, I would venture to say the lower classes have better morals."

He didn't comment.

She continued. "All that's different between the two groups is the amount of money the upper classes have to waste and the fact they, themselves, believe they're superior. For the most part, they've inherited both their wealth and the titles they wear with such delight. Neither money nor rank makes them more thoughtful, kinder, or more caring. In some cases, they'd been made loathsome and vile creatures."

"I suspect you're not speaking in generalities, but in specifics. Do you truly regard me as a loathsome and vile creature?"

She turned her attention back to him and realized she'd said too much, revealed too much. How had that happened?

"What is your first name?" she asked, no doubt shocking him.

But he surprised her by answering almost immediately. "Robert," he said. "Do you think it proper we should address each other by our Christian names, Miss Dalrousie?"

"The world is not in this room. The only people here are you and I. You are about to tell me the story of your wife, which is probably a very tender tale, if not a difficult one to recount. What does it matter what I call you?"

He didn't speak, and she found herself a little disappointed in the silence.

"Are you the kind of man," she asked, "who is defined by his title? Are you not Robert McDermott? Are you *only* the Earl of Linnet?"

He considered the question for a moment.

"Can I not be both? If your question is must I hide behind my title, no. I have met a great many people in my life to whom I have not presented myself as the Earl of Linnet. They know me as Robert or McDermott. I do not find it necessary to bandy my title about as if I'm a better person because of it. But it is who I am."

"Then I shall call you McDermott," she said. "It's not at all improper."

"And you? What shall I call you, Miss Dalrousie?"

Tilting her head, she regarded him for a moment. "Anything you choose," she said as she reached into the satchel, retrieved a folded length of cloth, and carefully draped it over the canvas.

"I'm done for today," she said, stepping out from behind the easel. She grabbed her satchel and made her way past him, not looking at him as she headed for the door.

"You're done?"

How remarkably annoyed he looked. Did he

think she was going to follow some timetable he'd set for her? He might be an earl, but in this room she dictated the pace.

"Yes," she said. "I know how I want the painting to look. I know which pigments I need."

"And you'll not work any more today?"

"There will be days when I will stand in front of the canvas, McDermott, until I nearly faint from exhaustion. Today is not one of them. Do not concern yourself; you'll get your money's worth."

She left him then, feeling amusement at his frown. Was it evil to take such delight in McDermott's irritation? If so, then she was Satan's minion indeed, because she smiled as she left the room.

Chapter 14

Margaret Dalrousie didn't appear at nine o'clock as they'd agreed. Robert waited in Amelia's sitting room, his irritation growing as the minutes ticked by, and she still didn't appear. What was she doing that was so much more important than her new commission? Or was she simply indolent by nature? He hadn't thought so, but he was capable of making an error in judgment.

At least he hadn't paid her yet. He could still call back the instructions to his solicitor. She'd get no money from him if she proved to be too lazy to complete Amelia's portrait.

Complete it? She'd not yet begun.

He strode to the corner where she'd draped the easel in cloth, and peered beneath it. All that was on the canvas was a series of unintelligible lines and circles. He wasn't an artist, but this didn't look like art.

Another fifteen minutes passed, and he finally left the sitting room for his office, intending to send Miss Dalrousie a tersely worded note. He was not used to being treated in such a fashion, and he was also a firm believer in the adage that a man's habits reveal his character. If she was going to be habitually tardy, then they were going to clash from the beginning. Such actions revealed her as arrogant, careless, and uncaring for anyone's time other than her own.

He had better things to do than sit and wait for her.

There were more than enough duties to occupy him, a wealth of correspondence that had not been forwarded to him in France. In addition, he'd received a letter from Delmont he'd not yet read. In turn, he needed to write letters to all of those people who'd been so kind to him during his long convalescence. There were some he didn't know how he would ever begin to thank, but he should at least attempt to do so.

Were people really starving in the Highlands?

He'd been concerned enough about his mother's words to begin an investigation, but he'd not yet received answers to his letters. If they were truly losing people because of sheep, then something needed to be done. He still had enough influence to call attention to the problem, and he'd begun by writing his own steward and inquiring as to whether any of the crofters farming Glengarrow land had been displaced.

If so, then their fate was his responsibility.

The idea of returning to Glengarrow had been anathema, but now he knew he should have come home long ago—not for his sake, but for the sake of the people who depended upon him.

He looked around his office. The chamber had always been a cozy one, and the intervening years had not changed that fact. He was surrounded by books and warmed by a fire, and if he wished to sit a while and think, the two leather straight-backed chairs in front of the fireplace provided a comfortable place to do so.

Right now, however, he was going to compose an invective to Margaret Dalrousie.

The path to his desk necessitated he pass a series of windows. A flash of color caught his eye, and it was so unexpected to see crimson on the landscape he halted, and then walked closer to the window, unable to believe what he was seeing.

Miss Dalrousie, attired in that red cape with her ridiculous fluffy hat, was seated on a branch of a tree near the edge of the forest, earnestly involved in some task or another. What was she doing? And why did she choose to do it outdoors? Was the fool woman trying to freeze to death?

He grabbed his greatcoat from the hook near the back door and left Glengarrow by the rear entrance. As he marched through the pristine snow, his boots sank in a good six inches. At the rate it was snowing this winter, he didn't think the earth would ever warm. But here and there were shoots of green, as if nature itself refused to be daunted by cold and ice.

Robert headed in a straight path toward Miss Dalrousie. She didn't look in his direction, even though he wasn't quiet in his approach. Nor did she look distracted by the sound of the branches clicking together in the wind. Whatever she was doing was occupying her attention fully.

The forest around Glengarrow had been allowed to develop in its natural state. Trunks were not trained to grow in a certain way, and lower branches were not lopped off if they were displeasing to the sight. If lightning destroyed a tree, it wasn't removed.

Margaret Dalrousie sat demurely on the low-lying limb of an ancient oak. She leaned forward, her concentration intent on a stump in front of her, for all the world as if she were taking tea with the queen.

Instead of a cup, however, she had a mortar and pestle between her hands. Gloved hands, he was pleased to note. Even though she was out in the frigid weather, she obviously had some common sense.

She had painted nobility, but she wasn't noble. She had evidently associated with Russia's elite, but he knew nothing of her past other than the fact she was born in Fife. She'd been honored by associations that did not often honor women, and yet, she never spoke of her laurels. At the same time, she was the most arrogant individual he'd ever met, as well as the most irritating. She was a mass of contradictions, not the least of which was her appearance.

She was as far from beautiful as silver was from tin, but she had a singular way of capturing attention. Perhaps it was her habit of looking at other people with a direct and unflinching gaze. He'd found himself drawn into her stillness more than once, as if she'd woven a web to ensnare him.

Her face was average, neither too long nor too wide. Her eyes were green, striking, and too intent for his comfort, shielded by brows as dark as her black hair. Her mouth was never still. Even now, as she worked, it twisted into a myriad of different expressions: a grimace, a self-deprecating smirk, genuine amusement. Her chin was squared, almost obstinate. Altogether, a face that should not have been as arresting as it was.

She turned at that moment, regarded him, then immediately went back to what she was doing as if his approach was of no interest to her.

"You didn't come to the sitting room," he said as he neared her. "May I ask why?"

"You aren't allowed to ask," she said, neither looking up or otherwise acknowledging his presence.

Was she always so insufferably rude?

"I cannot even question your absence?"

She glanced at him finally. "I had other tasks to attend to," she said.

"You haven't painted anything. Only a few scrawls in charcoal."

She stopped what she was doing and looked up at him.

"Did you remove the cloth from the canvas?" she asked, her voice even.

Her eyes, however, were not so placid. They flashed at him, reminding him of the darkness before a storm, when lightning races from cloud to cloud. Except this lightning was green, and very irritated.

He couldn't help but feel a little pleased by that fact.

"I didn't remove it," he said. "But I did look beneath it."

"Then I cannot work with you," she said very calmly, releasing her grip on the pestle. She slapped her hands together as if done with the chore and him.

"If you don't want this commission, Miss Dalrousie, I can seek out another artist."

She looked up at that comment. "You are more than welcome to do so," she said. "But you must understand the next artist would spend the same time doing what I'm doing. We cannot simply wave a brush in the air and the canvas becomes tinted with color, McDermott. A great deal of effort goes into making the paints I will use."

"Is that what you're doing?" he asked, interested despite himself. "Why didn't you prepare a supply before the first session?"

She sighed deeply as if he were an ignorant and stubborn student. Because of that gesture, he was determined not to leave. Or to allow her to annoy him further.

"Because I didn't know what colors I was going to use," she said. "Every composition is different, every portrait is unique. I am not going to paint a white silk gown, so I have no use for Bismuth White. Nor is this painting going to be a partial landscape, so my use of Egyptian Brown will be less than if it were."

"You've decided now?"

She glanced at him again, a look filled with irritation.

"Yes."

"But you're not going to tell me," he said. "Does no one ever question you, Miss Dalrousie?"

She didn't even take a moment to consider the question. "No," she said tartly. "Not about my painting. Not about the technique, or my practices, or anything regarding the entire execution of the portrait from beginning to end. That is not your

province, McDermott, and I will not tolerate it."
She frowned at him. "I thought I made that point
perfectly clear."

"Even for the amount of money I'm willing to
pay you?" he asked, a little startled at the fierce-
ness of her expression.

"You are paying for the portrait, not my talent.
Nor my time. Granted, the portrait I'll give you at
the end is a result of my talent, but how I achieve
it is my concern, not yours. You have no part of
the process, McDermott. You only care for the end
result."

She began to close up the jars on the stump. "But
it no longer matters. You looked at the canvas,
so our agreement is over. Find yourself another
artist."

Had he ever felt that passionate about anything
he'd created? Of course he had. He'd been known
as rash, perhaps even improvident in Parliament,
when a bill from the House of Commons irritated
him or pleased him. He'd felt the same the day
Penelope was born, when he'd held her in his arms,
seeing the future in his daughter's tiny face.

However, it had been some time since he'd felt
that sort of passion, or since enthusiasm strummed
through his blood. He could only look at her now,
envy her and because he envied her, he disliked her
more than a little.

"Very well," he said. "Do as you will."

He turned to walk away, and she spoke, the
words out of place for the rather brisk Margaret
Dalrousie he'd come to know.

"Perhaps you are buying part of my soul,

McDermott. If that's the case, am I not allowed to decide exactly how I deliver it?"

He turned back to address her. "I do not know much about art, Margaret," he said. "But I know my share about souls. When you give a piece of it away, it doesn't regenerate itself. The soul is an object one should guard with due diligence, lest you find yourself without one."

"You called me Margaret," she said.

"Was that not our agreement?"

"You hold some agreements, then, McDermott? Only yours and no one else's?"

"What do you want? An apology? A vow never again to look at your painting? If so, I'll give it to you. I erred."

He fully expected her to gloat over his admission, but she only nodded.

"If you do it again, McDermott, I will cease. I will never finish."

She turned back to the mortar and pestle and continued grinding up the yellow paste in the bottom of the bowl.

"Were you as imperious in the Russian court?"

"I had to be," she said. "Otherwise, I would have been treated with contempt. The Russian nobles are not an understanding breed. They have no patience for weakness, and they can scent it like a wolf."

"Is that why you're sitting here on one of the coldest mornings I can remember? Because you miss Russia?"

Her face changed, very subtly. "I don't miss Russia. I shall never go there again."

"Will you not come inside for a cup of tea or chocolate? Your lips are beginning to turn blue."

She stood abruptly, tucking her gloved hands into her cape. "It is safer for all concerned I do this out of doors," she said. "But I thank you for the invitation."

"Safer?"

She looked down at the mortar and pestle. "Some of these pigments are poisonous, McDermott. More than one artist has died because of contact with Kings Yellow, and Red Orpiment. I find that hideous. A man is expected to put his soul"—she glanced at him and corrected herself— "a piece of his soul on canvas. Most of the time, instead of recognition for his talent, he will die because of it."

"People die, Miss Dalrousie. Regrettably, it is a part of life."

"For beauty? A person should die for a cause, McDermott. Not by accident."

She looked suddenly stricken.

"I'm sorry," she said. "I do know how to carry on a conversation without being insensitive."

"Would it surprise you to know I agree with you, Miss Dalrousie? A person should not die by accident. Not without some sort of warning, at least. Life should not be so easily extinguished."

He turned then, and to ease her discomfort more than his own, left her to her chore. Only once did he glance back to find that she was staring at him, a look on her face that he couldn't decipher.

The young maid, the same one who'd caught the stove on fire, bundled up in a coat much too large for her, and made the journey from Glengarrow to Margaret's perch on delicate steps, almost toe first in the snow. A green-wool scarf was wrapped around her throat and covered most of her face. All that appeared of Helen were two inquisitive eyes and a forehead covered with curly red hair.

"Miss," the girl said, reaching Margaret. "I brought you chocolate."

Because Helen had braved the elements no doubt at the earl's bidding, Margaret didn't have the heart to refuse. Nor was it prudent to do so. Freezing to death didn't seem an entirely adequate response to the earl's peeking at her canvas.

Very well, he'd broken the rules. But he'd apologized. She'd countered with a bit of accidental rudeness. They were, if not even, then certainly matched.

She placed the pestle back in the mortar and pulled off her gloves. Only then did she reach for the cup proffered by the young girl.

The chocolate was, of course, delicious. Anything Janet cooked or prepared was superior. It was so cold the chocolate didn't stay hot for long. But by the time the liquid became chilled, it was gone.

"Oh," she said, sighing when she emptied the cup. "That was delicious, Helen. Thank you."

The young girl nodded. "I'm to ask you if you need any help, miss," Helen said. "I am to tell you, also, I'm not a foolish chit."

Margaret bit back a smile, hearing the echoes of Janet's irritation in the girl's speech.

"I can take orders well," she added, but the eyes exposed beneath the emerald scarf looked decidedly worried. "I've a beau in Inverness, miss, so I'm not wanting to poison myself."

"Did the earl tell you to say that?" she asked.

The girl shook her head rather vehemently. "He just said it was dangerous work. Mrs. Janet was the one who told me not to go and poison myself."

"Are you truly not a foolish girl?"

This time, Helen nodded, then added a comment. "I've a level head on my shoulders, miss."

"You haven't caught the stove on fire again?"

The girl smiled and then the expression immediately vanished, as if she were chastising herself for amusement.

"Mrs. Janet is a wonder, that's for sure. She makes one of the best bramble tarts I've ever eaten. Me, I've no talent whatsoever with food or stoves. But I can dust well, and I polish silver better than anyone I know."

"You'll have to have a level head about you now," Margaret said. "And a good pair of gloves."

To her surprise, the girl withdrew a pair of brown cotton gloves from her pocket. "Will these do?" she asked.

"As well as any, I suppose," Margaret said.

In truth, she was getting tired of this chore, and it looked as if she had a good hour or so of work ahead of her. At this rate, she truly would freeze before all the pigments were mixed. There was a chance she would need one or two of them tomorrow.

Once she was committed to beginning a painting, she liked to have all of her supplies around her. The very last thing she wanted to do was to be limited in working on a certain part of the composition because she hadn't prepared the right shade or tone for it.

Margaret showed Helen what she needed to do, demonstrating how to hold the end of the pestle as well as the proper twist and downward motion. The powder needed to be so finely ground that once linseed oil was added, no lumps would form.

She added two more teaspoonfuls of Egyptian Brown to the bottom of the mortar.

"Saints love us," Helen said. "It sure has a smell to it, it does. Like dead chickens too long in the henhouse."

"Try not to breathe of it," Margaret cautioned. "You'll begin coughing, and it will be weeks before you finish." She decided not to tell the young girl Egyptian Brown was also called Mummy because it was the ground-up remains of dead humans. The compound, however, produced a dark brown shade that could not be matched by any other pigment.

While Helen was occupied grinding the Egyptian Brown, Margaret carefully opened the jar of Madder, extracting the cork with care so as not to breathe any of the compound. Once the linseed oil was mixed, the pigment would become less toxic.

He'd sent her chocolate. What a very surprising gesture. None of the nobles she'd known in Russia would have shown such consideration. But then, they would've been amused at her reaction to the cold.

Just when she was certain she didn't like the Earl of Linnet at all, he'd surprised her. But then, it wasn't the first time he'd done so. She'd invaded his privacy in the worst way possible, and he'd apologized for his brutality and offered her a commission.

"Do you like working here, Helen?"

The girl looked surprised at the question.

"I suppose I do, yes. It's not a bad place to work. My knuckles don't get rapped, and nobody yells." She smiled. "Oh, Mrs. Janet gets annoyed from time to time, but she doesn't really yell."

Margaret wanted the girl to expand upon her comments, but questioning her further would only elicit Helen's curiosity. English servants had more freedom than those in Russia. If an English servant didn't like his position, he simply left it, choosing another household in which to serve. Russian servants were treated more like serfs.

A servant in the Empire also had a tendency to comment more openly. But that didn't mean, however, that the servants in Russia gossiped any less. Observing the behavior of those they served brought about endless amusement. Perhaps they were amusing, seen through the eyes of those who labored from dawn until dusk.

Margaret worked as hard as any scullery maid, but it was not easily identified as such. She stood for long hours in front of a canvas, staring at a blank spot, envisioning the depth and texture she wanted to see there. The translation of what she saw with her eyes and felt with her heart was always difficult to accomplish. Other people always thought it should be an easy process, that painting should be no more complex than simply wishing the image to appear.

Did authors feel the same pressure? Did they feel the same reluctance when viewing a blank page? Did they sometimes resent those who expected that the craft, their talent, would be so easy to achieve? In the case of a writer, however, their tasks to prepare for writing were so much easier than hers. They needn't obtain pigment from the four corners of the earth, or grind it for hours, or mix it with oil in small quantities so the paint was neither hard nor would take weeks to dry. A writer's only preparation was to sit in front of a blank sheet of paper and armed with a pen as his brush, await that instant when inspiration eased the transition from nothingness to a work of art.

Perhaps her life would have been easier had she been nothing more than a scullery maid. But there had never been a choice of that. She'd known, since she was a child, she was destined to scribble, as her mother called it.

Her talent had offered up some protection over the years. She was Margaret Dalrousie, favorite of the Russian court. If she had been nothing more than a scullery maid, she would have been at the mercy of any man above her station.

And she doubted if the Earl of Linnet would have sent her chocolate.

For the first time, she wondered at the Earl of Linnet's marriage. Had it been as happy as she envisioned? Had they been a pleasant couple to be around? For that matter, had they even encouraged visitors, or had they found themselves complete when alone?

She was rarely curious about the subjects of her painting, but perhaps this newfound interest in the

Earl of Linnet and his wife was the price she had to pay for the ability to paint again.

Did she have the ability to paint again, or was she just occupying her time with all these preparations to prevent testing her talent? What if she tried to work, only to discover that the same thing happened here as in Edinburgh?

Suddenly impatient with herself, she poured linseed oil into the bottom of the jar and signaled to Helen she'd pounded the pigment enough. For the next quarter hour, she concentrated on getting the consistency and the color just right.

Then, and only then, would she worry about whether or not she could paint.

Chapter 15

The sitting room was a bright and sunny place this morning. The snow from the night before had given way to a bright winter's day. The crystals of snow and ice glinted with the sun's rays, making the world a sparkling place.

He could almost believe in hope and joy on a morning like this.

Margaret was in place behind her easel. Today she was attired in a dark green dress, and he wondered if she'd selected it for the color. Did it bring out the hue of her eyes? Was she even that vain? Or was it vanity for a woman simply to accentuate her best feature?

Strangely, he would have thought her above such acts. The Margaret Dalrousie he was coming to know would simply disregard reactions to her appearance. Or dare those who disliked it to take their opinions elsewhere.

"McDermott," Margaret said, pointing at a chair beside the window, "if you will sit where you sat before, please."

"You're here early today, Miss Dalrousie. Are your paints all prepared then?"

She only nodded, once more pointing imperiously toward the chair with the end of her brush.

He did as she asked.

"Where did you meet Amelia?"

Surprised, he turned to face her, but all he could see of Miss Dalrousie now was the top of her head and portions of her skirt.

"Do you always appear like a disembodied voice?" he asked. "It's disconcerting."

"I can look at you, McDermott, or I can paint. I cannot do both." She stepped out from behind the easel, focusing her intent stare on him. "Which shall it be?"

"Painting, of course," he said, and sat back in the chair.

"In most cases I demand silence. But you would have me paint something not there, someone I do not know or cannot see. Consequently, I would like to paint a picture of her in my mind before I attempt to put it on the canvas."

She stepped back behind the easel.

"But I don't consider it conversation, McDermott. You are merely helping me define someone I can neither see nor touch."

Nor could he. Isn't that why he was here?

"Forgive me," he said. "For a moment I almost forgot. You are not merely a neighbor. You are Margaret Dalrousie, famous painter."

"While you are the Earl of Linnet, famous widower."

He stared in her direction. Did she say anything that came to mind?

"You were more than that, once. Well, weren't you?" She peeked out from behind the canvas, one hand resting on the easel, the other clutching a brush. She'd allowed her hair to do what it would this morning, and it curled in riotous disarray around her shoulders.

She was a gypsy, wasn't she? An *avant-garde* kind of woman. How very odd she was here at Glengarrow and that he was attempting to converse with her.

"You cannot mourn forever, McDermott. You will either wither and die yourself, or you will become such a hideous creature no one wishes to be around you." With that announcement, she stepped behind the canvas again.

"Have you become an Oracle now, Miss Dalrousie?"

"Where did you meet Amelia?"

He frowned at her, but because she couldn't see him, the expression had no use whatsoever. He turned back to the landscape, his mind recalling those moments seven years earlier. Was that all it had been?

"At a dinner party my mother gave," he said. "She was the daughter of one of my mother's closest friends. She was French. I'd heard her name before, of course, and I'm certain we probably passed each other at one entertainment or another. Edinburgh society is not that large, after all."

"What was your first impression of her? What did you think?"

"What an odd question, Miss Dalrousie. Would you rather hear what she looked like? What she wore?"

"Can you remember? It's been my experience men do not have the memory for wardrobe.

Women do, but then we are more fixated on such things. Take yourself, for example. You are wearing a white shirt and black trousers again. It's your common attire. I don't think you truly notice what you wear. If you had a valet, perhaps you would. Have you no manservant?"

"Which question shall I answer first?" he asked.

"What did you think of her?"

"I don't have a manservant, because I haven't had one since London. I live a different life at Glengarrow than I did at Parliament. There is no actual need for someone to tend to me."

"Did Amelia serve that purpose?"

Anger was a strange emotion. Just when he thought he was not capable of it, it bubbled free from its restraint and coursed throughout his body like a wave of heat.

"As in tending to me?"

"Don't wives do that?" she said blithely. "It has been my experience on observing marriages that women tend to act like a manservant. How very thrifty that must be. Once you marry, you can dismiss a valet, a majordomo, perhaps even a housekeeper. For no more expense than a wedding, you have obtained a bevy of servants."

"I thought she was very sweet," he said, ignoring her comment. "Unprepared for the conversation at dinner, perhaps, but that was something that could be corrected with a little more experience of the world."

She didn't speak for a moment, and he was wondering what barbs she was going to throw in his direction next. She was the most irritating woman, but then he'd known that before he'd given her this commission. It was his own fault he was sitting here being pummeled verbally by Margaret Dalrousie.

"Why are men attracted to helpless woman?" she asked.

He frowned toward the canvas again. But the question wasn't directed toward him as much as the air itself. She didn't seem to expect an answer, because she went on. "I have seen Cossacks turn to trembling jelly at the sight of a lone woman's smile."

"Perhaps because such women make us conscious we are men," he said. "Or we have a need to be protective. Or perhaps they simply remind us we're stronger, more equipped to deal with the world. I do not expect any of your suitors felt the same, Miss Dalrousie. No doubt they felt their very manhood was in peril near you."

There, they were at least equals in insults.

She didn't speak, either to refute his claim or bristle with indignation at his comment. Her very silence shamed him. Words were powerful weapons, and he knew that only too well. He was considered a brilliant orator by some, capable of swaying crowds, persuading stubborn old men. But he didn't apologize for the remark. She was the one who'd thrown down the gauntlet, and he had picked it up and thrown it back at her.

"She was wearing a yellow gown, and I thought she looked like springtime. I thought at first she was too young to be there, and only later did I realize she was only a year younger than I was. She never appeared to age, Amelia. Sometimes, I would see her and Penelope together, and I could see the shadow of Amelia as a child in Penelope's face. I think, even as an old woman, she would have appeared youthful. She had that kind of face."

Margaret still did not speak, but he didn't allow her silence to affect him.

"She had pale blond hair and blue eyes. They weren't her best feature, however. She had a lovely smile, one that was almost always present. Even in the midst of a domestic crisis, Amelia could find a way to look at the bright side. So, perhaps you're right," he said, conceding a point. "She was peacemaker and housekeeper, and no doubt a great many other roles. But the one I recall the most was that of wife, companion. Friend."

"How tall was she?"

The comment came in a dull sort of voice, as if Miss Dalrousie was deliberately ridding her tone of any emotion at all. Had he truly offended her?

"The top of her head came to the level of my chin," he said. How very strange that the comment should cause so much pain. Was it because he remembered all those moments when she'd stood next to him, or sometimes at night when she'd stand looking out at the world and he'd come and put his arms around her and rest his chin on the top of her head?

"She was not as tall as you, Miss Dalrousie. She had a delicacy to her that belied her strength. She was not petite, but she was not an Amazon either."

"I'm not that tall, McDermott. I daresay I come to your nose. Or maybe your eyes. The tips of your ears, perhaps. But no more than that."

When they next stood together, he would have to see if she was correct in her assessment.

"What shall you paint her in? Most of Amelia's gowns were in the trunk we took to France. But there are some items of clothing still here."

He had forgotten, for a moment, that she knew only too well how many of Amelia's dresses were left behind. He'd thrown one at her, hadn't he?

"And you are willing to remove them from their shrine?"

He was prepared for her insult this time. He only smiled.

"Why were you traveling to France?"

He was not prepared for that question.

"My wife's father was French. She'd not seen him for some time. He was ill, and had never seen Penelope. When he invited us, it sounded like a good idea."

He heard his own voice and wondered at the lack of emotion. Strangely, it was the first time he had spoken of the journey to France to a stranger. Would she probe still further? Was this truly serving the painting, or only Miss Dalrousie's curiosity?

"Do you need me to find you a gown of hers?"

"Not at the moment," she said.

"Is it even possible for you to do what I've asked, Miss Dalrousie? I've given you an idea of Amelia's beauty, of how lovely she truly was. But can you paint that?"

"Did you never argue? Did you never once become impatient with her?"

"I'm certain I must have," he said. "Neither one of us was a saint."

"But you can't remember those moments?"

He shook his head, then realized she couldn't see him. "No."

Silence stretched between them, in which time itself seemed elongated. Strangely enough, the moments were not unpleasant ones. It was as if Margaret allowed him this time truly to remember Amelia.

Where he was sitting was a warm place, and the pain in his leg eased. He stretched out his hand, his fingers widening in the sunlight. He'd been so cold for so very long.

"I have never met a perfect person," she finally said. "I've met kind ones, and self-serving ones, and even cruel ones. But never a perfect person."

"The fact I cannot remember her imperfections does not render Amelia perfect, Miss Dalrousie."

"In your eyes, she is. And because she is perfect, because she is rare, because there is no one else who could ever measure up to her," she said, "you will never relinquish her in your memory. Amelia would not want that for you. Unless, of course, she was selfish and cruel in her own way."

He stood and faced her. Her face peered around the side of the canvas, then she stepped out from behind the easel. Brave Miss Dalrousie, capable of fending for herself. Courageous enough to face the Earl of Linnet in all his rage.

"Have you taken it upon yourself, Miss Dalrousie, to rid me of my grief? Do you think to reason me from it?"

"I think you are a rational man in the core of you, but I don't think you know what to do with your grief. So, you wallow in it like a pig in mud and think yourself virtuous."

He'd never come so close to wanting to throttle a woman as he felt at that exact moment.

"Have you ever lost anyone you loved, Miss Dalrousie? Are you that much an expert at grief?"

"I've never lost anyone I've loved, McDermott. But then I've never been in love. Must I experience either emotion before I comment on it?"

At the moment he was so enraged he wasn't certain he could reason. And if he could reason, he wouldn't be able to speak.

"You loved Amelia, and loving her no doubt brought you great pleasure. Her loss brings you great pain. But isn't that the price you pay for love?"

He took one step toward her, then cautioned himself, remaining where he was. He didn't want to get too close to Margaret Dalrousie at the moment. He might take her shoulders in his hands and began to shake her.

Damn her, she seemed to know it if that small smile was any indication.

"There shouldn't be a price to pay," he said, biting out the words.

She carefully placed the brush in the tray in front of the easel and took one more step to the side so he could see her more clearly.

"Why not? Why is love exempt from every other experience in life? There are always pluses and minuses to everything, McDermott. Why is love not the same?"

Perhaps at another time he might have agreed with her. Right at the moment, however, he would have done anything other than admit she had reason on her side.

"For all your pain, McDermott," she said, clasping her hands together and staring at him with that intent look of hers. "I think you were very privileged."

He turned and walked back to the window, clasping the sash with both hands.

"So if I have five years of joy, am I supposed to have five years of pain?"

"I haven't the slightest idea."

He glanced over his shoulder at her. "That's the first honest statement I believe you've made today. How admirable you are not to know all of the answers to all of the questions of the universe."

"If it makes you feel better to be angry at me, then so be it. I'm not the one who visited you with grief, McDermott. I am only questioning why you are so angry at the fact you're in pain."

He turned back to her.

"Isn't it better you feel loss than you feel nothing? Some husbands might even feel relief to be rid of their wives. Not you. There is pain in your eyes, McDermott. And I see the lights on at Glengarrow often enough to know you don't sleep well. For all your pain, I find myself envying you."

"Why in hell would you envy me?"

"Because you've known love. A great many people haven't. I don't know how long it will last, but this pain you feel now is an homage of sorts, don't you think? It's a way of bidding farewell to what you did know, and perhaps even preparing yourself for what the future will bring. It isn't something to fear as much as it is something to endure."

"And yet you've never grieved. How very generous you are with your advice. Do you ever ask yourself why you've never loved, Miss Dalrousie? Is it because you're not capable of being loved? It's an emotion that thrives on being reciprocated."

She clenched her hands together tighter, but that was the only reaction to his words. If she had flinched, if her skin had paled, her eyes narrowed, if she had made any response whatsoever to his cruelty, he would have ceased right there and then. But she looked impassive, almost resilient, and resistant to anything he might say, and that very stoicism irritated him and pushed his anger up one notch.

"Why does no one love you, Miss Dalrousie? Do they not find you feminine enough? You with your way of challenging the world, your ungainly stride, your coldness. Your hair is too black, and your mouth is too large. Your eyes are too color- ful for your face. None of your features seem to go with the others. And I suspect you bind your breasts, because sometimes they appear large and at other times barely there. Is that why you've had no suitors?"

"I've had my share, McDermott. And lovers, if you must know."

At another time, he would have been startled at her honesty, but now he was too intent on hurting her.

"Or is it your character, Miss Dalrousie, that sets you apart from other women? Is it the fact you see yourself as separate from the rest of society? You are not subject to rules and regulations that govern the behavior of others. You are Margaret Dalrousie, and the world must give you whatever you wish, including the right to say or do whatever you please."

She gripped her left wrist with her right hand. Her smile seemed unnatural, but he'd not seen it often enough to know for certain.

"I can see this was a foolish idea of mine, Miss Dalrousie, I am humble enough to admit I make a mistake from time to time. Hiring you was evidently one of my greater mistakes in a very long time."

"You cannot dismiss me," she said, and her lifeless announcement irritated him still further.

"I can and I have," he said. "Your services will no longer be needed."

"The painting will go on," she said. "Whether or not you give me permission to do so. I will paint what I want when I want, McDermott, and words will not stop me. Even yours."

He wished, suddenly, he knew more about her, that he knew her weaknesses, her frailties. He would have used the knowledge as a weapon in the same manner she did. She wielded words like a sword and remained dispassionate when the victim began to bleed copiously.

Yet what she had said was not altogether wrong, which was probably why he was so angry. He didn't like a stranger, especially Margaret Dalrousie, pointing out the error of his logic. But then, love wasn't logical, was it?

Neither was grief.

He had dismissed her, yet she refused to be dismissed. He couldn't banish her from Blackthorne Cottage, but he could refuse her admittance to Glengarrow. Yet, by her own admission, she'd continue to work on the portrait. Like it or not, he had set her into motion, and Miss Dalrousie's irritating presence was the price he had to pay for Amelia's portrait.

The scales would be balanced, then. Another instance of her logic proving correct.

He walked slowly back to the chair and sat, heavily.

"I do not like you very much, Miss Dalrousie. If you were on fire, I'm not entirely certain I would summon a bucket of sand to put you out."

"Then I shall endeavor never to find myself in flames."

Her expression wasn't bland at all. He couldn't define what he saw on her face, but it was emotion. Pleased, he sat back against the chair as she occupied herself in painting, feeling as if he had won this battle after all.

Why, then, was he so damnably irritated?

Chapter 16

Margaret returned to Glengarrow time and again, armed with tenacity and a sense of purpose. To paint again was a miracle. To be able to touch the brush to her canvas and feel a rush of joy so profound it seemed spiritual was worth any amount of difficulty McDermott gave her.

Some days, he would do nothing but stare off into space. Other days, he was cutting in his remarks. Either way, she simply ignored him.

A day passed in this manner, then a week. The room was a comfortable one, lit as it was by the winter sun. For hours, she could almost believe herself alone, becoming familiar with the sound of Glengarrow settling around her.

Janet saw to it that the room was aired every morning, and when Margaret arrived, she closed the window, went to her easel, and carefully removed the drape from the canvas.

The clean winter air banished the smell of linseed oil, leaving only the scent of the potpourri Janet left in a dish on the table beside the chair. Along with the dried flowers and patchouli, she could smell the faint ever-present scent of Amelia's perfume, as if Janet used it to sweeten the mixture.

Before the earl arrived, Margaret would prepare herself for her task of the day. She approached a painting in a methodical manner, directing her talent rather than allowing it to run amok. She began on the periphery of a canvas, working toward a focal point. Often, a portrait's background was complete before the subject had ever been started. Each day, she knew exactly what she would be painting, and she studied the canvas with an eye to the finished task.

When McDermott entered the room, she waited for him to settle into his chair before beginning, but after that moment, she ignored him other than to ask an occasional question about Amelia. What did she do with her hands when she spoke and when she sat in a chair? Did she have the habit of propping her chin with her hand? Or linking her fingers together? He always answered, but never continued the conversation.

Would that all her subjects were as silent.

After several hours, she came out from behind her easel, wiping her brush on the cloth soaked in linseed oil, a sign that she was finished for the day.

McDermott would stand, and without another word, simply leave the room.

Today, however, was different, and the hint of it came when McDermott began a conversation just as she was attempting the most intricate pattern of a Chinese vase.

"Do your other subjects object to hours of silence on end, Miss Dalrousie?" he asked.

She smiled at the canvas. Every person she'd ever painted had asked the same question. The only difference was the length of time it had taken to ask it.

"Yes," she said. "If you want a Dalrousie portrait, there is a certain price to pay."

"In addition to the outrageous sum you're charging me?"

"You can always do as my patrons in Russia did, Your Lordship," she said. "You can always refuse to pay me."

"On what pretext?"

"None," she said. "Simply because they deemed me unworthy of being paid, perhaps."

She was distressingly close to revealing too much to him again.

"I'm a man of honor, Miss Dalrousie. I pay my debts."

She could tell by his tone that she'd insulted him.

"Should I apologize to you again?" she asked.

"You should," he said flatly. "And perhaps I should apologize to you for all the comments I made that were offensive. Or even worse, perhaps I should just issue a blanket apology to you now, Miss Dalrousie, for anything I may say in the future that may be less than kind."

She put the brush down on the tray in front of the easel and carefully stepped to the side, regarding him with caution.

"What is it about us, the two of us, McDermott, that seems to rub the other raw?"

The question wasn't a wise one to ask, but where had she been wise in regard to him?

He leaned back in the chair, his smile without a tint of mockery. She was more comfortable with the grieving noble, a man whose soul was so obviously battered and bruised. This man, with laughter in his eyes and his lips curved in a smile, was a stranger, and a too-charming one at that.

"I haven't the slightest idea, Miss Dalrousie. It's foolish, don't you agree? We're neighbors, however unwillingly we might wish it."

Why on earth did that remark hurt when she'd been able to ignore his more cutting comments?

Annoyed, she returned to her canvas.

"I've actually laughed because of you, Miss Dalrousie," he said a few minutes later. "For that, I thank you. For taking on this commission, which I know cannot be an easy one to execute, I also thank you. Do you think you can even achieve it?"

"I'm a woman of honor," she said, tight-lipped. "I wouldn't have agreed to do it had I not thought I could."

She wished the canvas was bigger. Right at the moment, it could easily have been the size of a room and yet not be large enough.

"Shall we talk of Janet and Tom? Or the weather?" he asked. "The weather is always an amenable topic."

"I normally enforce silence on my subjects. If they push me on the matter, I will allow one visitor. Shall I call for one of the maids, Your Lordship?" she asked. "Or perhaps Tom?"

"Why not? We can discuss the stables, or the hunting around Glengarrow. I'm sure we could find more than one topic of conversation. Unlike the two of us. You are excessively uncommunicative about your past, Miss Dalrousie. And I find I don't want to discuss mine."

"I do not like poetry," she contributed, in direct violation of her own rule not to converse while she was working. "Although I find that the majority of books in my possession at the moment are those of poetry. I haven't the slightest idea why, and I cannot remember how some of them came to be in my library."

"Perhaps they were gifts from admirers. Or from your many lovers."

She sent him an exasperated look, but of course he couldn't see it through the canvas.

"Feel free to borrow from Glengarrow's library. There is a large section of novels you might find to your fancy."

"Thank you."

"I expected a retort from you, Miss Dalrousie. I expected you to say something like: do you think me only capable of reading novels, McDermott?"

He so adeptly mimicked the tone she might have used that she found herself smiling again.

"Instead, you only thank me, which leaves me feeling like a boor."

She remained silent, her smile broadening.

"If you had no money, how did you purchase Blackthorne Cottage?" he asked abruptly.

"Is it any of your concern?" she asked.

"Yes," he said, surprising her. "Blackthorne Cottage used to belong to Glengarrow."

"I didn't purchase it," she said. "It was a gift."

"A gift?"

She moved from behind the easel. "I had a bene-factor," she said, "but I don't know who it was."

"How was this benefactor made known to you?"

"My solicitor came to me," she said. "He wasn't my solicitor at the time, of course. He agreed to work on other matters for me later. But Mr. Tapin said that the cottage had been given to me as a gift from someone who admired my art."

"Tapin?"

"Augustus Tapin. His firm is quite well-known, I understand."

"I know them well," he said, sitting back in the chair. His smile was back, but the look in his eyes was coolly assessing. "Are you certain you have no idea of the identity of your benefactor?"

"Mr. Tapin was very reticent on the subject. He would not divulge the information."

"How very fortuitous a gift," he said.

"But you would prefer that I be anywhere but near Glengarrow."

"Have I appeared that inhospitable, Miss Dalrousie?"

"You have," she said, stepping back behind the easel once more.

"You were reared in Fife, you said."

"Have you the gift of perfect recall, McDer-mott?"

"No, but I am capable of remembering facts that interest me."

She didn't answer him for a moment, curious if she interested him. That was *not* a question she'd ask.

"Yes," she finally said, "I was born and raised in

Fife. I come from a very poor family, McDermott. I had six brothers and four sisters. What else would you like to know?"

"I hear France in your voice sometimes. Sometimes a touch of an Italian accent."

"I lived in Paris, and I speak French and Italian."

"No Russian?"

"Yes, I speak Russian."

"You've achieved a great deal, Miss Dalrousie. Evidently, some of your previous lovers were influential, if not moneyed men."

"On the contrary," she said calmly. "I've never depended on anyone else for either my livelihood or any achievements I've accomplished. What I've done, for good or ill, McDermott, has been on my own."

"Ah, but there is your fallacious argument." He clasped his hands together and leaned forward, staring at the carpet beneath his feet. "No one ever accomplishes anything without the assistance of someone else. Either accidentally, or deliberately. We are a society of human beings, Miss Dalrousie, and as such, we interact and depend on each other. You may think yourself independent and alone, but if you will stretch your mind back through the years, you'll see your achievements were not solitary at all."

"Spoken like a politician, McDermott, but not as a man who has ever had to fend for himself."

He didn't respond to that remark. Were they both attempting to be civil? How unlikely of both of them.

"How well do you know Paris?" he asked.

"I know Italy better," she said. "I studied there for three years. My first lover was Italian. A count. Once we were intimate, I realized it was a mistake."

"Why?"

"Because I had nothing more to learn from him. And I could only hurt him by that admission. It taught me a lesson. It is not a good idea to mix pleasure and work. So, from that point on, when I did take a lover, he was neither a subject nor a teacher, or anyone involved in my work."

"Princes or dukes," he guessed.

Her silence was assent enough.

"How many lovers have you had, Miss Dalrousie?"

Did he expect her to blush or stammer at the question.

"As many as you, McDermott."

That comment evidently rendered him speechless, because he didn't say anything for several long moments. When he did speak, however, she almost wished she hadn't yielded to the temptation to needle him.

"Yet, for all your lovers, you've never known love."

"Is it necessary for one to have the other? I've felt affection for the men I've invited to my bed, McDermott. I longed for them, I wanted them, and when it was over, it was time."

"I know why you've never loved, Miss Dalrousie," he said. "I don't believe you're capable of it. You're cold and calculating, and about as warm as a Russian winter."

"Perhaps you're right," she said.

She stepped out from behind the painting and regarded him.

"I've always tried to be honest with others. I've wanted a great deal in my life, but what I wanted wasn't the same as what other women wanted. I wanted someone to be able to see a creation I did with my own hands." She stretched out her hands palms up, as if she had never before seen them.

"A painting will not last forever, McDermott, but it will last for a significant number of years. Enough time that someone will stand in front of it and be in awe. He will wonder how an artist had the skill to capture a person so perfectly that a moment was preserved for dozens and dozens of years."

She dropped her hands.

"That's what I want. That's what I've always wanted. I wanted that recognition more than I wanted love. But it was a trade, McDermott. I never fooled myself it would be anything else. I've never felt love, the anguish or the ecstasy of it. But if it's anything like I feel when I'm painting, then it's not something to be taken lightly or to be treated with disdain."

"Why do you practice shooting every day?" he asked abruptly.

"To practice," she said.

"Why?"

"To get better, of course. To be able to shoot a target. To at least shoot what I'm aiming for."

"For what purpose? Are you going hunting, Miss Dalrousie? You don't own enough land for game to be plentiful. And I take great umbrage to people hunting in my woods without permission."

"Your rabbits and deer are safe from me, McDermott."

"Then at whom are you aiming?"

"Perhaps a former lover," she said smiling again. "Or a subject who refused to pay me. Or one who refused to remain silent."

He stood and began walking toward the door.

"I have not finished for the day," she said.

"I have, Miss Dalrousie. It is one of my rules, one I've had to institute with only you. When I become sufficiently irritated, I leave the room."

"Will you be here tomorrow?" she asked.

He glanced at her over his shoulder. "Will my mood have mellowed by then? My irritation dissipated? I don't know, Miss Dalrousie. In fact, I haven't decided exactly what I'm going to do in regards to you."

Just what was that supposed to mean? Irritated, she stared after him.

Chapter 17

Margaret awoke, knowing she was screaming, either in her dream or in her mind. She
sat up abruptly, clutching the pillow to her chest
and rocked back and forth, a gesture not unlike
that of a child. But had her mother ever comforted
her? With so many children was there ever truly
enough time to croon to the oddest child among
her brood?

She lay back on the bed, curled into herself.
One day, the nightmares had begun. One day, they
would go away. All she had to do was endure them
in the meantime.

The physician she'd seen in Edinburgh did not
know the entire story. She didn't think she could
tell another soul about what had happened to her,
not after the reception she'd received in Russia
when she'd done that very thing. The physician had
counseled she walk and spend some time in reflection. She'd almost felt amused at his prescription,
but she followed it regardless.

Margaret stood and walked to the other side of
the room, turning the key at the base of the gas
lamp and increasing the flame. She never slept in

the dark anymore. Darkness, the night itself, encouraged her nightmares. Why was it that horrible deeds were never done during the day? Why was it that night seemed a more propitious time for evil? When darkness shrouded the earth did it obscure goodness as well?

She donned her wrapper and debated going downstairs to make herself some tea. Tom and Janet slept on the third floor, so she wouldn't have to worry about disturbing them. But she didn't like walking through the cottage in the darkness.

Instead, she stoked the fire, added some more coal, and sat at the window in the overstuffed chair where she normally read during the day. A moment later, she stood again and walked to the bed, grabbing a pillow before returning to her chair. She wrapped her arms around the pillow even as she mocked herself for finding comfort in such a silly object.

She pushed open the drapes with one hand, unsurprised to see that ice had formed on the inside of the windows. She leaned close to the glass, blew on it, then traced a pattern with her nail.

Margaret drew up her legs and turned in the chair, laying her cheek against the back, still clutching the pillow. The lights of Glengarrow were a beacon for her eyes and her thoughts.

She'd lied. Would he know? Would he also know she'd told him the absolute truth? She'd never fallen in love, unless what she felt when she was painting was love. That much was true. But she'd lied about taking a lover.

That night had been chill and damp, a harbinger to spring. The weather was an impetus to stay abed until the dawn sun warmed the bite of the air and turned the mist into fleeing tendrils of fog. Not that the nobles of St. Petersburg needed an excuse to avoid morning. Unless, of course, they were still celebrating from the night before, as Margaret had been.

She remembered smiling gratefully at the young maid who'd fetched her cloak and let her assist in the placing of it around her shoulders. Even the cloak could not warm her—it seemed as though the night air seeped into her bones. She shivered again, nodded in the affirmative when the majordomo asked if she wanted her troika summoned.

The ball had been interminable. Her face ached from smiling fatuously at her dance partners, her wrist felt permanently bent into a fan-holding position. Her corset, a torturous device lined with whalebone stays, felt embedded in the tender flesh of her torso. But most of all, she wanted to sit down, to dispense with the tattered and worn slippers covering her aching, swollen feet.

She sighed, glanced at the departing guests, and smiled slightly in greeting. She cupped one hand over her mouth to stifle her yawn and wished there was a retiring couch somewhere in this stuffy, crowded foyer.

A few moments passed and she yawned again, then glanced around to see who might have spied her rude gesture before smiling at herself. Half the guests were nodding off—she was just one of many who yearned for her bed. She stood on one foot, then the other, like a graceful stork, knowing her birdlike gestures could not be seen beneath the flowing skirts of her gown.

Suddenly, the lure of solitude and relief for her aching feet was something she could not resist.

The stone steps bit into her tender feet, and she could feel the fabric of her slippers falling away as she walked to the corner where the carriage stood, waiting its turn before the entrance to the magnificent mansion. She would have called up to her driver for assistance in mounting the carriage steps, had not a hand swooped around her neck and pulled her backward into bushes as tall as the wheels of the carriage. She would have screamed then, in shock, or sheer surprise, if a gloved hand had not been clamped over her mouth.

Her first reaction was anger. Nor was it tempered by the harsh, grating laugh behind her as another hand snaked around her waist. She twisted in her captor's grasp, rage adding an impetus to strength that came from youth and health. She kicked backward, but her barely shod feet encountered legs as strong as trees, and her flailing movements did nothing but bring another chuckle from her assailant.

Within moments she was covered by a suffocating cloth, dark and smelling of horse. Muscular arms clamped around her tightly, a band of flesh and muscle and bone she was powerless to dislodge. Hands grappled at her legs, pushed up the floor-length gown, and gripped her ankles tightly as she was hauled through the bushes like a hog, trussed and kicking. She screamed, but the blanket was quickly forced between her open lips by a ruthless hand, and the only sound emerging was a stifled moan.

Two sets of hands hefted her up into a carriage, and she was roughly dumped upon the floor. She spat out as much of the foul blanket as she could, enough to draw in deep gulps of air through her mouth. Her lungs felt near to bursting. Margaret knew, in that moment, that she was in grave danger.

She remembered everything. How could she ever forget?

She'd been a virgin, perhaps past her prime, but a virgin all the same when she'd been attacked. They'd taken her virginity, but at least they had not given her a child or the pox, and for that alone she'd learned to be grateful.

All they had bequeathed to her was a series of memories, and the ever-present nightmares. In her dreams, she was attacking them, she was fighting back and winning whereas in reality it had not happened that way.

She'd been blindfolded so their faces were unknown. Nor could she recall anything they said, words not being important anyway. The physician who'd been called by her maid also treated the Russian court, and he'd said nothing at all while he'd treated the scratches on her face and her bloodied fingers. She'd been a mass of bruises for weeks, and sometimes, even now, she thought she could see the shadow of them still on her skin. It had taken months until she could touch herself and not recall the intrusive fingers of strangers who'd used her body as if she were more no more than a receptacle.

How many baths had she taken? Enough that the maids had commented on how many buckets of hot water it had taken. Enough that the footmen had to summon more wood for the fire. Enough that her own maid had looked worried.

She couldn't wash the attack away, however.

Somehow, it had pleased her to play at being more worldly than she was. Let the Earl of Linnet think she was a shocking woman, a woman given to taking a great many lovers, then abandoning them. Let McDermott believe she was cold and fearless, that she had no compunction against saying what she wished and doing whatever she wanted.

He didn't need to know about her nightmares or the fact she was terrified more often than not.

Terror, however, had an immolating effect, and she refused to give in to it. Instead, she practiced her shooting until the day came when her solicitor reported he had, indeed, found the owner of the signet ring she'd sketched and given him.

A light blinked out, and she concentrated on Glengarrow again.

She'd been too direct with him. Mostly, she held her tongue, restraint coming not naturally, but a lesson learned after a number of years. Only with McDermott had that bond been loosened, and she'd allowed her opinion and her comments free rein.

But she'd spoken too candidly, revealing too

much of herself. For that revelation, he'd labeled her cold. Perhaps she was, in a way. She'd fought long and hard for what she wanted. In Paris and Italy, she'd denied herself affection, friends, and relaxation. When others danced and laughed, she was practicing the slant of an eye or the eternal damnable nose. Noses were her difficulty, and she'd practiced them endlessly until they were right.

"You have a great deal of internal strength, my dear," one of her instructors had said. "After all, it is not many women who would throw away a certain future for an uncertain one." He'd been speaking, of course, of becoming a wife versus her future as an artist.

She'd not known, then, how to articulate that painting was the one thing she very much wanted to do in her lifetime. Even a sliver of a chance was enough, and worth more than a hundred guaranteed futures. In the end, she'd been one of the fortunate ones. She'd attracted the attention of the Grand Duchess, and she in turn, had mentioned her to the Empress Alexandra Feodorovna. After that one commission, her future was assured.

Another lesson she'd learned—life changed, sometimes too rapidly to understand fully. Nothing was ever guaranteed or promised forever.

She knew that only too well.

The four men who'd attacked her had not felt lust as much as a sense of entitlement, a greed overwhelming any human feeling. Perhaps they hadn't even wanted her but had settled for any woman. She'd been available. Never mind that she'd screamed until her voice was hoarse. Never mind that she'd gouged at them until her own fingers bled. Never mind that whenever she thought of any of them, she wanted to be sick.

No, futures could be changed, couldn't they? Sometimes, they could be altered by a single act.

The Earl of Linnet understood that, didn't he?

Another light blinked out, as if Glengarrow agreed.

He was not the only one awake on this winter night. Why was he unsurprised to see the light on at Blackthorne Cottage?

He shouldn't have called her cold. If anything, she was restrained. She rarely smiled, and when she did, the expression was half-surprised, as if amusement was the last thing she expected to feel. From the moment he'd met her, she'd been an enigma. The only time she'd appeared alive was when she was angry. Perhaps he should endeavor to anger Miss Margaret Dalrousie more.

Evincing curiosity about another woman made him feel as if he were being unfaithful to Amelia. The logical side of his mind understood only too well that what he was feeling was idiotic but probably normal. Another oddity, that her death had felt so new when he'd first returned to Glengarrow. As the days passed, he was only too aware of the fact it had been three years since he'd lost Amelia.

All he could remember clearly was the sound of her laughter.

*   *   *

"It's been long enough," Janet said in the darkness.

She reached out and grabbed Tom's hand. When he squeezed it in return, she smiled. They had an affinity in their wakefulness, it seemed.

Being married twenty years eliminated the need for questions. Tom didn't ask the meaning of her comment. All he did was turn his head and look at her.

"He's grieving, lass, leave him be."

"If he doesn't let her go soon, Tom, he never will. The painting isn't helping."

He sat up, began to argue with the pillow as he did every night. Try as she might to convince him, he would not trade his old pillow for a new one or new stuffing either. She thought he'd liked the ritual he went through every night pounding it into shape with both fists, then shaking it in the air only to fold it in half beneath his neck as he looked up in disgust at the ceiling.

"I'm thinking the painting is helping Miss Margaret more than him," Tom said.

She sighed and turned to him in the darkness. "She's grieving too, Tom, but I don't know what for. She holds her thoughts inside so tightly it's like they're locked."

"Perhaps they're good for each other. Besides, how long would you have him grieve? How many years does it take? How long would it take for me to get used to you not being around, Janet?"

She smiled. "I'm not saying you get used to being without me. But you begin to believe it's true, that death has come between us. Sometimes I see him look up when I come into a room, and it's like he expects Amelia to be there. She isn't, and she's not going to be."

"Don't you think he really knows? I think it's a game he plays with himself. He's a smart man, Janet, and we knew his coming back to Glengarrow would not be easy."

"Do you hate him, Tom?"

"For our wages?"

She shook her head. "No, for the other."

"Janet, how can you ask that? Of course I don't hate him."

"Still, he didn't treat you the best."

Tom nodded. "I understand it, Janet. He had no time for thoughts of anyone else."

They lay quiet next to each other. Finally, Janet spoke again. "If it's a game, Tom, it's a foolish one. He's alive and should be among the living. Even Amelia would want that for him."

"Aye, lass, and it's probably why he came home. Not to revel in his pain as much as to say good-bye."

She turned to him in the darkness and placed her hand on his chest, needing the connection between them, and feeling grateful for the life she felt beneath her palm.

Chapter 18

"**I** have always loved this room," Janet said, entering Amelia's sitting room. "Did you know it was called the Winter Parlor? No doubt because the sun warms it most of the day."

"I imagine there's a room that's known as the summer parlor?" Margaret asked, carefully arranging her brushes for the day's work. She would be concentrating still on the background, a little delaying tactic on her part. She was approaching her subject very cautiously, giving herself enough time to actually think about how she wanted the portrait to appear in its final state.

She'd never before been so tentative with her work, but she'd never before tried to paint a ghost, either.

Janet only smiled at her comment.

"Amelia liked the conservatory on warm sunny days. It was always cool, what with all the plants there. But she was good at growing things. I never saw anyone like it."

Margaret peered around the canvas. "Is there anything she didn't do well? Was she ever impatient or inattentive?"

Janet's smile grew wider. "She wasn't a saint, Miss Amelia, but she had a way about her. She made people want to be around her. You would have liked her, I think."

"I find saints too virtuous to endure for long."

Janet only shook her head, as if Margaret's comment was laced with amusement.

She was truly tired of hearing about Amelia the angel. Granted, it was an all-too-human characteristic to ascribe virtues to those dear ones who'd died. But surely someone could think of a moment when Amelia had been annoying, or when she'd been insufferable.

"How is your painting coming along, Miss Margaret?"

Normally, she never answered questions about a work in progress, but she didn't want to be rude to Janet. So she answered as vaguely as she could.

"It's going well," she said.

"His Lordship has tasked you with a difficult chore, I'm thinking. To paint something you can't see, I mean."

"The task would be easier, if His Lordship were less tardy."

Janet looked surprised. "Are you waiting for His Lordship, then? He's not here, Miss Margaret."

She put down her brush.

"Has he gone to Inverness again?" she asked calmly.

Janet shook her head. "No, he's off to Edinburgh, miss."

She knew better than to ask Janet for details. Janet would smile and be amiable, but she wouldn't divulge any more than the earl wanted Margaret to know. Since he hadn't told her himself he would be away, he evidently didn't want her to know anything.

And in the meantime, her painting would suffer.

She really shouldn't be angry, but the swiftness of the emotion took her by surprise. How dare he leave. How dare he go without saying a word, without even so much as a note of explanation.

He'd violated her rules. Again.

"Very well," Margaret said, taking all of her brushes, one by one, and placing them in the leather case where they were stored. She folded the flap over them, then rolled them into a tight tube she tied with the enclosed ribbon. "I see no reason why I should remain here."

"Why ever not?" Janet asked. "He's made Glengarrow at your disposal. This room, especially." Her gaze encompassed the room, touching on the various pieces of furniture with more than a housekeeper's perusal. Margaret couldn't help but wonder if she saw Amelia reclining on the chaise or sitting in the chair beside the window.

If so, she sincerely hoped Janet wouldn't mention it. Margaret had no difficulty whatsoever picturing Amelia as the ghost of Glengarrow.

Despite what the older woman said, she and Amelia would probably not have suited well at all. She would have been slightly derisive of Amelia, and Margaret might have been a curiosity for the Countess of Linnet, or God forbid, an object of pity.

Single women were always excessively pitied by happily married women, and only envied by those miserably wed.

Each of them would have probably thought herself vastly superior to the other woman.

Did Amelia have the power to see Margaret as she stood here now? Was she angry that life had been taken from her and perhaps wasted on a woman like Margaret? A woman who, in the last year, had sometimes wished that life had been taken from her as well?

Margaret said, "I would be happier back in the cottage, I think. I'm less likely to be interrupted."

Janet's smile cooled. "Whatever you wish, Miss Margaret."

They both knew the chance of her being interrupted in the Winter Parlor was negligible. With only two servants employed in addition to Tom and Janet, Glengarrow was not overrun with servants. In fact, each of them had a full day of work just to maintain the large house.

Janet left the room, and the moment she was gone, Margaret wanted to call her back and apologize. Her anger was at the Earl of Linnet, not Janet.

Why was she surprised he was gone? After yesterday's conversation, it was a wonder he hadn't banished her from Glengarrow.

She placed the brushes in her valise, looked at the palette of colors she'd already arranged, and sighed inwardly. Pigments cost money, money she couldn't readily spare. It would be better not to waste what she'd already prepared for today's work.

The least he could have done was explain he was leaving, that he would be unavailable. How long was he going to remain in Edinburgh?

She scraped off the brilliant red Dragon's Blood pigment with her palette knife and put it into the jar set aside for the mixture. After she carefully wiped off the knife, she repeated the process with the Orpiment, Egyptian Brown, and Alizarin Crimson. Once the pigments were stored, she placed the jars back in her satchel and studied the work.

Every morning when she was actively working on a portrait, she stood in front of the canvas, whatever state of completion it was in, and closed her eyes, envisioning the final painting. She remained there however long it took to fix the image in her mind. Once she opened her eyes, it was as if she knew exactly what brushstrokes were needed to complete the work to fit her vision.

This portrait, however, was different. This was more challenging than anything she'd ever begun.

No one looking at the canvas would be able to discern the final product. Even the background was barely formed. Still, it belonged to her now, a product of her imagination and her talent, something infinitely personal and private.

She'd never before carried an unfinished painting back to her quarters, trusting, instead, in the rules she'd set down before a commission began. There was a time when she'd had more potential commissions than she could possibly accept. People had clamored for her to paint their portraits. Those who were fortunate enough to engage her were also wise enough not to disobey any of her rules.

The Earl of Linnet, however, had freely admitted to looking at the painting. He was an arrogant, stubborn, independent man, and reveled in any opportunity to prove that fact. Therefore, it was better simply to remove the painting and keep it close beside her.

She grabbed the canvas with her right hand, and her satchel with her left, leaving the Winter Parlor with a feeling too much like relief. At the doorway, she had the strangest feeling she should turn back and look at the empty room. Instead, she refused to do so, telling herself there was nothing there. No ethereal body wafting in the air, wings fluttering, an enchanting smile bidding her farewell. No disembodied presence hinting at life but smelling of the grave.

There was nothing of Amelia there.

Why, then, did she feel so much better after leaving the room?

The satchel was heavy, and the canvas cumbersome. She took her time walking down the corridor, studying the landscape murals painted on the walls. Were they of Italy? Or the south of France, perhaps, with their stunted trees and rolling hills. A peaceful vista, each of them, nothing garish or unsettling.

When she'd first arrived in Russia, she'd been assaulted by the magnificence of the Russian court, and their many palaces. Toward the end of her stay, however, she'd been surfeited by the excess.

There was too much gold and gilt, too many Florentine cupids and Raphael-like statues. There had been too much of everything, and it had jaded the palate.

Glengarrow wasn't a palace, but it was lovely in its way. Beauty was there in unexpected places, like the carved cornices and the detail of roses and thistles on the wainscoting.

Even the doors were carved, and she hesitated at one featuring trailing vines around the outside of the frame, culminating in a large rose at the handle. She placed the satchel and canvas on the floor, and traced the petals of the rose, amazed at the skill of the wood-carver.

Each door in this corridor was graced with some type of decoration, and she began to wonder if the rooms themselves were decorated to match. Was the room with the rose patterned door called the Rose Room, and were all the furnishings pink?

At the end of the corridor, she was surprised to find a door adorned not with flowers but animals. A small raccoon sat beside a log and in a pond in front of him swam three baby ducklings. A young fox peered furtively between tall fronds of grass.

Once again, she placed the canvas up against the wall and set her satchel beside it. Slowly, she tried the handle. The door wasn't locked but swung open easily. Margaret entered, keeping the door open behind her.

Although the room was dark, the light from the corridor made it possible for Margaret to see the draped bed, the dolls arranged on the shelves against one wall, a rocking horse on the carpet in the middle of the floor. A series of blocks had been carefully stacked together near the fireplace.

This was a child's room, a little girl's room, a room no longer occupied. She noticed the door in the far wall, but she didn't move, didn't cross the floor to open it. No doubt it led to a nurse's or governess's room. How old had Penelope been? She wasn't entirely certain. Young, from the arrangement of the toys, and small bed.

She'd never had a child, and it occurred to her she'd never been one, being a strange and solitary little girl. In her family, she'd always been the odd one, the different one. But the painful experience of her childhood was a very long way away.

This child had been loved and cherished, and probably would have been loved for the whole of her life no matter her nature or her character. Children died, that was a fact of life. A great many children died in infancy. But this child had not died of illness. This child had died in an accident, something that shouldn't have happened.

She could almost hear Penelope's laughter, could almost envision the little girl with long blond hair shaking her head when her nurse would have put her down for a nap.

"Truly I'm not tired. Why must I sleep?"

"Because it's time," the nurse would have answered, a patient smile on her face. And despite

Penelope's protests, the room would be darkened in the middle of the day, just like now.

Penelope's upbringing wouldn't have been relegated solely to a nurse. No doubt Amelia was a devoted mother and would have cared for her daughter herself.

Did she select the little girl's wardrobe, standing in front of the armoire every morning?

"I think you should wear the pink, Penelope," she'd say. "And don't forget that apron. You have a tendency, my love, to become more than a little dirty during the day."

"Could you read me a story, Mama?" Penelope would have asked her mother at bedtime. Together they would have sat in the overstuffed chair beside the table with its little lamp topped by a pink-and-green lampshade. Penelope would have sat beside her mother as Amelia read, and perhaps Robert joined them, and perched on the end of Penelope's bed. Or perhaps the roles were reversed, and Robert was the reader.

Did the shadows in the room move? At that moment, Margaret wouldn't have been surprised to smell Amelia's perfume. There were ghosts in this room. Ghosts that pulled at the heart and tugged at her tears.

How did McDermott bear this?

She'd never met Amelia, or Penelope, yet somehow their deaths weighed on her heart as strongly as if they were dear friends. How did McDermott endure this pain day after day?

She'd spoken to him so foolishly about grief, mentioned idiotic words such as payment and envy.

Was it any wonder she'd angered him? She hadn't known what she was saying. She'd never experienced the depth of his anguish.

Turning, she left the room, closing the door behind her. She grabbed the canvas and her valise, intent on her cottage.

Why did it feel as if she were running away?

Chapter 19

"**I**t's the potatoes," James Nottingham said. "Damn blight." He took a sip of his wine and sat back in the chair, solemnly regarding Robert. "The whole damn crop's touched by a fungus. Never seen anything like it, myself. Been going on for the last three years."

Robert had known the other man most of his life, had respected him as an able legislator. Now, however, the other man's look was almost chiding. Even if he'd returned to Glengarrow three years ago, Robert couldn't have saved the lives of his fellow Highlanders single-handedly.

"Has anyone done anything to feed the starving?"

Nottingham stared off into the distance, took a sip of wine, and resumed his stare. Robert waited, his impatience curtailed only by a desperate need to know. The silence ticked by for long moments.

The sitting room was a comfortable chamber, one he knew well from his childhood. His father had loved this house, preferred it over living at Glengarrow, but then, his father thoroughly enjoyed the company of others. The sixth Earl of Linnet had loved parties, even more so than Robert's mother. The two of them were renowned in Edinburgh for their entertainments, and this town house was almost a landmark in the city.

He knew his mother retained a full staff both in Edinburgh and Inverness. Although he hadn't yet reviewed any bills for the London house, he was hoping that residence was in good order as well.

Nottingham seemed to know the house well. The majordomo had greeted him by name and taken his coat as if the man had been a constant visitor. The most telling circumstance, however, was that after they'd greeted each other, James had led him unerringly to the back parlor.

A few minutes later, a maid entered bearing a tray filled with tea and a selection of biscuits and cakes. Nottingham thanked her by name, and sampled the offerings as if they'd been chosen with him in mind.

Just how acquainted was Nottingham with this house? Had he ever visited the bedrooms, for instance?

Whom his mother entertained was not a thought he wanted to hold in his mind for long.

Nottingham finally placed his cup down on the table beside him.

"Sir Edward Wallingford tried," Nottingham said. "Used his own ships to bring in oatmeal and other supplies." His mouth turned down. "Problem was, he expected the poor blighters to work a nine-hour day for what they received. Some of them could barely stand up. In the end, it's easier for a man to agree to go to Canada or Australia than to build a road to nowhere." He sighed. "At least the clerks don't starve."

"A great many of them are reduced to living on the streets of Inverness."

That was a mystery explained, then. His mother would have known of their conditions. No wonder she was so incensed. Regrettably, this wasn't the first time Highlanders had been pushed to the edge of the sea. Sheep now outnumbered crofters. But the combination of smaller plots of land and their staple crop rotting in the ground was a death sentence for the men, women, and children living in the Highlands.

"Some landlords have offered their people free voyages to Canada rather than see them starve. The newspapers are taking them to task."

"And the landlords working to lessen the effects of the famine? Tell me there are some of those."

"Most of them have refused to accept any responsibility, McDermott. Those who have are, unfortunately, in the minority."

Robert leaned forward, selected a biscuit more for something to do than from hunger.

"I might have been one of those," he said. "I don't know yet. I haven't received word back from my steward."

The other man nodded.

"And Parliament? Do they give a flying farthing about starving Highlanders?" It felt wrong to finish the biscuit in his hand when discussing his starving countrymen, so Robert put it back on the plate.

Nottingham looked uncomfortable. "They have other things on their minds."

"Which means no."

Nottingham nodded. "But you could."

Robert glanced at him.

He didn't think he could go back into politics. He lacked the stomach for it. Nor did he have any desire to compromise with idiots or meet in darkened corridors with the opposition to wrangle over some idiotic word in an obscure law that wouldn't alter people's lives one whit.

"You were very persuasive, McDermott. Your speeches could sway the hardest Tory heart."

He didn't want to talk about the past.

"What can I do now, Nottingham?"

Nottingham looked doubtful. "Use your influence with some of the larger landowners. Perhaps you can do what others have not."

"Short of buying enough food to feed a country, I'm not as certain of my influence as you."

The two men looked at each other. What a damnable mess. He might as well have spared himself the effort of coming to Edinburgh.

The whole trip had been a nightmare, and this discovery didn't make his journey any easier. Instead, he had the oddest feeling he would have been wiser to remain at Glengarrow and face Margaret Dalrousie head-on. She, at least, was not an insurmountable problem, just a woman with an annoying penchant for remaining in his mind too long.

What would Margaret say if faced with this situation?

And why the hell did he think she would even have an opinion? No, he was foolish to think Miss Dalrousie would be free of an opinion about anything.

"What do you find so amusing, McDermott?"

At his look, Nottingham explained. "You're smiling."

"Not about starvation, Nottingham," he said. "Simply a thought."

That was all she was. A thought, and an errant one at that.

Two hours later, Robert was in his solicitor's office, waiting for the man to return. Impatient, he stood, walked to the window, staring out at the Edinburgh street. Carriages crowded the streets; the cobblestones were wet and shiny in the evening light.

He turned at the entrance of the older man, waiting impatiently for Augustus Tapin to read through a sheaf of documents he'd brought with him into the room.

The minute Margaret had said his name, Robert had known the identity of her benefactor. Augustus Tapin was the head of the firm employed by the McDermott family for generations. His mother hadn't sold the cottage at all. She'd simply given it to Margaret Dalrousie. The question was: why?

"It is indeed true I agreed to perform the transfer as requested by your mother, Your Lordship," Tapin said now. "She had the legal right to do so, conveyed by your own hand."

He simply regarded the older man for a few minutes until the solicitor looked away. This was the man to whom Robert had entrusted his estate while he remained in France. The same man who, on his mother's wishes, had withheld funds to Glengarrow, and by extension, Janet and Tom.

"Do you have a personal interest in this matter, Your Lordship?" Tapin asked.

"If I said I did, would that inspire you to redouble your efforts? Or shall I send my mother to plead my case?"

Instead of angry red spots appearing on the man's sallow cheeks, Tapin grew paler. His hunched frame, more inclined to accountancy than the law, seemed to shrink even farther.

"Your Lordship," Tapin began.

"Spare me your protestations of innocence, Tapin," Robert said. "I'm not entirely certain that your firm will continue to represent me. It's entirely up to you."

"What can I do, Your Lordship, to justify your faith in me?"

"I understand that you've agreed to act as Miss Dalrousie's solicitor in other matters. The amount of money due her from Russia."

"I have done so," Tapin said finally, peering over his pince-nez at Robert. "However, Your Lordship, the task is a Herculean one. In fact, I might even say it is an impossible one. Relations with Russia are not exactly amenable at the current moment, what with the situation in the Crimea."

"Then you've been unable to acquire any of her funds?"

Tapin drew himself up, his bony shoulders squaring beneath his ill-fitting black suit. "I have not, Your Lordship. That is not to say, however, that I will cease in my efforts."

"What is the amount owing Miss Dalrousie?" Robert asked, taking a chair near the desk.

Tapin returned to his desk, consulted yet another sheaf of papers and named the amount.

The older man smiled when Robert made no comment. "It is indeed an enormous amount of money, Your Lordship. Almost impossible to conceive Miss Dalrousie being owed such a sum."

"She's reputed to be a famous artist, Mr. Tapin. Do you not think her deserving of her fees?" How very odd that Tapin's remark irritated him.

The expression on the solicitor's thin lips was more a smirk than a smile. "Your Lordship, she's a woman. A rather shocking one, I gather. What could a woman need with such an amount of money?"

"To live her life?" Robert asked. To his great satisfaction, Tapin frowned in displeasure. "Do what you can to assist Miss Dalrousie. So, yes, you can say that I have some interest in the matter."

The older man nodded. "I will do what I can, Your Lordship."

Robert stood. "As for the other, you will see to it with dispatch?"

"Ten ships, yes, Your Lordship. Stocked with food. It will be done as you wish."

"There will be no recompense, Tapin," he said. "Not one penny charged. Not one single compensating effort. No one is to have to pay for food. Do you understand?"

Tapin put down the documents on his desk and regarded him somberly. "I do indeed, Your Lordship."

Was there a way to intimidate the other people

in his life as easily as Tapin? Perhaps if they had as much to lose. Tapin was attempting to make up for his previous poor judgment and stay in his good graces. But how the hell did he intimidate Margaret Dalrousie?

She had to leave, that was all there was to it. She had to leave Glengarrow and go somewhere else.

Amelia's portrait was suddenly not as important as Margaret Dalrousie's absence. She was too much on his mind. He thought of her when he awoke at night, curious to see if her light was on as well. He thought of her when he awoke in the morning, oddly energized at the thought of sparring verbally with her. Too many occasions, he'd been seated only a dozen feet away from her, watching her skirt as she moved from side to side behind the easel. She sometimes tapped her toe, her skirts bouncing forward, the movements fascinating him almost as much as her thoughts.

He found himself listening for her soft exhalations of sound, the clucks of her tongue, almost as if she chided herself in the execution of a brushstroke.

What was she doing living in the Highlands of Scotland anyway? She needed the excitement of other people. She needed to be around laughter and joy. She was too somber a woman, too controlled, and she had an effect on him that was disturbing. So disturbing, in fact, that the idea of buying Blackthorne Cottage from her suddenly struck him as being particularly apropos.

The minute she was gone, he would raze it to the ground and stand in the shadow of the flames and watch as the memory of her burned away also.

He wouldn't be able to recall her. He wouldn't be able to remember that she had a way of walking, almost sauntering, that he found disconcerting. She made a parade of it, one hip going up, then the other, her derriere no doubt pert and round beneath the hoops of her skirt.

Did she walk like that on purpose to entice him?

The squeak of hinges called him back to himself. Tapin stood beside the open door, his lined face appearing too eager to please for comfort. Robert felt oddly sorry for the man his mother had charmed and used so capriciously.

"Women can sometimes be dangerous creatures," he said to Tapin.

The older man just nodded.

"We think they should be protected, but I'm beginning to think that we should be protected from them."

Tapin's lips curved in what might have passed for a smile in another man.

"Quite so, Your Lordship."

As Robert left the office, the thought kept niggling at him. How the hell might he intimidate Margaret Dalrousie? Or perhaps that wasn't the correct word. How did he prevent her from affecting him as she did?

Ah, that was the question, wasn't it?

Chapter 20

Margaret took aim, closed one eye, and cautioned herself about the recoil. She was becoming used to the sound of the pistol, the horrifying noisiness of it. The stench from the burning gunpowder didn't bother her as much—years of breathing linseed oil had inured her to odors.

She squeezed the trigger and was pleased to note the shot was not far off the mark. Each day, she became a little more accustomed to the gun in her hand, and with the familiarity came a little more skill. Shooting a gun had some similarities to painting. The act of pulling the trigger didn't require dexterity, but there was a certain connection between the eyes and hand.

Would she be able to shoot him? Of course she could. Even if it meant her soul was in damnation forever? She didn't believe that. The God of her belief allowed for retribution. Wasn't there a saying: an eye for an eye? In this case, the life of someone who'd wasted it, who preyed upon the weak and defenseless, who delighted in the suffering he caused or didn't notice it at all.

Could she kill him?

Oh yes.

If it meant she was damned to Hell, at least it would be warmer than Russia or Scotland.

Margaret reloaded, another task at which she was becoming proficient. Instead of seeing *his* face at the end of the barrel, she saw the Earl of Linnet, his eyes filled with pain. The image changed to become a man enraged, his face stiff with anger.

The rage on his face was better than his stoic expression of pain. She would rather have his eyes blazing at her than be encapsulated in grief.

Did he ever smile? When was the last time he'd laughed? She'd made him laugh, he'd said. When?

She was spending entirely too much time in thoughts of him, but perhaps that was natural, considering the painting was taking up so much of her energy. She woke in the morning filled with enthusiasm, entering the tiny trunk room immediately after breakfast to begin work. Sometimes, she'd paint until just before the light faded, unaware until dusk the entire day had elapsed.

She'd found herself again, and it was because of the Earl of Linnet. Fate or circumstance had led her to this magical spot in the Highlands to heal. The last year had been a time of reflection, months in which she'd been forced to relinquish the frenetic life she'd been living. With her basic necessities seen to by the small bequest she'd received, she no longer feared for her very survival. She hadn't had to paint in order to make money.

Was that why this portrait was a labor of love?

In all the years she'd been painting, all the sittings, all the practice and experimentation, she'd never felt what she did now. Perhaps her compassion was engaged, her need to express to McDermott her understanding of his sorrow. Perhaps it was her own sadness about Amelia and Penelope making her so careful about each stroke of the brush.

She had always cared about her work, but she'd never cared this much.

How very odd that McDermott had that affect on her.

Why had she told him so much about her life? She'd never done so with another human being, not even her rather intrusive maid in Russia. Another few moments, and she might have divulged even more information about herself. Why? What was there about the Earl of Linnet that made her want to confide in him, when she'd never before felt the need? Was it because she saw in him the same loneliness she felt?

She lowered the pistol, surprised at the thought.

When she awakened in the middle of the night, it was hard not to feel alone. She had no friends nearby. Never mind that she'd made a point of not cultivating friendships for years. She'd been a woman on the fringe of society, someone not subject to the rules but not wholly exempt from them either.

She was *not* lonely.

Granted, it was sometimes difficult to witness Tom and Janet's devotion to one another and know she would never be privy to such an emotion. Perhaps her fame might attract a man's attention, but the shame she'd endured would push him away again.

She raised the pistol, and this time she envisioned *him* at the end of the barrel. With great deliberation, if not a little pleasure, she pulled the trigger.

"Whoever you're aiming at is certain to be dead."

Of course the Earl of Linnet would be here at this exact moment.

She turned to face him, biting back her smile. What did she care he'd finally returned to Glengarrow?

"You've moved the painting. Have you stopped working?"

He was dressed in his greatcoat, his face windburned, his hair askew, looking fierce and annoyed.

"Well?"

He folded his arms and frowned at her. In the next moment, he would begin to tap his foot imperiously, she was certain of it.

"You are a very autocratic man, McDermott," she said, turning her back on him. "I do what I wish, when I wish."

"Not as long as I pay you, Miss Dalrousie. A not-inconsiderable sum of money, I might add."

She glanced over her shoulder at him. "Worth every pound, McDermott."

He looked as if he wanted to say something, then hesitated. "I've no doubt, Miss Dalrousie. Which is why I question why you are not working."

She turned. "Am I allowed to question why you whittle away your hours in Edinburgh?"

"I was there on serious business."

"No doubt," she said, lowering the gun to a stump nearby.

"I was in Edinburgh to discover whether or not the rumors I heard were true."

"You don't appear to be the type to follow rumors," she said.

"I do when they speak to starvation."

She held herself still. "Who is starving and why?"

"Highlanders, and I haven't the slightest idea why it continues."

"You must do something."

He frowned at her.

"I know what it's like to go hungry and to be afraid, even as a child, that there would be no more food. You must do something."

"Why do you think I can change what a country hasn't altered?"

"You're McDermott. Of course you can change it."

Something struggled between them, either irritation or attraction, some emotion difficult to qualify, but present from the very beginning.

"I'm sending some ships," he finally said. "It might not be enough."

His eyes were not haunted today, looking merely tired instead. Anyone looking at him would know he hadn't slept well. The lines around his eyes had deepened in the week he'd been gone. Had he ridden all the way from Edinburgh? In this weather? Foolish man. He would not see it that way, of course.

She wanted to reach out and trace one finger across a particularly deep line, coax his face back into youthfulness. He was too young to wear such marks of grief and pain.

"I haven't changed my mind," she said, answering his earlier question. "I simply wanted the canvas close."

He nodded, and would have turned away had she not stepped forward.

"I am not cold," she said. "Because I fail to express every emotion doesn't mean I lack them. Must I weep at a sunset to prove I see its beauty? Or cry at a tale of unrequited love in order to demonstrate I have a heart?"

"The fact I angered you is proof you're not cold. Forgive me for that."

"You don't have to apologize in order for me to continue to work on the portrait," she said. "I've been working every day."

"I thought I needed to be present?"

"That was hardly possible, McDermott, if you were in Edinburgh. And if you believed that, why did you question whether or not I was working?"

They stared at each other for a moment, neither speaking.

"Why are you here?" she asked softly.

"I'll be damned if I know," he answered. He advanced on her, his eyes fierce, his mouth thinned to a grim line. "To tell you I'd returned. To question you about the painting."

"You could have sent word through Janet."

"Oh, but Janet doesn't annoy me, Miss Dalrousie. You do, possibly more than anyone I've ever met. Do you do so deliberately?"

She stood her ground, tilted her head back, and smiled. "What would you say if I answered yes?"

Good, she'd startled him.

"It is an amusement taunting you, Your Lordship. You rise to the bait only too well. You, too, are an annoying man. Aristocratic, arrogant, autocratic. You are the equal, easily, of any prince I ever met in Russia, any count in France, and any earl in England."

His emotions seemed so close to the surface one errant word might cause him to erupt in anger. Strangely enough, she was neither afraid of him nor frightened of this confrontation. Instead, her blood raced, and her skin warmed.

She deliberately turned her back on him again, staring at the target. "Go away, Your Lordship," she said, uncaring if she was rude.

When he placed his hands on her shoulders and turned her, his strength evident in that one small gesture, it felt as if she'd been waiting for him to do exactly that for a very long time.

When his mouth lowered to hers, she made a sound of startled surprise, then was swept away in a sensation she had never before felt.

Long moments later, she was aware she was walking, and that his hand was guiding her back to her cottage. Suddenly, they were in the kitchen, the warmth causing her cheeks to sting.

He kissed her again, and she forgot about everything but the feel of his lips on hers. His face was warm, the stubble on his cheek abrading her palm. He smelled of bay rum and the patchouli that filled all the potpourri jars and bags at Glengarrow.

Her whole body felt as if it were glowing. Excitement spiraled up her spine. Her hands flattened on his chest as she stood on tiptoes to deepen the kiss.

Don't end this.

All too soon, it was done, and they pulled apart, each breathing raggedly. She stared at his chest. His hands rested on her shoulders. Thought was impossible in that moment, as was censure.

"Where's your chamber?" he asked softly.

She glanced up at him.

At this moment she should protest, should tell him she was not as easily overwhelmed as this. Oh, but she was.

She told him, and in moments, he'd mounted the stairs, his hand pulling hers like two conspirators about to engage in wickedness for the sheer fun of it.

In seconds her scarf was on the floor, and then her cape, then one by one her garments discarded as easily as pieces of paper fluttering in the wind.

She was cold and unprepared for the feeling of vulnerability as he stood there still dressed in his snow-dusted greatcoat.

She should've covered herself, should have reached out with modest hands and shielded her breasts or her womanhood from him. Instead, she fought back both the cold and her shyness or modesty and stood there unashamed and unafraid.

Like it or not, she was who she was. Nothing, not wishes or dreams or prayers could change that.

Silently, he led her to the bed, and she went, releasing his hand as she sat on the edge of the bed as if he were a courtier and she a queen.

McDermott dispensed with his own clothing as quickly as he'd rid her of hers.

When he was done, she lay back on the bed, her arms braced behind her, hands flat on the covering.

He was magnificent. His clothing had not hinted at such a masculine physique. If she ever painted a naked male, he would be the one she chose, his penis jutting out magnificently, erect and ready. Everything about him was perfect, from his muscular arms to his lean stomach, to hips that led to beautifully shaped buttocks. His legs were muscular as well, and hair was sprinkled over his body. He was not so much hirsute as all male.

Two scars marred the perfection of his body—a long vicious one nearly transecting his torso, and a fainter line from his right hip almost to his knee.

Strangely enough, the scars didn't take away from his utter beauty. Instead, she looked on them as she might a masterpiece defaced by a saber cut. The painting wasn't judged lacking.

His anger had faded, and there wasn't a hint of sadness in his eyes. Instead, he looked as confused as she felt.

He kissed her.

She didn't understand how she could lose the sense of herself, so easily. She wrapped her arms around his neck and buried her face in the shadowed space, hearing the harsh rasp of his breath, nearly as fast as hers. Was his heart racing as well?

He pulled back, tipping her head up for another kiss. She closed her eyes. She, who had never admitted defeat to anyone, who'd defied the world itself, readily surrendered to McDermott and his kisses. Dear heavens, how he kissed. He pulled her mind and soul free of its body, and it went soaring away, leaving only pleasure behind. She made a sound in her throat, and he deepened the kiss in response.

She stroked a hand from his shoulder down across his back, feeling the tightness of his muscles, the strength of his body.

Her body warmed, heat pooled in secret crevices, readying her for him.

Somehow he seemed to know, because he gathered her up tightly in his arms and rolled with her.

A grimace of pain shadowed his face.

She didn't break the spell with words, only placed her hand gently against his hip on the worst of the scar and rested her cheek against his chest.

With words that sounded like an apology, he laid her back on the bed and lowered himself over her. Suddenly, he was inside her, thick and full, invading her and stretching her. There was no pain in this coupling, no discomfort, only a sense of completion she'd never expected.

She'd wanted to ask him to be gentle, to be considerate, to understand this would be difficult for her. The quickness of his invasion made that point moot, while her compassion had easily banished any fear. She was lying with a man, and she'd never thought it would happen. She was lying with a man, and all she felt was a giddy sense of delight.

She wanted him to touch her breasts, to suckle on her nipples, to touch her skin and stroke his hands over her body. The sound of his breath was harsh in her ear. Softly she whispered, "Will you not kiss me again?"

He raised his head and stared down at her. "Do you orchestrate even your lovemaking, Margaret?"

Her hands reached up to grip his shoulders, and she traced a line down to his elbows and back up again, feeling the strength of his arms. Her fingers had never before been so talented, able to discern the dusting of hair on his arms, the angle of bone, the flexed muscles, the texture of his skin. When her fingers reached out to trace the taut column of his neck, her thumbs brushed his jaw. And then slowly, with great care, she allowed her fingers to rest on his hollowed cheeks.

If she had the ability to communicate by touch, she'd press her hands against his face and allow all of what she was feeling to be transmitted to him. Gratitude, perhaps, that she wasn't afraid or in pain. On the contrary, what she was feeling was the most delightful heat winding its way throughout her body. Confusion, that he was the one to bring her pleasure. But the strangest feeling of all was this odd desire to hold him close and comfort him, give him her body to use as he would.

She pulled his head down for a kiss, silencing her thoughts for several long moments. When it ended, she opened her eyes and looked up at him.

The sadness was back in his eyes.

"If you regret this, if you're chastising yourself even now, McDermott, then you should end it now. Leave me and go back to your celibate life." She frowned at him. "Are you celibate?"

"Do you always issue demands of your lovers, Miss Dalrousie?"

"Since you're my first lover, yes, I guess I do."

His look of confusion did not match well with his scowl. "What do you mean by that remark?"

Instead of answering him, she wiggled beneath him, a movement that had him narrowing his eyes at her. He hadn't diminished in size, even though he'd not moved in the last few minutes.

"I think you hate yourself because you're human and alive. I don't think you want to feel what you're feeling, and the greatest punishment you can give yourself is to refuse to feel anything. If that is the situation, I would appreciate it if you left now."

"I was giving you time," he said between clenched teeth, "to accustom yourself to me."

"I'm accustomed, McDermott. I'm practically eager."

"Then prepare yourself, Miss Dalrousie," he said. He thrust his hips forward. "Is this what you want?"

Her vision grayed, all sensation narrowing to the one spot where they joined. Utter delight mixed with wonder.

She pressed her hands against his buttocks, urging him to move. He made a sound like a growl deep in his throat and began to thrust, slower at first, then with greater speed, transporting her to a destination she'd never before gone. She gripped his shoulders tightly, wrapped her feet around his calves, and held on to him as if he were the only support in a world suddenly foreign and unknown.

Pleasure mounted from where they joined and spread throughout her body, little flecks of flame dancing across her arms and down to her toes.

He kissed her again, and this time she didn't bother trying to hold back her moan of delight.

He lowered his head, trailing a line of kisses over her collarbone to her shoulder, then to her breasts. Please, her breasts. Her hands gripped him at his sides, thumbs measuring his ribs as he suckled her.

She'd never felt what she felt now, a burning ferocity, a need flogging her heart and shortening her breath. She was both cold and hot, sweaty and chilled. She wanted his hands on her, his body on hers. But more, she wanted the pleasure hinted at in the power of his kiss, in each slow movement of his body in hers.

His teeth nipped at her shoulder. She gripped his hips and pressed her hands flat on either side of his buttocks as his thrusts became longer and more rhythmic. He smiled against her mouth.

She was on a precipice, the sensation one of ice and heat and frantic desperation. Her body knew before her mind understood. Her breath caught, and she gripped McDermott tightly as a sensation like lightning began to travel through her limbs. When pleasure came to her, and the world seemed to darken, then sparkle with a thousand stars, she began to weep, startled and surprised.

McDermott gave a great shuddering gasp and stiffened in her arms.

She held him there, not a little confused, and more than a little stunned.

Margaret lay staring up at the ceiling, clutching the sheet to her chest. What had just happened? Oh, she knew what had happened only too well. She just didn't know *how* it had happened. She had allowed a man into her bed. Not simply allowed, but acquiesced when he'd led her up the stairs. That wasn't right, either, was it? She had not only acquiesced, she'd been a willing participant. What had happened to them?

She had never before felt such attraction to a man, such explosive energy. She'd never before felt anything like it, and in the aftermath, she was still shaking.

How very odd to realize that, at her age, she liked kissing.

She wanted him to kiss her again, craved the tentative exploration of it, the sensation of one person melding into another, then surrendering slowly and delicately like the unfolding of a new leaf.

But this couldn't happen again. She'd been taken unawares, that was the reason. She'd not understood the power of passion or desire.

Had she ever felt it before?

Once or twice, perhaps, but she'd never acted on it. Nor had she done anything as foolish as couple with a man on the strength of a kiss.

McDermott sat up on the edge of the bed, his naked back as perfect as his front. She wanted to reach out with her fingers and slowly trace a path up his spine to his shoulders. Worse, she wanted to kiss him at the nape of his neck, where his hair tapered, press her cheek against his shoulder, and wrap her arms around him.

She'd allowed a man into her bed, and she'd felt nothing but tremulous delight. When he'd touched her, she'd not thought of anyone but him. Russia had been a distant memory, something that had happened to someone else.

"Miss Dalrousie," he began.

She shook her head as she stared at the ceiling. "At what point in our relationship do you think you should begin to call me Margaret?"

He glanced over his shoulder at her. "Do we have a relationship?"

There were a dozen comments she might have made, but none of them seemed correct or proper. Not that she had acted in any way proper.

In Russia no one had looked askance at the affairs of wives and husbands. Only the most jealous husband made it known that dalliances weren't acceptable. Of course, he was free to engage in whatever behavior he chose, but his wife was not.

But she wasn't in Russia anymore, but Scotland, a country renowned for its conservative beliefs, for its staunch morals and upright leaders.

Men like Robert McDermott, a man no doubt suffering from an excess of guilt at this exact moment.

"Should I have fought you?" she asked, and the question was not directed solely at him, but also at herself.

Her virtue had once been tattered, but not by her own actions. But this act had been of her own volition. Was she sinful because she'd felt desire? She was not a Puritan, nor had she ever been. Nor—if the truth be told—did she want to be now. Nor did she have any desire to be a hypocrite.

She'd enjoyed him. There, a bit of honesty. She'd enjoyed the act so much that she'd forgotten herself and moaned. Thank heavens Janet and Tom hadn't been in the cottage. Her duennas kept her chaste at night, but no one had done so this afternoon, had they?

"Margaret," he said, and her name was an admission of sorts. She drew the sheet around her, wishing she didn't feel as naked—no, as vulnerable—as she did.

She'd never expected to act the way she had, uncontrolled and driven by her passions instead of her logic. Had he felt the same way? She wanted to know, but the question was too intrusive. How very odd she'd felt free enough to lie with him in the middle of the day, and too constrained to ask him a simple question about it.

That would not do. That would not do at all.

"I've never behaved in this way," she said, pushing past her natural restraint to offer up the truth to him. "I've never felt this way. Did you not notice something different between us? A certain madness?"

He stood, and her artist's gaze scanned his skin, the broad and muscled chest with its dusting of hair growing in an arrow pattern as if to pointing the way for that lovely penis, now flaccid but still perfectly formed. Perhaps it wasn't her artist's eye as much as a womanly one that lingered on his hips, waist, chest, and shoulders.

All during her inspection, he returned her gaze steadily, as if he were accustomed to being studied in such a fashion.

He hadn't answered her, and she would not ask again. Words felt forbidden, captured and caught in a locked box. The same box held delight and possibly affection and all the emotions she'd felt in this room only minutes before but that seemed strangely forbidden now.

Turning his back on her, he began to gather up his clothing.

Was it better, then, to pretend that they were back to what they'd once been, simply neighbors, accidentally so. He was a widower, and she a shocking artist. Her life was not as proscribed as his. Both of them, however, had been touched by tragedy, his more lasting and deeper.

He halted in the act of picking up his clothing, and for a moment he remained standing there, his back to her, his head bent. His hands were clenched and his back muscles rigid.

She knew, suddenly, that he was regretting what had happened between them. Before he could speak and, no doubt, annoy her—or even worse, hurt her—she propped herself up on one elbow and addressed him.

"Do you hate me or yourself, McDermott?" she asked. "If it's me, is that entirely fair?" At his silence, she continued, "If you hate yourself, that doesn't seem right, either. You cannot be unfaithful to a ghost."

He glanced at her over his shoulder, his expression one of bone-deep contempt.

She sat up and faced him. "I know you loved her, McDermott. But Amelia is dead. Must you die along with her to prove that devotion?"

"You don't know what you're talking about."

"Or will you insist on punishing yourself each time you feel human and alive?"

He began to dress.

"I don't regret what happened. In fact, it was the single-most-freeing experience of my life."

He glanced at her, his expression confused again. She stared back at him defiantly.

"I wasn't a virgin, but not because I've had lovers."

He remained still, the moment frozen. All that she need do was to refute what she'd just said, he would be on his way, and her secret would remain hers. But she found herself talking again, giving him the truth, a truth she'd never thought to divulge to anyone, let alone McDermott.

"I was attacked," she said. She turned and dropped her legs over the side of the bed, drawing up the sheet to cover herself.

He still didn't speak, and she didn't know whether to be grateful to him for his silence or wish he was questioning her.

She didn't look at him, focusing her attention on the floor. "In Russia," she said. "By a group of vile thugs all bearing titles, all with noble blood. Aristocrats, all of them, and exempt from any sort of justice."

She forced herself to face him.

"For the last year, I couldn't even countenance the idea of a man touching me, let alone inviting one into my bed." She smiled. "Not only did you come into my bed, McDermott, but I liked it."

At his silence, she continued. "Because of this afternoon, I've been freed of terror. And for that, I thank you."

"Margaret." Just that, just her name.

If he meant to apologize, he didn't continue with it. If he meant to explain, no explanations were forthcoming. What could he say?

They'd been unaware of anything but each other. It wouldn't have mattered to her if Janet had been in the kitchen when they'd entered the cottage. She would have led him up the stairs if he hadn't been the first up the steps. And if he hadn't undressed her, she would have thrown her clothes off with delighted abandon.

Should she apologize for that? Probably, but she wasn't going to do so.

She watched him don his jacket. His movements were swift, economical, and had an utterly charming flow about them. Of course, he dressed every day of his life, and he did so now unself-consciously, as if the perfect beauty of his body and the symmetry of his limbs was something he took for granted.

"You are truly magnificent, you know," she said.

There, she'd managed to startle him again.

His cheeks were deepening in color. *Now* he chose to be embarrassed and not when he was naked? Sometimes, men were very strange.

She didn't ask if he'd be in the parlor the next morning. She didn't want to hear him refuse. Nor could she bear it if he banished her from Glengarrow again. Right or wrong, wise or idiotic, this painting would be finished. Not because she'd been commissioned by the Earl of Linnet, and not even because she was fascinated with the subject, but because it was a celebration of sorts, proof that she had not, after all, lost her talent.

People might disappoint her or even terrorize her. Circumstances—or a vengeful Fate—might alter her future. She might never make close friends, or have another lover. But if she still had her talent, her life could be an adventure, a challenge. With her talent, she had a reason to want to live.

How strange McDermott had unwittingly given her another one.

Chapter 21

The next morning, Margaret gathered up the canvas, her satchel, and wrapping herself against the cold, left the cottage for Glengarrow.

Janet had delivered a tray to her room the night before at her request, neither commenting on the fact Margaret had changed the sheets on her bed or that the kitchen had been meticulously clean when the older woman had returned to the cottage. Margaret had even mopped the kitchen floor so there were no traces of the snow and ice they had tracked in on the way to her bedroom.

The two women had not spoken much at all, a fact for which Margaret was infinitely grateful. She'd come to like Janet and trust in her judgment. The very last thing she wanted to see was disapproval in the other woman's eyes.

When had she become so attuned to the approval of others? When had she begun to care? When had she begun to care for *them*?

In truth, her life had begun to change the minute she'd returned from Russia, from those horrible three months in Edinburgh when she'd been unable to paint, to here in the Scottish Highlands.

She wanted to smile, but it was too cold, and her
teeth would freeze. She wanted to laugh, but it was
much better to stay bundled beneath the scarf. But
she stopped and did a tiny little jig, knowing she
probably looked the idiot.

There was a time for silliness, wasn't there? How
very odd she'd never taken much time for it before
today. How very odd that she couldn't remember
the last time she'd laughed.

She stopped by the gates of Glengarrow and
nodded to the lions.

Would McDermott be there? Would they carry
on as before? She really should have sent him a
note, but she was afraid he would cancel the commission. Yes, the money would have been a blessing, allowing her to buy more pigments and linen
for canvases. But more than the commission, she
wanted to know about him. Wanted to sit across
from him and study him in a way few women were
privileged to do.

She wanted to know about Robert McDermott,
and if that were a typically feminine thought, then
so be it. She was feeling typically feminine at the
moment, which was why she had taken extra care
with her hair, brushing it until it shone, then arranging it in one long plait arranged at the back
of her head. The style was rather antiquated, but
it suited her.

Today, she'd worn her favorite dress, a deep red
that flattered her complexion and contrasted in
a lovely way with the blackness of her hair. The
bodice was snug, marked with twelve jet buttons,
and she'd only worn two petticoats, one of them

taffeta, causing a slight swishing sound when she walked.

She opened the door to Glengarrow's kitchen, nodded to Janet and the two maids who were sitting at the table.

"You're painting, then," Janet said, a note of surprise in her voice.

"I am if the cold hasn't frozen the paints," Margaret said. "I'll need to put my satchel closer to the fire, I think. At least until they've warmed."

At the door to the corridor, she turned. "Will you let the earl know I've arrived?"

Janet nodded, her face expressionless.

She left them then, entered the main part of Glengarrow, and slowly climbed the stairs to the second floor. Without looking in the direction of Penelope's room, she walked toward the Winter Parlor. Once there, she placed the canvas back on the easel, opened the drapes, and stood looking on the bright winter morning.

Margaret opened the window just a sliver to allow some of the cool air in to refresh the room. Once she uncapped the pigments, the smell of linseed oil would be the most prevalent odor. Now, however, the scent of Amelia's perfume was heavy in the air. Did it never dissipate? Or were there sachets in all the drawers?

Did Amelia's ghost linger here at night? Or worse, did McDermott come here, spray his wife's perfume as if to summon her presence?

She pushed that thought out of her mind and went to stand behind the canvas. After arranging her brushes just so, she uncapped three jars of pig-

ment, spreading a little on the oiled wooden palette with her knife.

Would McDermott come? Or would he avoid
her because of embarrassment, or regret? What if
he preferred to pretend yesterday had never happened? She would act the same. Nor would she
make of the encounter more than it was.

The Earl of Linnet was a man with rich ties to
their shared country of birth. He was a politician,
a wealthy man with a proud heritage, a showplace
of a home.

She was a painter, itinerant and landless, tied
to people only in the most transitory way. She
had no antecedents featured prominently in her
country's history. There was no one in her family
to brag about or to point to with pride. They
were simple people, making their way through
life as best they could. Some had been honest
and hardworking. Others had not been, but the
shame they might have brought to the rest of the
family was augmented by an understanding of
how difficult it was simply to make it through
life sometimes.

McDermott had been touched by greatness from
his birth. She'd been touched by greatness because
of drive and ambition and refusing to accept what
the world thought she should have chosen for her
destiny.

He was proper.

She was slightly scandalous, a woman painter
who was autocratic enough in her way. She had a
reputation, deservedly so, for being a perfectionist.
Not once had she ever acted as if she were beholden

to anyone, even though there were many times
when she was, especially if a commission wasn't
paid in time to keep the bill collectors at bay.

But for an hour, they'd used each other, hadn't
they? For an hour, the loneliness was kept away.
She'd felt closer to another being, and for that
hour, she'd pretended, to herself, and perhaps to
him, there was some feeling between them.

The Earl of Linnet was as autocratic in his way
as she was in hers. He was dedicated, and had a
reputation for being determined to do the right
thing. She knew he had loved his wife, probably
loved her still at this moment. No doubt he'd been
a doting father as well. What more could a man
want to be? Devoted to his family, to his country,
to his heritage—wasn't that enough?

Such a man would regret what they had done.
She would be, for him, a reminder of his fall from
grace, a reminder he wasn't a paragon of virtue but
a human being with human frailties.

He would, if she guessed correctly, be more
difficult on himself than he would be on her. He
would dislike the fact he'd succumbed to a man's
needs.

Very well, if he wouldn't join her here, she
would continue to paint what she could. She didn't
actually need his presence to paint Amelia. In her
mind, she had already envisioned the woman, and
the pose.

Her palette arranged, she stepped into the middle
of the room, turning slowly in a circle. Perhaps it
was because this morning felt ripe for foolishness,
but she spoke to the air itself.

"You loved him, I know you did. And when you love someone, do you not wish the best for him or her, even if it does not meet with your plans?"

Amelia didn't answer. The light in the air remained as bright. Thankfully, the scent of her perfume wasn't stronger.

"I didn't take him away from you. But I did give him pleasure, if only for an hour or so. Don't make him sad because of it."

There was no answer, only the gentle wafting of the curtains from the open window. How odd that the room felt less constrained by sadness.

"Are you there, Amelia?"

"Who are you speaking to, Miss Dalrousie?"

His voice was low, his tone modulated. She glanced in his direction and felt her cheeks flush. Being naked in front of him had not made her feel as vulnerable as what she was experiencing right at this moment.

He was dressed in his ubiquitous black trousers and white shirt, and he'd never looked more handsome. Unbidden, the image of him naked came to mind as well as the touch of his hands on her skin, the sound of his breath, harsh and rasping.

"Margaret?"

She'd laced herself too tightly in an effort to appear virtuous, and it felt as if her corset bound her lungs. She couldn't breathe, and her heart was beating much too quickly.

She looked up at the ceiling, but there was no answer there, and the gesture didn't give her any more time.

He approached her, his footsteps muted on the soft carpet. With one hand, he reached out and closed the window. The curtains immediately stilled.

"To a ghost," she said and glanced at him. "Do you not think Glengarrow is haunted sometimes?"

"If it is, there are a variety of ghosts present. The house is three hundred years old. A great many people have lived here over those three centuries. If a building carries the memories of the life experiences of those who lived within its walls, Glengarrow would have many ghosts indeed."

He knew quite well she'd been addressing Amelia, but his wife's name was not mentioned. She shrugged and returned to stand behind the canvas.

"I didn't expect you to be here," he said in answer.

"I have a portrait to finish."

He nodded as if he expected her answer.

"Had you no one to speak for you?"

She knew, immediately, to what he referred. "It wouldn't have mattered," she said. "I suspect one of them was a royal prince. That meant all of them would be protected."

He hesitated for a moment, and she could almost predict his thoughts.

She took a step forward and held up her free hand. "You did not overpower me, except with sensation, Your Lordship. You did not hurt me, and it was not rape."

"Are you certain?"

Her laughter burst free, and she almost kissed him for the joy she felt at the moment.

"Were you not there?"

"Margaret." Once again, that was all he said, as if her name were either a chastisement or a sound of exasperation.

He stepped to the side so he could see her. "What do I say to you? Do I thank you?" he asked. "Do I assure you it will never happen again?"

She gestured toward the chair beside the window.

After a brief hesitation, he walked toward it. Once seated, he glanced toward the corner.

"Are you certain apologies are not in order?" he asked.

How very careful he was in his tone.

"Must we discuss it?" she asked.

"I think we must."

She stepped out from behind the canvas again, one hand still resting on the easel.

"We were hungry for each other, Your Lordship. Nothing more and nothing less. We had a hunger, and it has been appeased."

"Appetite, Miss Dalrousie?"

"Either that, or loneliness, Your Lordship. I would prefer to call it appetite."

"Did I hurt you?"

She shook her head. "You did not."

"Tell me about that night."

She stared at him incredulously.

"Why?"

He didn't answer, only focused his attention on the view outside the window.

"Please," he said, and she neither understood the request nor his politeness.

"Why do want to know?"

He focused his attention on her once more, and she felt pinned by his gaze. "If it disturbs you, of course we don't have to discuss it."

"I didn't say it disturbed me," she said, but it did. She hated remembering that time, and she'd never discussed it with anyone, not even the physician who'd treated her.

"Is that why you practice your shooting every day? You're planning on retribution?"

She really didn't want to have this conversation, but McDermott had a stubborn look on his face, one that promised he would not give up the subject.

"Tell me about that night," he said again, and his tone wasn't gentle or encouraging. Nor was it filled with anything remotely resembling pity. If it had been, she wouldn't have spoken.

But because he sounded interested, curious in the way two people often want to breach gaps between them, she answered.

"What do you want to know?"

"All of it."

She moved to sit at the end of the chaise facing him.

"I was quite the darling of the Russian court," she said. "I would have been busy from dawn until dusk for months and years if I'd allowed it. But I had my pick of commissions. Emperor Nicholas I and the Empress Alexandra Feodorovna recommended me to the court. Anyone who wished to be considered part of society commissioned Margaret Dalrousie for his portrait."

His smile was barely there, but it was a sign of amusement nonetheless.

"It isn't immodest to state the truth, McDermott. I was not only famous, but I was well on my way to becoming quite wealthy. Perhaps that's what made me think I was invincible, and inviolate. The world was what I wanted it to be, not as it was. I hope I never forget the lesson I learned, because to be that foolish again puts me at my peril."

He didn't respond, and after a moment, she continued, "I was used to taking my own troika from my studio to the night's entertainment. Depending on the rank of my subjects, I often made special arrangements for them. As long as the place was airy enough and had enough light, I had no objections to setting my easel in the rooms of their choosing. I've found that people were more natural in their own homes." She glanced at him. "But I'm digressing, aren't I?"

"Yes," he said, and the word sounded absurdly gentle.

"I'd been attending a ball in honor of the Grand Duchess's birthday. It was late, and the night was beautiful, cold but with a hint of spring. Spring comes so quickly in Russia. One moment you're certain the winter will never end, and the next it's upon you. The snow melts and the grass shoots up and the flowers come. It's like a great surprise God has provided as a reward for surviving the winter."

How very odd that suddenly she felt afraid. Not of him, but of the memories cascading into her mind, one after the other, recollections that she'd not had before. As if they were waiting for permission to surface, and now they were nearly drowning her with sensations.

"Are you all right?"

She could barely breathe, and panic squeezed her chest like a tight band. After a moment, she nodded.

"They'd all been drinking. I knew that almost immediately. But it was hard to find any young noble in Russia who hadn't been drinking."

"You knew them?"

"I'm sure I knew them," she said softly. "I never saw them, but their voices were familiar."

Thankfully, he didn't want to know exactly what happened, because she had no intention of telling him. Instead, he asked her a question she didn't expect.

"Is that why you left Russia?"

"In a way," she answered. "I made a mistake, the very worst kind of mistake," she said.

He didn't comment. Nor did he ask, simply waited, silent in that inexorable way of his.

"I was certain I recognized the voice of one of the young men. I knew he was the grandson of the Grand Duchess. I went to her and told her what happened. Two errors on my part, actually. One, to admit such an attack actually occurred, and I was the victim of it. Two, to accuse her grandson. I was twice condemned."

She looked down at her clenched hands, released them, and placed them flat on her skirt. "I was an artist, a woman viewed with some suspicion despite my popularity. I was forgiven my talent because of it. Because the royal family had approved of me.

But I was a woman of loose morals now, someone who'd lured these young men to unspeakable acts. Even if such a horrible thing had occurred, I was to blame. In addition I had darkened the name of her grandson."

"I have some knowledge of Russian society, they're very close-knit. If one hates, the others do as well."

She smiled at him. "That's exactly what happened. Those who owed me money simply took advantage of the situation and stopped paying me. My work was no longer sought after, and consequently within a matter of months, I was in dire financial straits. The very people who'd summoned me to Russia turned their backs on me."

She took a deep breath. "I didn't know who they were, but I suspected I had met one or two of my attackers in society."

"What can I do?" he asked.

"Do?" She stood and moved to stand behind the easel, then took pity on him, returning to his question. "There is nothing you can do. Why is it men always want to solve a problem, even when a problem cannot be solved?"

"Because it gives us the illusion we're in control," he said without hesitation.

"Even if you fail in your quest?" She peered at him.

He smiled, one of the few times she'd seen him smile. "It doesn't matter if you fail," he said. "It only matters if you don't try."

"So if there was something you could do about the situation I found myself in, what would it be?" she asked, genuinely curious.

"Justice, certainly. Although I'm not certain how that could be accomplished. The relationship between Russia and the Empire is deteriorating every day. At least you are well away. Can you not put it behind you?"

"One of them was English."

He didn't move his gaze from her face.

"What is his name?"

"Do you think to find me justice, McDermott? Is that why you want to know?"

He didn't answer, remaining implacably silent.

She turned to look out the window. "I don't know who he was. I always hoped that circumstances would change, and I'd no longer need the charity of others."

"What circumstances?"

She sighed. Had he always been so tenacious? One did not tell a new subject she'd been unable to paint until this very commission. For all their previous intimacy, McDermott was still her employer, at least for the time it took to complete Amelia's portrait.

"I left Russia with a great many people owing me money, McDermott," she said, stepping back behind the easel again.

"Why do I think those aren't the circumstances you mean?" he said.

Was he still staring in her direction? She didn't look.

"I suspect the circumstances you're talking about have a great deal to do with practicing your pistol."

She didn't answer him. What could she have said, after all?

Chapter 22

Long moments stretched between them. Neither spoke, and yet it was a comfortable silence, a companionable time. Finally, she peered out from behind the canvas to find him looking not at the view, or surveying the tips of his boots, but directly at her.

Startled, she smiled at him, and amazingly, he smiled back.

"How did a poor girl from Fife become an artist?"

"How?" she asked. It was his fault if she sounded idiotic at the moment. He really shouldn't smile—it rendered him even more handsome.

He nodded. "I suspect a man was at the heart of it."

"What makes you think it was a man who guided me?"

"It wasn't?" He sat back, his smile still in evidence.

"It was the Duchess of Burford," she said.

"Indeed."

Should he look so very pleased? Jealousy wasn't

an emotion she'd ascribe to the Earl of Linnet, especially not in regard to her.

"And how did the Duchess of Burford recognize your talent?"

He leaned back against the chair, his hands resting on the arms, a very aristocratic pose. She was not intimidated by his fixed look. The Emperor of Russia had stared at her just so, and she had simply stared back.

How much did she want to tell him of her past? She'd already told him more than anyone else in her lifetime. What were more revelations after the tale of what had happened to her in Russia?

"As I told you, my family was desperately poor," she said, careful not to allow any emotion into the words. She would not reveal any of the desperation of her childhood, of the very real fear there would never be enough to eat, that she would never be warm enough, that she'd never be able to sleep the night, six of them crowded into one bed.

"The Duchess of Burford did good works," she said. "I was one of her charity cases, you might say. One day, she was distributing a basket of food to my family."

The duchess had not exited her coach but had directed a footman to the door of their home, a squat, horrid, dark little hovel. Something captured her attention, and she'd first opened the window, then the carriage door, and finally emerged, an angel dressed in green silk and smelling of perfume.

"What are you doing, child?" she asked, coming up to Margaret squatting in the corner at the front of the house.

Margaret had ignored her, being intent, instead, on venting her rage on her oldest brother by rendering his image in the dust. He'd eaten her breakfast, and she was so hungry her stomach hadn't ceased its grumbling for hours. The picture in the dirt was recognizable, and very malicious, and she'd be hit if anyone else in the family saw it.

"Child?" She looked up to find a woman staring down at her, then tilting her head to see the picture she'd drawn of her brother. When she would have reached out and smoothed the dirt, the woman stayed her hand.

"It was she who arranged for me to be given instruction," she said now.

"At her home?"

Margaret smiled. "I don't think the Duchess of Burford wanted me anywhere near her home. I didn't see her again until three years later. No, she arranged for a retired teacher to instruct me. I went to his home three days a week."

"And after that? Were you expected simply to return to your . . ." he paused, and she completed his question.

"Hovel? Squalid living conditions? Poverty? If I was content to do so, yes. The duchess never tried to sway me one way or another. She only offered possibilities.

"I was hungry, then. Not just for food, but for knowledge. I wanted to know what the world was like, and the duchess did that for me. She opened an entire universe in her way. My instructor was a good man, patient and knowledgeable. The day he announced he could no longer teach me, I was devastated. I sent word to her, begging her to change his mind."

"And she did, of course."

Margaret smiled. "No, she didn't. She sent a carriage for me and received me in her sitting room." She glanced at him. "Have you gone anywhere and known, immediately, you didn't belong?"

"Yes," he answered, surprising her. "The Imperial Court of Russia."

She tucked that information away to think about later.

"I was too dirty for the sitting room," she said. "I didn't know where to sit, what to do. When the duchess entered, she told me to sit down on the davenport, never to appear uneasy regardless of the circumstances. She also told me she was going to send me to Italy, that my instructor had said I'd learned everything he had to teach, that I needed to study with someone more skilled."

"And so you went. What did your parents have to say?"

She smiled. "I'd actually earned some money by that time. I'd painted the portrait of a rich man's child, and he paid me something for it. I think the prospect of my being able to earn money was more valuable than my presence. Getting rid of one more mouth to feed must have been a relief."

"How many years did you send money to them?"

She glanced at him, surprised. "How did you know?"

He shrugged. "A guess. The same way I'm guessing you've never been back since."

She nodded. "I've not spoken to them since the day I left for Italy," she admitted.

Her mother was a lass with a winsome way, her father had always said, telling the story of their courtship with a grin and a gulp from the tankard of ale never far from his hand. The fact the lass had a fiery disposition to match her lovely sunset-colored hair was something never mentioned in the fairy tale her father spun. Nor did he ever comment on the fact that husband and wife rarely talked, and only then through their children.

Margaret had walked away from the tiny cottage and the sight of her mother's face pinched with age and bitterness, slitting her eyes at her as if gauging the weaknesses of a particularly loathsome enemy.

Punishment by silence was her mother's way. They had clashed from the moment Margaret could speak. The biggest rift, however, was one words would not make right between them: Margaret's strangeness. Margaret had wanted more than her mother had, more than she'd settled for, more, perhaps, than her mother thought she deserved, and for that, her mother would never forgive her.

Above all, she'd dared to aim too high above herself.

"What about the Duchess of Burford? No doubt she's proud of her protégé."

"I hope that's true," she said. "I went to her house in Edinburgh only to discover that she'd died when I was in Russia. I've always regretted that I didn't correspond more often with her."

"Have you never gotten your fill of the nobility, then?"

"More than once," she said. "But they're the only ones who can pay to have their portraits painted. Who want to immortalize themselves. The poor simply want to endure their lives. They don't give very much thought to posterity. Perhaps that's the biggest difference between them, the freedom to think about the future."

She moved behind the easel again, finding the shelter of it reassuring and protective.

"But that is enough about me," she said.

"Was I truly your first lover?"

She stared at the canvas, unseeing.

Her body heated as she contemplated not answering the question. But McDermott would not cease until he'd obtained an answer—she knew that much about him. He was persistent and dogmatic, Scottish-stubborn.

"Are you going to answer the question?"

"I am intent on my work, McDermott. I normally do not let anyone speak while I'm painting."

"Surely you do not object to a simple answer."

"Yes, you were my first lover." She waited for him to accuse her of lying, of questioning why she'd made up stories, but he surprised her with another question on another topic.

"What would you do to help our starving countrymen?"

She peered from behind the canvas. At the rate they were going, she wouldn't finish anything today. "Why are you asking me?"

"Why shouldn't I? Is there any reason you shouldn't be consulted as to your opinion?"

"Send ships of food to them," she said. "Wagonloads. Not for long. The Highlanders are proud.

They don't want to be cosseted, they want only what is necessary."

He nodded as if he agreed.

Why had she come today? Would it have been better if she'd remained in her cottage? Perhaps he would move back to London or visit Edinburgh extensively, leaving her in peace as she had been before he arrived. Was it peace? Or was it only half living? She wasn't entirely certain she wanted to know the answer to that question.

Granted, he annoyed her, even infuriated her, but he also incited her curiosity and her compassion. Nor could she, however much she might wish, discount the passion that flared so quickly between them.

"You've stopped asking questions about Amelia. Why is that?"

She sighed. "I do not wish to discuss Amelia because I'm not a saint," she said. "I find being around extreme virtue to be rather tiresome. I am not without faults, McDermott, I know that only too well about myself. Even you know that about me," she said, recalling her lies about her lovers. "But I do not need to be reminded on a constant basis that Amelia was a paragon of virtue. The woman is dead and can sin no more. She cannot do something foolish or stupid or inattentive. She can only become, as time passes, an even more virtuous figure."

"I am not speaking of her character, Margaret, but her appearance. Do you not require more information about her appearance?"

"I have all I need at the moment."

She picked up her brush again and tried to con-

centrate on her work. To her consternation, however, she was all too aware of the man seated on
the other side of the room.

The silence ticked by, one ponderous second at
a time. She didn't speak, and neither did he. This
time, it wasn't a restful quiet. Instead, the air
seemed filled with questions, curiosity, and something else, a feeling pulsing between them and
almost shouting to be released.

Finally, he stood and approached her, but this
time, he wasn't content to stand at one side of the
painting.

"How do you do it?" he asked. "I tell myself to
stay away from you, and instead I find myself listening for that damned gun of yours. I tell myself
you are a bohemian, an iconoclast, almost a gypsy,
but it doesn't stop me from climbing the damn roof
for a sight of you. You annoy me and confuse me,
yet I find I enjoy our conversations more than any
I can remember in a very long time."

He circled the easel, took another step toward
her, and another. She stood her ground, holding
her brush in front of her almost like a knight would
a shield.

"I tell myself to have nothing to do with you,
but I cannot help but remember your mouth. That
damnable mouth of yours. And I want to kiss it
again."

One more step, and he was so close she had no
choice but to step backward.

Her hand was squeezing the brush so tightly she
was afraid she'd break the handle. She dropped the
brush in the tray as he moved closer, his sheer size
nearly overwhelming her.

Suddenly, she was against the wall and he was there, so close her bodice brushed the linen of his shirt. Her breasts pressed against his chest.

"Damn you," he said softly, the words so softly spoken it was almost a caress.

"Damn your martyr's soul," she whispered.

"I hate your mouth."

"No, you don't."

She gripped his shirt with both hands and pulled him to her. Without the slightest hesitation, she linked her fingers behind his head and stood on tiptoe, closing her eyes and tilting her head back.

His kiss was like hope to the hopeless, wine to the thirsty, pâté to the starving. Aquamarine, teal blue, crimson, gold, all the bright and brilliant hues of the spectrum swirled beneath her eyelids as she succumbed to the sheer joy of kissing McDermott.

She, who'd always thought herself such a private person, suddenly wanted to be naked in front of him. The morning sun would illuminate all her flaws, but she didn't care. Let him measure the ugliness of a birthmark low on her abdomen, but let his fingers stray toward the nest of curls guarding her womanhood. If his hands cupped her breasts, marking them as too full for a woman her size, she would not demur, but please let his fingers stray across her nipples, and perhaps his lips. Her knees were particularly bony and were an embarrassment, but she would not protest if his palm strayed upward from ankle to thigh.

A sound emerged from deep in her throat, a sound of such yearning she was instantly embarrassed by it. She pressed one hand against his chest but he didn't release her. Instead, he deepened the kiss as if the sound she'd made urged him toward seduction.

But, oh, it wouldn't be seduction, would it? How did you seduce a partner? How do you urge capitulation on a woman who was already envisioning the sheer joy of being taken by you?

She moved her hands up between them and pressed her palms flat against his chest and pushed him away. Just as earlier, he didn't move. Finally, however, he lifted his mouth from hers and stared down at her, his cheeks bronzed, his eyes glittering darkly. She pressed against his chest again and took one small step away.

"You mustn't see the painting," she said in a hoarse voice. When had it become difficult to speak? Reaching out, she covered the painting with the cloth.

"Even now, you think of your painting?"

He was not the first man to ask that question. The answer, however, was one she'd never given before. "One of us must be sensible."

"Sensible?"

Oh dear God, she didn't want to be sensible either. The sadness in his eyes had been burned away by passion. She reached up and kissed him again, knowing as she did so it was foolish, knowing it would lead to more because she couldn't forbid him. Or herself.

He was too much of a temptation. He was like chocolate, or the finest wine, or a French pastry. But overindulgence was always a bad idea, and coupling with McDermott again would be hedonism of the worst kind.

Suddenly, she was free. She looked up at him, bemused, but he didn't say a word. Instead, he pulled her out from behind the easel and walked to the middle of the room, to a large square patch of golden light on the carpet.

"Now," he said, and there was no refusing him. Nor did she try, captivated by the feelings that were already spreading through her body.

His hands reached out and began unbuttoning her dress. She returned the favor by doing the same to his shirt, marveling at the expanse of chest she revealed.

He unbuttoned the bodice of her dress, placing small kisses on each inch that was bared. She was wearing too many clothes. She wanted to pull off everything and allow him to see her naked and flawed.

Amelia might have been beautiful. Margaret wasn't.

Her fingers pressed against the broad expanse of his throat, trailed over his collarbone, and pushed the shirt gently from his shoulders. When the sleeves were caught at his wrists, she unbuttoned his cuffs one by one, smiling up at him when she finished.

He bent down to kiss the upward slope of her cheek at the corner of her eye, a strange caress that had her smiling again.

"Margaret," he said, and her name was no more substantial than a whisper dancing on a sun mote.

"McDermott," she said, making him smile.

How like children they were in that instant, silly and amused, yet at the same time intense and passion-filled adults.

It was easier to undress him than her, and he toed off his boots, before helping her with his trousers. In moments he was naked and she was down to her chemise, her hoops tossed in the corner, her corset lying in a jumbled heap at her feet.

She stood on tiptoe and brushed a kiss against his cheek. In seconds, he'd turned and pulled her into his arms, deepening the kiss and the embrace. His hands gripped her bottom, pulling her up against him. It wasn't the cold that caused her trembling. The look in his eyes, and his harsh breathing as the kiss ended had the power to destroy any poise she might still have possessed.

She laid her head against his chest and felt the most curious sensation, almost as if she were holding back tears.

In Russia, it would have been easy to manage a liaison with any number of devoted admirers. Had she found a man who interested her as much as her art, she would have planned a dalliance, perhaps. Her lover would have been invited to her home, after she'd indulged in a long soaking bath, had the maids change the sheets, placed flowers and beeswax candles in her boudoir, and sprayed the air with perfume from France.

Not once had she ever envisioned that passion would come on the trailing end of amusement on a sunlit winter's morning in Scotland. Nor did she imagine she would be so impatient to rid herself of her clothes she'd toss them to the other side of the room, uncaring. Not one time did she think she would be laid down on a prettily patterned carpet and be uncaring about her trysting place.

Never did she imagine she would leave her painting for passion and feel as if she'd gained the better of the moment.

He kissed her, and she let him. No, more than let him. She participated, she enjoyed, she savored. Her mouth opened to allow the invasion of his tongue. Her breath mingled with his, her hands smoothed his chest. She felt herself go weak as her blood heated, almost like fire traveling through her body. Her breath escalated, her heart pounded furiously. Her body warmed, readying itself for him.

Suddenly, he was gone.

He stood, leaving her. She felt bereft without him, as if she were not totally whole unless he was there, touching her. How very odd that she'd acquiesced to such dependency. How very unlike her.

When had she begun to rely on McDermott? When had being with him become more enjoyable than being alone?

"What are you doing?" she asked, raising up on one elbow. How very strange that her voice trembled. She wasn't afraid of him, but her entire body was shivering. Is this what passion did to you?

According to society, she skirted the edges of proper behavior, living just barely within the boundaries of decorum. She'd heard her name whispered by more than one giggling miss. More than once, she'd received a new visitor to her studio and watched as her guest looked around the space, disappointed, as if expecting to see satyrs and nymphs frolicking naked in the corners. More than one woman had asked her, over the course of her career, exactly what it was like to live such a daring life.

They would have all been shocked to learn that in actuality she was chaste, unlike the titled wives in the Russian Imperial Court.

Now, however, she was going to lie with the Earl of Linnet in the middle of the day, and do so without hesitation.

She watched as he unrolled the leather pouch holding her most precious brushes.

"Be careful with those," she said. "They're very costly, and it took me months of waiting until they were done."

He smiled and nodded, but otherwise didn't respond.

"I am not as wealthy as you, Your Lordship. If you damage one, I will not be able to replace it."

He looked at her again, and she was pinned by the intensity in his gaze. It wasn't sadness she saw, only a strength and power that rendered her silent.

"I have no intention of damaging your property, Margaret," he said softly. "On the contrary, I was marveling at how fine your brushes were. What are they? Sable?"

"Those are. I have a mixture of brushes," she said, feeling odd about conversing with him while she was lying naked on the floor. "Hog hair for the larger areas, sable for more delicate work. I've even experimented with mink." She sat, pulling her legs up and wrapping her arms around her knees.

"Is this gold?" he asked, pointing to the ferrule, the metal surrounding the joining of the brush to the handle.

"Yes. And the handles are mahogany."

"They're very long, but heavier than I expected."

"Designed especially for me. I like them weighted for my hand. They're not as long as most," she said.

"How very convenient," he said, smiling.

He was up to something, but she wasn't sure what.

The trembling was back in full force. How could she possibly endure the wicked provocation of his smile? Her nipples tightened, and the rest of her body warmed in preparation for his return or in longing for it.

She lay back down on the floor and stared up at the ceiling, attempting to sound nonchalant. "I didn't like the mink," she said. "The hair is different. I didn't like the effect."

He came and stood above her, a position of power, one of command or perhaps challenge. But McDermott did not subjugate. Nor did he overpower. Instead, he cozened her along for the adventure, urged her to share what he was feeling. They were conspirators in passion, equally at blame and equally pleasured.

His gaze encompassed her from the top of her head down to the tip of her toes. She returned the look, marveling at the perfection of his body.

Slowly, she raised her arms to him.

Somehow, in the intervening minutes, they'd ceased to be earl and artist. They were simply human, wanting and elemental, like fire and water and the air itself.

Kneeling beside her, he unrolled the leather case. In each of the ten separate pockets was one of her precious brushes, each designed for a different technique.

"What are you doing?" she asked.

"Anticipation is an integral part of pleasure, don't you think?"

"I haven't enough experience at pleasure to answer that question with any intelligence."

He halted in the act of pulling a brush free from its pocket and looked at her, his eyes suddenly somber. "You haven't, have you? So all that blather about your many lovers? It was all a lie, wasn't it? Why?"

She looked up at the ceiling again. A mural should have been painted there, something interesting to study. But then, she doubted if the builders of Glengarrow had envisioned this scene of seduction.

"Does it matter?"

He pulled her fan brush free, his finger trailing across the featherlike hairs forming the semicircular brush.

"What is this used for?" he asked softly.

"Lace, fabric rosettes, anything delicate with a pattern."

Slowly, he drew the brush across her skin, beginning at her throat. He stopped between her breasts, and twirled the handle, all while his gaze remained on hers.

"Why?" he asked again, and she didn't bother to avoid the answer this time.

She turned her head to look at him. "Because it's easier to pretend to be the person someone thinks you are than demand he look at you differently."

He stroked the brush beneath one breast, then the other. "Because I thought you worldly and shocking?"

"Didn't you?"

"You've confused me from the first moment I met you," he said, his gaze on the action of his hand. "You've been unpredictable and challenging and maddening."

"So have you," she said softly.

The look they exchanged in the small yellow room was so intent that if the world had stopped outside, neither of them would have noticed.

She reached out and touched his wrist, then the back of his hand with her fingers. His skin was so warm.

He swept the brush up the slope of one breast, circling a nipple with a tender stroke. His smile was soft and almost predatory, wicked and not a little promising.

How could she possibly resist him?

"Do you like that?" he asked, as the fan gently caressed the very tip of her nipple.

"It's a very interesting sensation," she said.

"Is it?"

He moved to lie beside her on the floor, propping himself up on one elbow. He was drawing concentric patterns around each breast, then softly tapping at the nipple with the hairs of the brush.

"Tell me how it feels," he said, his smile still firmly in place.

"Like air. As if you're breathing across my skin."

"Like this?" He blew across one breast and the nipple puckered even harder at the sensation of his warm breath.

"No," she said, hearing the tremulousness of her own voice. "Even more delicate than that."

"Barely a touch, then. A whisper of a touch, you might say," he said.

"Yes."

She closed her eyes at his smile. Was her body capable of bursting into flames? She felt it might, especially from the inside out. Even though she lacked experience in passion, she suspected she would never feel more wanton and needy than at this moment.

He kissed her, but not as deeply as she wished. When she reached up with both hands to pull his head down, he pulled back and shook his head.

"Not yet," he said. "I lose myself in your kisses, Margaret. I think it's your mouth."

"It's too large," she said. Was that her voice? When had it become so husky?

He pulled another brush free of her leather case. This one was more substantial, one she used to apply gesso to a new canvas.

Slowly, he drew a line from below her lips, over her chin, and down her throat to rest in the well there. Her skin was so sensitive and so attuned to his touch that she shivered when he bent his head and replaced the brush with his lips.

When the kiss ended, he didn't meet her gaze. Instead, his eyes intently followed the path of the brush as it trailed down her skin, following the slope of her breasts and gently beneath them. He circled her navel with the brush, then across her abdomen to touch first one hip, then the other, as if he were planning a painting of her nude and wanted to mark her features on some mental canvas.

He turned to look at her, his eyes filled with heat. "Open your legs for me, Margaret."

He was erect and hard against her thigh, and instead of answering him, instead of being compliant and meek, she stretched out her hand and touched him.

How very shocking she was supposed to have been and wasn't, and how very proper he was rumored to be and how shocking in actuality. Something in her nature long suppressed, possibly ever dormant, rose to the surface and curved her lips in a smile as wicked as his.

His penis nestled into her hand like a bird come home to its nest. She stretched her fingers around it, marveling that she couldn't encompass the whole of the organ in her grip. How very substantial he was. How very manly.

"Open your legs."

"And you'll touch me with the brush? Shall I like it?"

"I think you will."

He laid the brush on her abdomen and trailed his fingers through her intimate curls. She bit her lip against the sensations flooding through her. What she was experiencing was not only physical pleasure but mental delight as well. They were being wicked, lying in the morning sun, playing at passion as if it were a game given to them for their amusement.

If he felt any regret, it wasn't in his gaze.

Unexpectedly, he leaned forward and surrounded one nipple with his mouth, the heat of it
drawing a gasp from her. Then he played with the
nipple with his tongue, darting back and forth over
the sensitive tip before doing the same to her other
breast.

Sometime in the last minute, he'd picked up the
brush again, and it traveled down one leg, inciting
shivers in its wake. Down to one knee, and slowly
back up one thigh, then across her abdomen and
down the other thigh to her knee, a semicircular
pattern slowly driving her mad.

She played with his cock, her fingers trailing
up and down, following the same pattern, up and
down. His flesh was as hot as a brazier, as if there
was fire in his blood. Was he feeling as crazed as
she?

His lips met hers, and she sighed, almost in relief.
The kiss deepened, his tongue touched her lips,
darted into her mouth to tease hers. She angled her
head and lost herself to the sensation of it.

The brush suddenly stopped, and his fingers
were there again, combing through the soft, curly
hair between her thighs. He explored lower, parting and gently tracing the line of her swollen folds.
A finger gently entered her as his thumb pressed
against her. She made a sound in the back of her
throat, and he pulled back, smiling.

"You're ready for me," he said softly.

A stroke of a finger through her swollen folds
proved his comment was true. She closed her eyes
on an indrawn breath.

"Yes," she said, the assent more of a sigh. A

second finger entered her, gently, slowly, but it wasn't enough. She wanted him. All of him.

She opened her eyes and turned to him. "Now," she said, echoing his earlier command.

The heat in his look arced higher, almost as if he enjoyed her sparring. Or her refusal to be meek and well mannered. On this floor, in this room, both naked and needy, neither one of them had a role or a title or a past. This space and time, marked by four walls and a door, was their own, and she was free to be anyone she wanted to be, even herself.

"Now," she said again.

His cheeks turned darker, as if passion gave him a ruddy glow and made his eyes sparkle.

"Later, perhaps."

"Not too much later," she said. "You're driving me mindless. "

"If you have enough composure to speak, it's not mindless enough."

She felt as if she should clench her muscles, hold tight the sensations he was evoking. She truly couldn't concentrate on anything other than what he was doing with his fingers.

She wrapped her left arm around his neck. "Do you want me to beg?" she breathed against his skin. She was more than willing to do so.

His chuckle was unexpected, wicked, and utterly delightful.

"That would be nice," he said.

"Please," she said. "Now."

But he didn't move, content to let his fingers stroke through her folds, play with her dampness. Somehow, he knew where she longed to be touched and how. She tensed in anticipation but every time she wanted him to concentrate on one spot, his fingers would move.

Beast.

She retaliated by gripping him tighter with her right hand and beginning a gentle, unrelenting movement of her hand from base to tip. An inchoate sound emerged from between his lips, and strangely enough, the sound of it made her blood race even faster.

Suddenly, he was over her, his cheeks darkened, his eyes smoldering, his smile gone.

"Now," he said.

"Are you very certain?" she asked, feeling a disconcerting tenderness.

He only smiled.

She placed both her feet flat on the floor and pressed up to welcome him as he entered her.

Her hips rocked as he thrust again and again. There was no hesitation in this lovemaking, no regret. Instead, they were both impatient and mindless.

His mouth was on her breast; and then he was kissing her. She gripped his shoulders, reveling in the touch of his skin. She wanted him, wanted to feel what she had before and surrender to a fog of delirium. When all was lost to her but the sensation of her own body's delight, her hands fell limp to the floor.

His cheek was against hers, his breath was loud and harsh in her ear. She turned her head slightly and placed a kiss on the curve of his ear. Her hands reached up, her arms enfolding him. He was still inside her, so she rocked her hips gently to keep him there, needing him to remain. Just simply needing him.

The sudden joy she felt was as confusing as the tears peppering her eyes. Margaret didn't know what to say, even if she'd been able to speak.

McDermott lay there for long moments, his breathing calming. The slow drip of icicles outside the window was testament to the warming of the day.

Would he regret this interlude now that it was over? Would the pain be back in his eyes now that passion was burned away?

Please, no. She didn't think she could bear that.

Finally, he stirred, raising his head and looking down at her. Bracing himself on both forearms, he brushed tendrils of hair away from her face.

"Are apologies in order again?"

"No," she said, smiling.

His lips were against her forehead. Not a kiss as much as the promise of one.

"I always lose my restraint around you," he said, in such an offhand tone it was as if he spoke to himself. "My words are improvident, my actions equally so. I'm not myself around you."

"Or perhaps you are," she said. "More than you've ever been."

He drew back, his smile amused and self-deprecating.

"Shall I apologize?" she asked. "For what, I don't know, but I'm more than willing to do so if it will ease your mind."

"For being a sorceress, perhaps? Do you use some magic potion in your paints? Perhaps you've bewitched me."

"If I knew any spells, McDermott, I would certainly have used them before now. I am simply myself."

His smile grew broader. "Ah, but that self is Margaret Dalrousie, inimitable artist, beloved of the Imperial Court of Russia, exhibited at the Royal Society of the Arts."

"How did you know that?" she asked, surprised.

Instead of answering, he said something else startling. "I've never seen any of your work. I very much wish to." He placed a finger over her lips when she would have spoken. "Not to assure myself of your skill, as much as to understand you."

She blinked several times, but couldn't speak. Finally, she closed her eyes and turned her head away, overwhelmed.

No one else had ever known that. No one else had ever figured it out. She worked when she was miserable, sick, alone, and desperate. She worked when she was ecstatic, amused, happy, and silly. She worked when another woman might have sobbed into her pillow, cursed her existence, or laughed with joy.

Who she was could be seen in each portrait, in the curve of a cheek, the loving eyes of a favored pet, or the sweet smile of a child holding his mother's hand. How she felt about tyranny or children or her own preference for colors was to be discovered in each successive painting. She was there along with the subject, and no one else had ever discerned that before now.

He left her, rolling over to gather up his clothing. She felt the drape of cloth on her stomach, and opened her eyes, her equilibrium once more restored. He was staring at her, at her half-open thighs.

She clenched her legs together tightly, but it was too late.

"What is that?" he asked. His tone was calm, but not naturally so. He'd said he wasn't restrained around her, but at the moment, he was. She could tell by the muscle clenching in his cheek and his unblinking gaze.

"What is it?" he asked again, and she closed her eyes once more.

The past was back again, however she might wish it gone. The past might well mar the beauty of this morning, bury the memory of the exquisite pleasure they'd felt together beneath its sheer weight.

He placed a hand on her thigh, and one corner of her mind marveled at the gentleness of his touch even as she flinched from it.

She knew better than to pull away, however. He would simply reach for her again. He was resolute, stubborn, and willful. What McDermott wanted, he no doubt always achieved.

"A coat of arms," she said. She didn't look at him, but at the ceiling, instead. She couldn't bear to see his expression.

"Tell me about it," he said softly.

"There's nothing to tell," she said. "It's a coat of arms."

"What's it doing on your leg?"

Margaret turned and looked at him. "Can you not forget what you saw, McDermott?"

She knew the exact moment he understood. Comprehension lit his eyes and thinned his lips.

"Someone branded you, Margaret. How did he do it?"

She had a choice—to tell him or keep silent. For nearly a year she'd kept the secret, never telling anyone. Even the physician who'd treated her hadn't known the extent of her injuries.

What difference did it make now? He'd seen, and he wouldn't forget, no matter how much she wished she'd been more careful.

"He heated his signet ring," she said, careful not to allow any emotion into her voice.

For some time it was silent in the room. He didn't comment, only retrieved their clothing and slowly began to dress.

She did the same, grateful for the respite, knowing the silence was only a prelude for the questioning to come.

"What you're describing is torture, Margaret," he said finally. "There's no other word for it."

"I didn't know what it was at first," she said. "The burn took some time to heal. At the beginning, I thought it was just the end of a poker he'd used. It was only later, when the swelling went down that I saw it was a pattern. A shield topped with a knight's helm. I think there are lions on either side, and a banner at the bottom."

"Who did this to you?"

"I don't know."

She'd used all her skill and spent days on the drawing, taking it to her new solicitor when the drawing was done. He had two tasks, only one of which McDermott was familiar—that of finding her benefactor. The second, and more important, was to find the owner of that particular coat of arms.

"Don't trouble yourself, McDermott," she said blithely, sitting up, and donning her chemise. "It's not your concern."

He didn't answer, and she managed to ignore him until she finished dressing. Only then did she glance in his direction. He was not looking at her as she'd supposed, but was staring out the window, toward the lane, an expression on his face she couldn't decipher.

He annoyed her, he irritated her, and he also had the power to elicit her compassion, a fact she chose not to share with him. Most importantly, he was the only man who had the power to seduce her from her work.

He was regretting their interlude. But at least, this time, regret had not been his first thought.

"There will come a moment when you want to smile," she said softly. "Even despite yourself, you'll begin to live, to want to. The human heart finds a way through the darkness."

He turned his head and looked at her.

"You talk about things you don't understand, Margaret. If you've lost no one, how can you know?"

"I've lost myself," she said.

Without waiting for him to respond, she turned and left the room.

Robert sat at his desk, staring down at the note that Janet had delivered to him this morning.

Was Margaret Dalrousie two people in one? She was, no doubt, simply an unstable artist. Weren't

they supposed to be temperamental and volatile?
One moment she was smiling sweetly at him, the
expression oddly tender, and the next, she sent him
this damn note.

*I am unable to continue the sittings at this
time, finding myself indisposed.*

What the hell happened?

Had he said something wrong? Done something
wrong? For that matter, did she regret what had
happened between them, not once but twice?

Twice now, he'd been overwhelmed by sheer
lust. He'd never before experienced such searing
pleasure or its confusing aftermath.

He hadn't lied to her—should he have? He'd
told her the truth, bare and unadorned as it was.
He'd tried to banish thoughts of her. He'd tried to
stay away from her. She was like a pebble in his
boot, annoying and constant, and doomed to be a
constant irritant until he rid himself of her.

Was it because of her scar? Was she shamed
by it? Had he been too insistent on hearing the
story?

He couldn't very well unsay the words, could
he? And there was no way in hell he was going
to forget her explanation. Nor could he banish
the rage he felt whenever he thought of someone
branding her.

A few minutes later, he stood as a knock sounded.
He came around the desk, crossed the carpet, and
opened the door to Janet.

She entered, bobbing a small curtsy, and staring
intently at the floor as if spying a speck of dust.

Her hands were twisted together in front of her, and her teeth were worrying her bottom lip.

"Sit down," he said, pulling out one of the two chairs in front of his desk.

She sat in the chair to the left while he sat next to her. There was no need for him to sit behind the expanse of mahogany that was his desk. He wanted Janet to confide in him, and reinforcing his role of employer would not accomplish that aim.

He smiled at her, but she looked away, intent on the view outside the window.

Undeterred, he waited until she looked back at him.

"You were with the Duchess of Burford for a number of years, weren't you?" he asked.

She nodded.

"In fact, that's how you met Tom, was it not?"

Again she nodded, gripping her hands tightly in her lap. Her glance encompassed him, his desk, and the windows to the far side of the room.

"He worked for your mother, as you know, Your Lordship. Is there a reason why you ask?"

"I imagine that you still have friends working for the duchess."

"The duchess passed away three years ago, Your Lordship."

"But her Edinburgh house is still open, isn't it?"

"Her son spends a great deal of time in the city, I understand," she said.

"Who was it who told you that Miss Dalrousie came to call on the duchess?"

She stared down at her hands. Robert waited patiently.

"Someone told you, didn't they?"

She finally nodded. "The housekeeper and I are friends. She thought I should know."

He circled his desk and took his chair. "What did you do then?"

She sighed, sat back and regarded him levelly. "Tom and I talked about it. For a few days we did nothing, but the more I thought about it, the more I knew what the duchess would have wanted."

"And what was that?"

"She believed in Miss Margaret, Your Lordship. She wanted the best for the girl. She would have stepped in to help Miss Margaret if she could have."

"Therefore, you went to my mother?"

"They were friends, you know. She and the duchess. Great friends."

"So my mother made a gift of the cottage to Miss Dalrousie. Why didn't you take advantage of your meeting to remind her to pay you?"

She looked shocked.

"I didn't go to see her, Your Lordship. Tom did. And he wouldn't have mentioned our pay for anything." She took a deep breath. "He found out where Miss Margaret was living, Your Lordship. It was a place not fit for rats, although there were plenty of those. I think she was close to starving. When she first came to the cottage, a sorrier sight you never saw. We never suffered like that, Your Lordship. Glengarrow always provided."

What had he ever done to inspire such loyalty?

"Thank you, Janet."

His housekeeper stood and walked toward the door. She turned and faced him again.

"Are you going to tell Miss Margaret? I hope not, Your Lordship. Russia was not kind to her." She hesitated a moment. "She thinks she doesn't need anyone, Your Lordship, but we all need someone. She's beginning to realize that, in her way. Still, she's a proud woman."

"Thank you, Janet. For caring for her. Even before she knew it."

Janet studied him for a moment. A smile curved her lips finally.

"She's a lovely person, Your Lordship. But I expect you know that already."

With that comment, she left, making him wonder exactly how perceptive Janet had become.

Chapter 23

"**I** think you'll find the service is very uplifting, Miss Margaret," Janet said. "The presenter has a beautiful voice, and the sound of the congregation singing is enough to send your heart soaring."

Margaret glanced at Janet, but she didn't comment on either the older woman's uncustomary poetic words or her enthusiasm for church.

"Will you be coming to service with us, Miss Margaret?" Janet asked, and every Sunday except for this one, Margaret would respond claiming a malady. *I have a headache. I'm feeling a little tired. I have a cough that has kept me up all night.* Anything but agree to go to the village church. Janet never said a word when Monday came, and Margaret was mysteriously cured.

"It's glad I am that you've finally decided to come with us, Miss Margaret. I know you will enjoy it."

If there was any truth to the idea that God knew each sinner, then she might well be crushed in the doorway as she entered. After all, she'd been a loose woman, guilty of the worst kind of sin. The truth of the matter, however, was that she was heartily tired of her own company, and the confines of the cottage seemed to be growing smaller and smaller.

Even if *he* were at the services, he would not be able to bedevil her. Surely God would see to it that she wasn't struck dumb with lust in church?

She tied the emerald green ribbon of her best bonnet below her chin, put a smile on her face with some degree of desperation, and resigned herself to several hours of acute boredom.

But at least she would have left the cottage.

She willed herself into a calm frame of mind, and followed Janet out the door.

The carriage was a beautiful creation of black lacquer with a soft blue interior. Tom had borrowed a carriage from Glengarrow. She wanted to ask if he had inquired of its owner for permission, but she decided that it was best not to mention the Earl of Linnet under any circumstances. What would she do if Tom replied in the affirmative? She'd be inspired to inquire as to his health. She didn't want to know if he fared well.

A large compartment rested beneath each of the four windows, and curious, Margaret opened one to find that it was equipped with a mirror, a clock, a crystal flacon of ink, and an ingenious pen comprised of a wood handle and a quill that could be inserted at the end. The entire compartment could be twirled on its side to serve as a flat space on which to write or even to play cards.

Evidence, again, of the Earl of Linnet's wealth. There was nothing ostentatious about the carriage, but it had been built for comfort and a certain touch of luxury.

She sat back against the seats, fiddling with her gloves. They fit perfectly, but she kept pulling them even tighter. A sound called her back to herself and she realized she was tapping on the carriage floor with one foot.

Years had passed since she'd gone to church. Even longer since she had attended a Scottish service. As if she had heard Margaret's thoughts, or could somehow interpret her nervous habits, Janet reached over and patted her on the arm.

The gesture wasn't the least reassuring, but Margaret pinned her smile in place for Janet's sake.

North Linten Village was comprised of a dozen or so buildings dating back to medieval times. Inserted among them were new houses and shops, not appreciably different in size or construction, only their pristine brick marking them as new neighbors.

Tom drove them through narrow winding streets, curiously well occupied for this Sunday morning. There were even a few fishermen standing beside the Tenye River, testament to the fact that the Kirk's influence in this part of Scotland did not mimic that of her childhood. Evidently, here in North Linten, dishauntening of ordinances— avoiding church services—was not punished.

At the top of the steepest road was a large square pillar with four taps mounted on each of its sides. For hundreds of years goodwives had drawn water here, and the adjoining road had been named Teapot Lane in their honor.

The carriage halted in Ramartin Square, in front of a building proudly proclaiming itself St. Munto's Episcopal Church. Another change from the religion of her childhood. The church she'd attended as a girl had been a plain box of a structure, little to recommend it in the way of artistry or beauty. This building was gabled and topped with a towering spire, accentuated with carved naves and scrollwork.

North Linten Village was a surprisingly prosperous village, and its Episcopal church no less so.

Reluctantly, she left the carriage, following Janet down a red-gravel walk bordered by now dormant flower beds and to the front door of the church.

She waited with Janet while Tom parked the carriage, then accompanied the couple to a pew midway and to the left of the altar. She sat closer to the aisle and studied her hands on her lap, the better to ignore the looks of the parishioners.

Anyone looking at her might have thought she was devout. Instead, she was wondering if her bonnet was truly as ill flattering to her complexion as it had looked in the mirror this morning, and whether or not she was the only one dressed so garishly in red among the more sober blues, browns, and black coats.

A whisper began, and was carried through the congregation. She looked up to see everyone craning their necks and turning around and facing the door.

She knew, even without turning, who it would be. Of course it was the Earl of Linnet. And of course he looked absolutely magnificent in a very somber suite of clothing. His hair was a little mussed by the wind. Did he never wear hats? He was tall and commanding as always, and as always, when their eyes met, she felt a jolt of something inexplicable right down to the soles of her feet.

Evidently, God did allow lust to occur in His church after all.

He strode down the aisle, and hesitated beside the pew, nodding at Janet and Tom. His glance toward her was cursory, no more important than a dust mote.

She frowned at him, but he didn't look at her long enough to note it. Instead, he kept walking until he reached the front pew, the one with the carving on the side, resting just below a massive stained-glass window. He hesitated at the end of the pew and took a seat, his shoulders straight, his gaze fixed on the altar.

"It's the first time he's been back," Janet said. "Poor thing. It's not been easy on him."

He sat alone in the pew built for a family. She could almost see the missing ones. Amelia would be sitting close, and his little girl might be peering over her shoulder at the congregation. A place of honor that pew, and now the site of speculation. She was not the only one staring at the Earl of Linnet and wondering at the depth of his pain.

She wished, not for the first time, that she was the type of woman who could push aside society's rules and regulations with alacrity. If she were to be as shocking as people thought she was, she would stand, walk down the aisle, and join him in his isolation. She might even take his right hand in her left, and hold tight to it, the better to help him endure the sudden swell of memory.

How many times must he be reminded of his aloneness? On how many occasions must he mark it, solitary and in public?

She wasn't an unconventional type of woman. Instead, she was simply a woman who loved to paint, who found the meaning of her life in something the world thought shocking for her to pursue. She was less a bohemian than simply labeled one.

Still, she wanted to ease his apartness somehow.

At that moment, he turned and glanced over his shoulder at her. She didn't look away. She didn't even blink. For a long moment, an hour or an eternity, they looked at each other. She was no more certain of his thoughts than she was of her own. Instead, she only existed to feel at that moment. Finally, he nodded, just once, but it seemed to be an acknowledgment of her empathy, a bit of thanks from him for her caring, or simply his reception of it.

When he looked away, she stared down at her hands, wondering why it felt as if her heart hurt.

Janet bent closer to Tom and then leaned over to speak to Margaret. "He shouldn't be alone, Miss Margaret."

"You and Tom should go and join him," she said.

"And leave you alone? I'll not think of it."

Ask me to come with you, she wanted to say, but Janet didn't. Margaret's joining the Earl of Linnet in the family pew would be cause for village gossip.

"Go on, Janet, I'll be fine."

The older woman hesitated for a moment, biting at her lip in indecision. She glanced at Tom, then at Margaret again.

"Are you certain? We would just be a few steps away if you need us."

"Of course I'm certain," Margaret said, the duplicity of being polite pulling at her. She didn't want to be left alone any more than she wanted the earl left alone. The sad fact was that in any contest between McDermott and her, Janet and Tom had already chosen their loyalties.

She twisted to the side so Janet and Tom could exit, then watched as they walked to the front of the church. McDermott stood to allow them access and glanced back at her. There might have been a look of disappointment on his face, but he faced forward too quickly for her to determine it. Of course there wasn't. How very foolish she was being.

The service was shorter than she recalled, or else the child Margaret had thought it endless and the adult had seen it as it was. She did try, in all earnestness and remorsefulness, to concentrate on the service. But no matter how many times she was required to sit or kneel or stand, her attention repeatedly returned to the Earl of Linnet.

Her upbringing came back to her in strict remembrance as if her mother sat beside her tapping at her hand or arm. Behave yourself, Margaret, she would say, when Margaret's attention wandered. Why was she always reprimanded when her brothers were so much worse behaved than she?

Blessedly, McDermott didn't turn to look at her once, not even when the presenter stood up and led them all in song. True to what Janet said, the congregation had a lusty voice, and it was a pleasant few moments.

When the service was over, she meant to make her way to the front of the church and wait for Janet and Tom. However, she didn't have the chance. In a gesture reminiscent of noblesse oblige, the Earl of Linnet stood, the first person in the congregation to do so, and slowly turned to face the door. The rest of the congregation stood as well, but no one moved from their pews, waiting instead for the earl to pass. Anyone else would probably have marched straight through to the doorway, authoritarian footsteps marking his passage, but McDermott took his time, nodding at more than one person, taking the opportunity to shake several men's hands Twice he bent down to speak to a child who hid his face in his mother's skirts.

He hesitated beside her pew, but didn't say anything.

For a second, a flash of an instant, the flitter of a butterfly's wings, she actually contemplated holding out her hand to keep him in place. To be in his company, to breathe easier, to feel his arm beneath the trembling fingers of her left hand seemed altogether forbidden, exotic, and wonderful.

When he walked away, she took a deep breath.

She didn't want to be around McDermott. She didn't want to share the same air, or even look in his direction. She wanted nothing to do with the man, even if it meant not finishing the portrait. Never before had she reneged on a commission.

Even if the subject was unpleasant, or the sitting environment unbearable, she'd always finished every painting.

This, however, was unbearable. She couldn't be around him without making a fool of herself. A needy, foolish woman who only existed to *feel* and nothing more.

Had she absolutely no restraint when it came to the man? Was she simply a creature of passion? Had she no sense, no decorum?

Where had Margaret Dalrousie, Margaret Louise Dalrousie, Miss Margaret Dalrousie gone? She'd disappeared, leaving behind this panicked, emotional, flustered, confused woman.

At this moment, she was no more capable of doing what she did three years ago than the flightiest of women. Traveling to Russia, arranging for her own lodgings, and taking up her career thousands of miles from her home and her culture would simply be beyond her. She was too inept, too idiotic.

She had lost her mind. That was the explanation. She had become one of those true unfortunates touched by a brain fog. One night, not too long ago, when was sleeping, she'd suffered a storm in the brain, and when she awoke all was as it normally was, except instead of being unable to move one side of her body, her judgment was gone. Disappeared. Vanished. Poof!

Were women afflicted by passion? Was that why society guarded their virgins with such great care? That would certainly explain why women of the court hadn't been the least discreet about their illicit affairs. Their minds had gone.

To make matters worse, Margaret couldn't stop thinking about him. The nightmares that used to visit her with such regularity had disappeared, and in their stead dreams of McDermott. When she bathed, her washcloth lingered, imagining his touch. When she sat in the parlor at night, she stared at a page for an hour or more, unseeing. Instead, her vision was turned inward, her mind replaying that afternoon, then the scene in the Winter Parlor. She often put her fingers against her lips, remembering his kisses.

If other women were not afflicted with passion, she most certainly was.

What she felt in McDermott's company was different from anything else she'd ever experienced. When it was happening, she didn't care. Propriety? Hah! Sanity? What was that? Only let her touch him, feel the texture of his skin, the strength and flexing of his muscles. Let him smooth his fingers over her body, please, and feel where she was warm and where she welcomed him.

She was mad for him.

Only when need was satisfied did she come back to herself. Only when passion was momentarily spent could she marvel at the fact she had lost both her inhibitions and her mind.

It must *not* happen again.

She was not, after all, a fool. She was still young enough to bear children, and each time she lay with him, it was as if she dared God, Himself. McDermott had taken no precautions, and she'd not used a sponge soaked in vinegar that was all the rage in Russian society. Even now, she might be with child. She could barely keep herself—how was she to support a baby? A baby with his eyes, his nose, and her mouth?

Dear God, not her mouth.

She pressed her hand over her mouth. One way or another, her mouth was always getting her in trouble. Either it tempted McDermott to kiss her and led to other delicious occupations, or she was guilty of saying too much or saying the wrong thing.

Nearly a week ago, she'd sent him a short note. *I am unable to continue the sittings at this time, finding myself indisposed.* That was all. Any longer note, and she might have inadvertently revealed her utter panic.

She simply had to disregard him. Easier said than done when she could still remember exactly how she'd felt when he'd touched her. And his kisses. Dear God, the man kissed like a satyr. Nor would she ever be able to look at one of her brushes again without blushing.

The only reason she found herself entranced with the Earl of Linnet was because she was lonely. She was not immune to handsome men, after all, and McDermott was a very handsome man, naked or clothed. The last year had been difficult for her. Was she to blame for seeking a little comfort where she could?

There was something about his eyes, something about the way they seemed to look right through her as if seeking out the essence of her soul. She felt as if she should confess all of her deepest, darkest sins.

Oh, how silly. He *was* her deepest, darkest sin.

He continued greeting members of the congregation, then he was at the church door, where he was introduced to the minister. She moved off to the side, slipping from the doorway and walking down the graveled path.

Toward the east was the last resting place of a hundred or more souls of North Linten Village, all laid out with hands over their chests and their feet toward the sun in order to stand at the resurrection. To the west was the road leading to her snug little cottage nestled within the shadow of Glengarrow.

A small grove of trees clustered in the corner, and it was there she walked. It had been cold in the church, but she had not felt it as much as she did now. Perhaps because her attention was directed on something other than her own discomfort. Now, however, she was conscious of the winter wind, and snow crunching beneath her boots.

How very strange that she felt like weeping all of a sudden. Was it the proximity of all these small gravestones? Or did it have something to do with the fact that the Earl of Linnet was holding court behind her, nodding at the villagers, speaking softly to some, allowing himself to be touched, his hand to be held, promises of baked goods and prayers accompanying him?

She had held him. She'd pressed her cheek against his and allowed him to feel the dampness of her tears. She'd brushed her eyelashes against his skin and pressed her lips against the firm softness of his. When life became too much for him, when the brashness of it, the certainty of it, and the fe-rociousness of it became too harsh, she'd held him within the circle of her embrace, and rocked him back and forth to comfort him, to ease him.

None of those sweet matronly ladies could give that to him. And although from the looks in their eyes, the younger women wished to be closer to him, for now he was her lover. Her lover.

A tear fell. How utterly foolish she was being, but it wasn't the first time she chided herself in regard to the Earl of Linnet.

All these here are sinners, and sinner you be. One day, you, too, will rest in this place. She could almost hear the words whispered in the wind, along with another caution. *Enjoy your life, for it is fleeting. Waste not one single hour or day.*

"I never thought to see you at church, Miss Dalrousie. I'm surprised you were not too *indisposed* to attend."

She turned to find that McDermott had followed her. She began to walk again, making her way to the side of the churchyard, beneath the shelter of a tree that looked to be as old as the village itself. She studied the bare branches above her head, conscious that he was right behind her.

"Are you not going to answer?" he asked.

"I had not thought to see you here today, either, McDermott."

"Else you would not have come?"

"Else I would not have come," she said, glancing at him.

There was that look in his eyes, the one he'd worn when he'd made love to her.

Being on the fringes of society had given Margaret the ability to discern society from the vantage point of an outsider. She was all too conscious, now, of the speculative looks being given her and the outright curious ones directed

at the Earl of Linnet. No sooner had he come to
church for the very first time than he had pub-
licly aligned himself with the odd woman in the
neighborhood.

Why had he done so?

Out of pity? Or simply to bulwark himself
against the eternal questions others would raise?
*Have you managed to put your sorrow behind
you? What was it like coming home after all these
years? Is it true there are ghosts at Glengarrow?*

Well, he had certainly put those questions to
rest, hadn't he? Yet now he'd involved her in the
speculation.

*Exactly what is Margaret Dalrousie to you, Your
Lordship? Why did she not speak to you or look in
your direction once? Was it for fear that she might
reveal something in her expression? Why do you
bedevil her now?*

Despite the coldness of the day, the congregation
huddled outside the church steps in small groups.
People conversed, and more than a few looked in
their direction. Little children tugged at their moth-
ers' skirts, a group of men walked off together to
light their pipes. Life in North Linten Village was
marching on without their participation, but not
without curiosity from its inhabitants.

"I would like to know what is it about me that
inspires your disappearance?"

Slowly, she turned and faced him, wishing in the
intervening days that he'd grown uglier somehow.

Silence stretched between them. His gaze encompassed her hair, her face, her dress, and even
her ugly boots before sweeping back up to rest on
her face again.

"You haven't been sleeping," he said.

She shook her head.

"You haven't been painting, either."

"How do you know?"

"There's a look of contentment on your face when you're working. I've come to watch for it."

No one had ever said anything like that to her before, and she was flummoxed by his knowledge of her.

"Do you study me, then?"

He only smiled, the question remaining unanswered. Could true honesty exist between them? And if it could? What would she ask of him? What would she tell him?

Take me to your bed. For as long as circumstances warrant it or we wish it, we shall be lovers. Apologetic to no one, explaining our actions to no other soul.

But life was not that easy, was it? Not for painters, and certainly not for earls. There were too many people to gauge and weigh and measure and judge.

Twice now, they had lain together. Twice and it wasn't enough.

There, a little bit of honesty to give him, forbidden and inappropriate in this place of God and recompense.

"Have your ships arrived yet?"

His face darkened and his eyes glittered and if they had been anywhere else, she would have placed her hands on either side of his face and brought his head down so that she could press her lips against his. But they were in a churchyard, being observed by dozens of people.

Dear God, she didn't care. It did not make one whit of difference to her. The world had judged her for years and years, and all she had ever done was pursue her art and her ambition. Let them judge her for something she wanted, something forbidden and delicious. Let each person who stood there talking enrobed in their scarves, and their best hats and coats look at her in her threadbare woolen cape and wonder at the look of hunger in her eyes. Let them judge her and know that she was a harlot, a fallen woman.

She might well be that, but she was also deliciously intoxicated with the touch of his fingers on her flesh, and the promise of his kiss, and the soft, low words he murmured against her skin. She was drunk with it, sotted with passion, and she wanted more.

She turned away. "People shouldn't starve. Not in Scotland, at any rate. Not if they're free."

"Did you care for the plight of the serfs with such diligence, Margaret?"

"No," she said, wishing she could give him another answer. "I barely noticed them. I was entranced with the canals, the view of the palaces, the balls and entertainments."

"Yes, my ships have arrived. Will they be enough? I don't know."

"And if they aren't? What will you do?"

He looked startled by the question, and well he might be. Who was she to demand he change the world?

Instead of answering her, however, he asked, "Did you come to church to ask forgiveness from God?" he asked.

Startled, she stared at him, wondering if he had the power to deduce thoughts.

"Or to petition God for the courage to carry out your plan?"

"What are you talking about?" she asked, confused.

"Your plan to kill another human being. Or have you given up your plans for revenge?"

She didn't answer.

"Will you be satisfied, once he's dead? Will everything be made right? The attack will not have happened; you won't have the scar? You'll be back in Russia and still the darling of the court, the magnificent Margaret Dalrousie?"

"A man should not be able to rape with impunity," she said. "Not in Russia. Not anywhere. A woman should not be attacked simply because she is a woman."

"A man should not be killed, simply because he's a bastard. Nor should a woman be given the power of life and death simply because she's filled with a sense of injustice."

"A sense of injustice? That's all you would call it?"

She turned her head and stared at him. "He branded me, McDermott. He laughed when he did it. He bragged of it."

"Death is final, Maggie. There is no return." His glance encompassed the churchyard as if to prove his point. "There is no second chance, no change of heart. You cannot wish a person back into existence or make a bargain with God to alter time itself so you can make a better choice. Dead is forever dead."

He should not have the ability to tear her heart from her chest with only words.

"You don't understand."

"Enlighten me."

"I can't." Words wouldn't be able to express the depth of her horror, the extent of her humiliation. He'd taken her talent, and her sense of self, and the future she'd struggled for years to create for herself. He'd used her body without her assent, and uncaring about her pain. She'd been weak and incapable of protecting herself, and the awareness of her vulnerability frightened her.

She had to find Janet and Tom. She had to leave.

Janet was standing in front of the small gravestone, Tom standing beside her. Both of them had their heads bowed.

McDermott reached out and cupped her elbow with his palm. "Give them a moment," he said.

She glanced up at him. His attention was on the couple.

"We used to have services at Glengarrow. It was more convenient in winter, especially. But Janet and Tom always came here to the village church, and it wasn't until several years ago that I discovered why."

She glanced at him, waiting.

"It's their child, there. The only one they were able to have. And every week, Janet and Tom stand just as they are right now. No one disturbs them, because everyone knows."

The two leaned into each other, slightly, as if braced against the wind. Their bodies met at arm, hip, and hand. Tom's head bent solicitously toward

Janet, and she curved toward him as if seeking his greater strength. They seemed to need no one, bulwarked against the world itself.

Margaret dropped her arm, and McDermott's hand slid to her wrist, remaining there, poised.

Were they, too, linked? Not by emotion or loss or by the simple act of sharing memory. If she and McDermott were joined, it was by shedding the restraints binding them to civility.

"Do you not have your own visit to make?" she asked, the words constrained and difficult to speak.

He glanced at her. "Amelia isn't here, Margaret." He turned back to look at Janet and Tom. "She's buried in France, along with my daughter."

Why did it feel as if she'd been spiked through with a hundred different lengths of splinters? She focused on her breathing, taking several deep breaths.

"It must have been difficult to leave them," she said finally.

"Yes."

Moments passed, during which they didn't speak at all. How did she retract the comment? How could she wish back her curiosity?

"It is not an easy thing they do," he said slowly, still looking at Janet and Tom. "To visit those you love. I admire their courage."

She took a step closer to him, wishing she had the freedom to touch him.

"The first time I stood over Amelia's and Penelope's graves, I thought the pain would break me."

If not for their being watched, she would have placed her hand on her arm, wordless comfort. She might have stood on tiptoe and pressed her lips against his wind-chafed cheek, the better to banish his memories. She did nothing, holding tight to propriety, not by the wish to be viewed as virtuous so much as a desire not to be rebuffed. The moment, like it or not, belonged to Amelia and Penelope, and she remained silent and motionless in deference to them.

The wish, however, and the wanting were there, strong, resilient, and intrusive as they always had been.

"It did not get easier the more often I went. Life does not acknowledge death with any comfort, and like it or not, I was alive."

She knew that he was remembering the last time he'd stood over his wife's and child's graves. How did she call such a memory back?

"How do you bear it?" she asked softly. She turned away, staring at the majestic tree in the corner of the churchyard.

"Margaret." He placed his hand on her arm, attempted to turn her, but she wouldn't move. Not to be deterred, he peered around her bonnet. "Are you crying?"

"No," she said, brushing her gloved hand against her cheek. "It's the cold. It's making my eyes water."

"Do not grieve," he said. "There has been enough of that. Amelia loved laughter, and Penelope was the embodiment of it. She found joy in each moment." He smiled. "That's how I bear it," he said. "By remembering who they were more than the fact they are no longer here. No longer with me."

She wanted to put her hand on his cheek, reach up, and place a kiss there. Or pull his head down to rest against her shoulder. A gesture of nurturing, one that she'd rarely felt before, and never as fiercely.

He placed his hand on her shoulder as if to offer her comfort. She stepped away.

"You mustn't single me out in public, McDermott," she said. "You'll only cause people to talk."

He studied her. "They will talk regardless."

She nodded. "True. But at least they will not talk about me. I am heartily tired of the world talking about me."

"Have you always been an object of speculation, Margaret?"

"Yes. I was unmarried, unaccompanied, and different."

"An artist."

"A woman," she corrected, "who refused to do what was expected of her."

"If you hadn't been an artist, would you have been the same?"

She glanced at him, startled by the question. "You mean, which came first, my rebellious nature? Or my art?" She considered it. "Art," she answered after a moment. "I was forever scribbling in the dirt, drawing pictures of my brothers and sisters. I wasn't rebellious back then. I was merely trying to survive, and to protect what I'd done."

"But you never could."

She glanced at him again. "How did you know that?"

"It's why you're so protective of your paintings

now. I suspect your reputation is secondary to your art, but tied to it. Without a good reputation, you cannot garner commissions, and without commissions, there is no one to pay you for your work."

She smiled. "I would still work," she said.

He took another step closer.

She pressed both hands against her waist at the front, a swift and stern admonition to herself not to show any reaction. He seemed to know how she responded to him if his smile was any indication.

"Go away, Your Lordship."

"Does it help?"

"Does what help?"

She turned, deciding that it was easier to converse with him if she didn't have to look at him. He was an extraordinarily handsome man, and even bundled up in his greatcoat, she was only too aware of his physique. Her body, traitorous and abandoned, seemed to know that he was standing close. Her hand ached to reach out and touch him. Her body chilled, as if requiring his to warm it. Even her lips felt lonely, as if longing for his to be pillowed against them.

"To call me Your Lordship? Does it distance me in your mind?"

"No," she said softly.

How foolish a woman she was to give him the truth. She felt his hand suddenly on her shoulder, and almost sagged in relief. In the next instant, she made herself stand tall, shoulders back as if not needing his touch, or craving it. Still, it seemed as if she could feel the warmth of his palm within his glove.

Margaret turned and began to walk, her hearing acute for his footsteps behind her. But he didn't follow her, remaining instead in the churchyard as she resolutely made her way to the carriage.

She didn't look back, even though she wanted to, even though she was desperate to do so. Instead, she faced forward and wished herself back in her snug little cottage, drawing comfort from her memories of him.

Chapter 24

The parlor was warm, the fire blazing. The wind had died down, and it hadn't snowed for three days. In the distance, spring was poised like a young girl, skirts gathered up in her hands, a blush on her cheek, and flowers in her hair, waiting for the demise of the hag of winter.

Margaret sat in a comfortable chair, near the fire, the oil lamp a constant and glowing friend. She could not, however much she wished it, become interested in the words of this Scottish poet.

> *Thence, countra wives wi 'toil an 'pain*
> *May plunge an 'plunge the kirn in vain;*
> *For oh! the yellow treasure's taen*
> *By witchin skill;*
> *An 'dawtet, twal-pint hawkie's gaen*
> *As yell's the bill.*

She set the book aside, staring through the windows, her gaze captured by the night. She didn't hear Janet until the woman spoke.

"Are you certain you are well, Miss Margaret?"

Janet asked, standing at the door to the parlor. "Can I get you some tea? A posset? I make mine with a little yarrow, mixed with slippery elm, and a half a glass of vinegar with crushed basil leaves. Mix in a little honey, more than a little pepper, some garlic, and you'll be feeling better in no time."

"You mustn't go to any bother," Margaret said hurriedly. "I'm feeling fine, Janet, truly." She brandished her book as if it were a flag, but Janet still looked doubtful.

"I can sit with you a while, if you'd like."

"It's not necessary, Janet," Margaret said. "Tom is waiting for you. Why don't you retire for the night? I know it's been a long day for you."

"No longer than any other," Janet stubbornly said. "And if you're ailing . . ."

"I can assure you, Janet, that I'm feeling fine."

Janet came to stand in front of her, gripping her shawl with both hands. "I would never call you a liar, Miss Margaret, but I think, perhaps, you haven't looked in the mirror in a while. Your face has gone all pale-like. You look as bad as you did when you first came to Blackthorne Cottage."

Margaret smiled, surprised at the comment. "You've never mentioned those days before."

"And why should I mention them?" Janet asked. "It does no good to bring up the past if all you can find there is sadness. I knew you were hurting the very first moment I saw you, and it took months for that look on your face to disappear."

"And it's back, is it?" Margaret asked.

Janet shook her head. "No, not so I can see. But

304　KAREN RANNEY

another look is there in its place, Miss Margaret. Something a little sadder, perhaps. But there's no fear in your eyes."

Margaret smiled. "You're the only one who would have had the courage to say that to me, Janet."

"And who better? I've known you near a year, haven't I? Besides, you're all bluster but no bite. You may scowl and look fierce, Miss Margaret, but you've a warm heart, all the same."

"I doubt many people would have agreed with you over the years," Margaret said. "I was quite the termagant in Russia."

"Why ever did you go to that place?" Janet asked, hesitating at the door.

"Because I could, I suppose. I'd become quite sophisticated, you see. I'd learned to talk correctly, to dress appropriately, to comport myself in a variety of social situations. I was Margaret Dalrousie, painter of important personages." Her smile held a touch of mockery.

"Deep in my heart, however, I've always been the lonely little girl growing up in Fife, the strange one who painted pictures and talked about colors and shapes as if they were a foreign language."

"I think I like that Margaret best," Janet said.

Margaret forced a smile. "Go to bed, Janet. I'm not ailing, and I think only time will banish the look on my face."

"I don't think time has anything to do with it, Miss Margaret," Janet said.

What on earth did she say to that? Thankfully, Janet didn't require a response.

"If you want me, you know where Tom and I are."

"Thank you for your care of me, Janet. I truly do appreciate it."

Janet only nodded and left the room. Margaret leaned her head back against the chair, listening for Janet's soft footfalls as she climbed the first set of stairs, then the smaller steps leading to her and Tom's garret room. Despite the fact the room was beneath the eaves, it was a spacious chamber. The construction of the cottage was such that she rarely heard the couple in the evening.

She couldn't help but wonder now if Tom sat in a comfortable chair reading and Janet sat beside him crocheting as she sometimes did in the parlor. Sharing lives, sharing their days, sharing the experience of living.

Three years ago, she wouldn't have thought about Tom and Janet. She wouldn't have envied them their shared looks of amusement, the casual touches in the morning as they passed in the hall, the glance Tom gave his wife as he left for Glengarrow. She wouldn't have thought about their shared grief and how it linked them together.

A few years ago, she wouldn't have considered Tom and Janet fortunate. After all, they'd hired themselves out as servants to other people, forever to be reminded of the differences in station. Yet they never saw the divisions, never acted as if McDermott was better. Although he was their employer, he was also a member of their family, in an odd and touching way.

Margaret waited until she was certain Janet had settled herself in and wouldn't return to the parlor. Only then did she stand and leave the room, ducking her head beneath the lintel. The door at the back of the cottage was framed by two windows. Both had been shuttered against the night.

She lit a lamp and opened the door, shivering as a wintry blast of cold air greeted her. McDermott slowly walked toward her, his footsteps making a crunching sound on the ice crusted grass. He wore his greatcoat, but no hat.

"Are you a fool to stand out in the cold without a hat, McDermott?"

"I'm a fool to be here at all. What does it matter my attire? How did you know I was here?"

"You've been here for the last four nights. Why?"

"I've long since lost the ability to consume the quantity of brandy necessary to sleep through the night. Alcohol and endless hours do not make for a well-matched couple. They mate with acrimony, toss epithets, and quarrel from the first glass to the last dregs of the bottle. In the morning, I'm left with a blinding headache and no sense of having rested."

"And you think I'm a tonic for your sleepless nights?"

"I think you're the reason for them," he said.

"Go away, McDermott."

Instead, he came closer, took the steps up to the door, and gently took the lamp from her hands. He stepped across the threshold, bent his head, and brushed his lips over her forehead.

"I need to get away from you," he said. "But every time I leave Glengarrow, you accompany me.

I go and visit God, and there you are, tempting me."

He was too close, too warm, and too masculine. Her body remembered him even as her mind warned her he was becoming addictive.

"Margaret," he said, and her name was both an entreaty and a promise.

"Go away," she whispered.

"Only words. Words seduce," he said softly. "Words have power, don't you think?"

She would say anything to banish him. "Perhaps."

"Touch me," he whispered against her temple.

She flinched.

"Tempting words, don't you think?"

"Yes. Go away."

"Unkind words, Margaret. Stay. A much better word, I think. Kiss me. Even better words."

She held herself still, waiting.

"I cannot sleep for wanting you."

He rubbed his cheek against her temple, moving closer still. They stood in the doorway, but she was conscious only of two things, the heat of McDermott's body and the fierce booming beat of his heart.

"I could bring you to satisfaction simply with words, couldn't I?"

She took a deep breath, felt her breasts press against the wool of his greatcoat. He was going to take her, on the kitchen floor, on the frozen ground, sitting in the parlor, and it didn't matter.

I am falling in love, and I most desperately do not wish it.

What would he say if she had the courage to address him with those exact words? He might pale. Or he might have a look of pity in his eyes. But most certainly he would understand why she avoided him at every turn. This emotion truly could not be allowed to fester. If it did, she would soon be even more miserable than she was now.

"Couldn't I?" he repeated.

"Yes," she said softly, surrendering completely.

His face changed, his features hardening. He placed the lamp on the table in the center of the room and returned to stand in front of her.

She placed both palms against his chest, slowly unbuttoning his coat. She wanted to feel the contours of his body beneath the linen shirt— the subtle ridge of muscle, the texture of his skin, the light dusting of hair across his chest. Brushing her knuckles against his coat, she brought her hands up, pressing herself against him, threading her fingers through the hair at the nape of his neck as she gently pulled his head down for a kiss.

At this moment she was again defenseless, feeling as if passion were a separate entity in this room, compelling them one to the other. As he deepened the kiss, catching her up in a tight embrace, she realized that surrendering to McDermott was so much easier than shielding herself against him, and so much more pleasurable.

Until this moment, lying beside McDermott, Margaret had never before considered that she might have been lonely for a very long time.

What would it be like to have someone who would listen to her secret thoughts? Someone who might *want* to listen to her confidences? Someone who might want to know her uncertainties, and her questions?

I have this need inside of me to be the best I can be. Each painting brings me closer, but I've not yet done my best work. What if I never can? What if I fail? Revelations she'd never made to anyone else. Questions she'd never asked a single soul. What would it be like actually to share such secrets?

She sat up quietly so as not to disturb McDermott, pulling the coverlet free from the end of the bed and wrapping herself in it.

The fire was banked, only a soft orange glow remained, but the room was warm enough.

She moved to the window, looking out at the landscape. The night was still and soundless. Smoke gently wafted up from Glengarrow's chimneys. The moon shone brightly, creating bluish gray shadows on the snow. Branches became elongated fingers stretching out from the forest. Hedges were transformed into small, snug, square-shaped cottages for elves and brownies.

There was magic in this night. She should have heard music, the sound of a violin perhaps. The piercing sweetness of the high notes, the lustful intonation of the lower notes—music that made her heart soar and sing.

The air, so crisp that her eyes watered and her nose felt assaulted, carried her breath, lifted each exhalation, and hung it suspended in the air as if to prove to her she was alive.

She brought her hands up, cupped them around her mouth, blowing her hot breath against her skin.

In the past, when she couldn't sleep, it was because a painting lured her from her bed. She would sit and sketch to keep herself occupied. If the sitting were in her studio, she'd go and stand in front of the canvas, trying to determine what concerned her, what had captured her attention, what kept her from sleeping. She thought of challenges she'd had in the past, the shadow of candlelight on ivory silk, caramel-colored lace with all its intricacies, tiny rosettes lining a hem.

A painting had not awakened her. Instead, the misery of her own heart kept her sleepless. The pain of knowing that what she felt would not be easily tamped down or banished.

Tears peppered her eyes. She was not a woman to whom tears came easily. Other women cried; she remained stoic. Other women wept; she expressed contempt for such weakness.

All the same, the tears fell freely.

There was so much she missed right at this moment. A family that might have loved her for all her strangeness. Friends who might have cared enough to brave the social stigma of being supportive to a woman in her situation. A lover who would have defended her, protected her, cared for her, who would have enfolded her within his arms and held her when she wept for the betrayal she felt. Someone who might have loved her as McDermott loved his Amelia.

At that moment, he stirred. She brushed the tears from her face and turned to face him.

"You're awake," he said, his voice without a hint of sleep to it.

"I couldn't sleep," she admitted.

"While my damnable leg woke me."

"At least we made it to a bed this time," Margaret said, smiling in the darkness.

"It's a bloody good thing." He sat up on the edge of the bed and began to massage his thigh. "My leg can't take the floor again. In fact, I'm limping more often than not, and I think the responsibility lies with you."

He turned his head and looked at her, a shadow with glittering eyes. His shoulder, left arm, and the side of his face were touched by the moonlight, rendering him an otherworldly creature. She wished, at that moment, that she had the skill to paint him just as he appeared. Mysterious, surrounded by darkness, but not part of it. He was alien to the night, but it succored and shielded him.

And her? She was his companion, if only for an hour or two. If only for this night. Why did that knowledge hurt so much?

"Are you blaming me?"

"While I'm not still convalescing, I'm to treat my leg with the dignity it deserves. Not coupling on the floor or racing up stairs."

She bit back a smile.

"You're following a pattern, McDermott. You're insistent and intent until you have me beneath you, and after it's done, you spend an inordinate amount of time regretting it."

"I don't regret it," he said softly. "I don't understand it, but I don't regret it."

"Must everything be understood? Must we comprehend all that goes on around us?"

"Life is more orderly when you do."

She smiled. "Life isn't orderly, McDermott. It's occasionally very messy, cluttered, a jumble of people and circumstances."

He walked to where she stood beside the window. She didn't comment that he had, indeed, been limping. He tipped his head back and stared at the starlit sky.

She followed his gaze. "I used to believe the stars were the eyes of angels. I always used to wonder if they saw everything I did."

He smiled. "Instead of angels, they were a chained maiden, a water bearer. Perhaps an eagle or a bear."

She glanced at him.

"Have you never heard of the constellations? Andromeda, Aquarius, Aquila, Ursae Majoris?"

She shook her head as she reached over and pushed a lock of hair off his forehead. Her fingers strayed across his cheek and down to his unsmiling lips.

"You never answered me, you know. In the churchyard. You're going to kill him, aren't you?" he said.

"Kill him?"

She lowered her hand. How odd that it felt as if her heart was surrounded by ice.

"Don't prevaricate, Maggie. You're too intelligent."

"Don't call me Maggie," she said. "No one ever has. I've only been Margaret all my life."

He ignored her comment, returning to his questioning.

"Why not all of them? Why not all the men who attacked you? Why settle for one? Because he marked you?"

His questions were not entirely unexpected. McDermott asked what he wanted and when he pleased. In that respect, perhaps they were too much alike.

She returned to the bed, sitting on the edge of it. Instead of looking at him, still standing by the window, framed by moonlight, she stared at the floor.

"You already know too much about my past, McDermott. Now you insist on knowing my future?"

"Will you have a future if you kill another human being?" His words were cutting, but his voice was soft. Did he think to spare her reputation, knowing Tom and Janet slept above them?

"But you don't want to be swayed from your task. No doubt vengeance has kept you focused, and without it you're afraid you'll have nothing. Is that it, Maggie?"

He began gathering up his clothes, dressing in silence. They were forever doing this, mad for each other, then summoned to reality when satiated.

"You're Margaret Dalrousie," he said, buttoning his shirt. "Who are you to feel remorse for your actions? To feel guilt?"

"I'm not as indestructible as you think I am."

"Next you'll be telling me you're only human,"

he said. "If that's the case, why are you playing at being God?"

"You ask impossible questions, McDermott. Why do you bother, when it sounds as if you already know the answer or don't care how I respond?"

"Because I expected more from you."

He stood and regarded her in the moonlight.

"Even worse, I wanted more from you," he said, and left her.

Chapter 25

"It's a fine day," Janet said, bundling herself up in her coat for the walk to Glengarrow. "Nearly spring, I'm thinking."

Margaret, too, was dressed and ready for the day. She hadn't slept well last night. But then, she hadn't slept well for weeks, ever since McDermott had left for Inverness.

"It's off he's gone again, on that fine horse of his," Janet had said nearly a month ago.

"Gone?"

"The earl, off to Inverness. It's better than being holed up in Glengarrow like a ghost, I'm thinking."

Margaret pretended great interest in the row of buttons down the middle of her dress. She really should sew the third one from the bottom on a little more securely. She didn't have a matching button and would have to replace them all if she lost one.

She looked over at Margaret. "He needs to make a life for himself, don't you think?"

"I haven't an opinion on the Earl of Linnet," Margaret said. She didn't want to discuss McDermott, not with Janet. Not with anyone. "I hope he enjoys his trip," she said, and managed to make the words sound almost sincere.

"Are you going on your walk then?" Janet asked.

"I think I shall," Margaret said, grabbing her cape from the peg by the door. She took her time buttoning the cape, donning her gloves, and wrapping the scarf around her throat.

All the while, she resolutely refused to think of the Earl of Linnet, as she did every day. And every day, thoughts of him flew unbidden into her mind, along with another image, the countess he would eventually bring back to Glengarrow. The woman would be petite and blond, and pretty, of course. She would be proper and wise and nurturing. She wouldn't be irritable or easily annoyed.

An angel, brought to earth. Not unlike Amelia.

Would McDermott be happy? Would he ever think of her? Would he ever stand at his window and gaze toward Blackthorne Cottage, wondering at her whereabouts or her fate?

Because she wouldn't be here. She couldn't bear it. That was the worst of it, wasn't it? Somehow, she'd become ensnared with the stern earl, the grieving man. She'd lost whatever independence she had. Even now, she could feel the skeins of emotion tying her to him.

Was it wrong, therefore, to wish him happiness but also wish he found it somewhere other than in her view? Please, God, let her find a life somewhere else.

Could she leave Glengarrow? She didn't want to leave her snug little cottage with its blue-slate roof and its ivy-covered walls, and that was another revelation.

Here, she'd found a home for herself, a place where she was accepted. She was Margaret Dalrousie of Blackthorne Cottage. Her idiosyncrasies did not seem to matter to anyone. She was simply accepted for who she was.

Could she take herself off to Edinburgh again and pit herself against the greedy men and women who so fervently wanted her talent but never remembered to pay her? She didn't know if she had the heart for it anymore. Or the stomach. Perhaps she should demand payment in advance. But there were other artists, those less talented, or too new to understand the financial pitfall of following a dream, who would gladly accept any promise to pay as long as it resulted in some type of recognition, some type of work. Once, she'd felt the same, before she became wiser and more practical.

What good was recognition when she was starving?

She opened the door and stood on the step, feeling the change in the air instantly. The air felt a little less damp, not as if snow were coming but as if it wasn't as cold, as if spring had waved in passing. The air struck her cheeks in a gentle pat. She could almost smell the scent of growing things and newly turned earth, so close did spring appear.

She began to walk, knowing her destination only too well. She nodded to the lions flanking the gates of Glengarrow, then stepped onto the path winding around the estate. Glengarrow seemed oddly lonely today, as if all the preceding months and years of desertion showed upon her façade like wrinkles appearing overnight on a beauty's face. Or it could have only been her mood, somber and nearly sad.

She felt a kinship with the house, one she'd never before felt, as if they mourned the same loss, as if they felt the same desertion. Over the last year, she'd grown to love Glengarrow, to know it, and appreciate its beauty. There were memories in Glengarrow's rooms, especially in the Winter Parlor.

The wind was not as fierce or as wintry as it had been weeks earlier. Now it felt like the touch of a ghost's breath, stirring her hair loose from its braid, swirling her skirt.

She sat on the bench in front of the urn, settling her skirts, and clasping her gloved hands together. For a long time she sat there, the sun beginning to warm the top of her head. She looked down at her clasped hands, removed her gloves, and gripped her hands together tightly. A supplicant's pose, perhaps. How did one entreat a merciful God, especially the God she'd ignored so very long?

She couldn't even frame the words—she didn't know what words to say. She was adrift in misery, and it was such a strange sensation she marveled at it even as she suffered through it.

"Help me," she finally said.

No celestial voice came to her aid. The clouds did not part for a gigantic finger to spear her to the spot. The world went on as it had been moments earlier, the day brightening. She heard the sounds of birds, another harbinger of spring. From deep in the woods came the cry of a fox, but it, too, quickly faded.

McDermott had left again, and Glengarrow seemed to know it. McDermott had left, and she knew he would never come to her again.

I wanted more from you.

As she sat on the bench in front of the wall and looked up at Glengarrow, she began to cry. If anyone chanced to look out a window, they would have seen a sight. A lone woman brightly dressed in a red cape, tears bathing her face.

How strange she didn't care.

She buried her face in her hands and began to sob deeply. Perhaps she cried for Russia, or for those horrible months in Edinburgh, or for the loss she felt right at this moment. Perhaps she cried because of the realization she was capable of love and it was not an emotion like others would have her think. Love was violent and catastrophic, torturous and invasive. This love had the capacity to wound her to the death, and even now she felt as if she bled from a hundred tiny pinpricks of doubt and sorrow and inadequacy.

For the first time in her life she wanted something she knew she couldn't have. No amount of effort, attention, or sheer work would accomplish this task. Nothing she did would make a jot of difference. Love was not something she could create. It existed without her cooperation and would live or die without her compliance.

In the interim, however, it would make her miserable.

*   *   *

Robert stood beside the refreshment table and wondered how soon he could politely excuse himself.

Why the hell had he agreed to host this afternoon soiree? Or any of the other entertainments in the past month? To prove something to himself? To demonstrate that he was putting his life back in order, that grief wasn't the predominant emotion he felt?

The predominant emotion he was feeling at the moment was searing pain. His damn leg hurt. The night before, he'd danced with girls not long out of the schoolroom, as well as women who'd known Amelia and held either too much compassion or speculation in their gazes.

He'd smiled until his face felt numb and conversed on a great many topics, including politics. He'd fended off the flirtations of a dozen women, all of whom were thoroughly charming and ebullient.

None of them annoyed him. None of them angered him. Not one of them made him curious as to what they thought or how they would respond to his questions. Nor did he feel desire for any of them.

What was she doing now? Still practicing her shooting, no doubt. Still taking her endless walks. Who did she talk to? Janet? Who did she argue with? Tom? Poor man. When he returned to Glengarrow, he would instruct the older man to simply walk off when she began haranguing him. Someone like Margaret could never avoid voicing her opinion. Did she ever walk into the village and give the shopkeepers any difficulties?

He hadn't been home in weeks, and now as he leaned surreptitiously against the wall, Robert wondered at his own reasoning. Did he somehow want to make her miss him? Or did he stay away from Glengarrow in order to purge thoughts of her from his mind?

She refused to leave. He could recall every conversation they'd ever had, envision every encounter. Try as he might—and he didn't try hard—he couldn't forget what loving her had been like.

She'd been shocked at the power of passion. At first, she'd tried to hide it, but surprise was there in her eyes, and in her reaction to her own body's delight. Nor could he ever predict how she would respond. One moment she was reluctant and a second later eager.

He'd never thought he could feel this way about another woman. He'd never suspected that someone other than Amelia could occupy his mind with such tenacity. Margaret—Maggie—wasn't beautiful, but she was fascinating. Looking out at the women crowded into his mother's home—any one of whom could surpass Margaret in appearance— he knew that he could spend a year in Inverness and not be able to forget her. What he felt for Margaret had less to do with her appearance than her character.

Was that why he'd remained in Inverness so long? To give himself time to come to grips with the idea that what he felt was an emotion he'd never expected to feel again? Not simple lust, even though that was certainly pleasurable enough. Margaret fascinated him, challenged him, made him smile, and even more disturbing—had the capacity to make him angrier than he'd ever been in his entire life.

He was not a man given to excessive reflection. Instead, he'd set out to achieve certain milestones, unsurprised when he'd achieved each one. After all, weren't goals to be accomplished? Why make them, otherwise?

For the last month, however, he'd spent some time evaluating his life honestly. What he saw didn't please him. Yes, he'd become a member of Parliament. Yes, he was the Earl of Linnet, and a fair steward for his inheritance. Yet there were so many other things he might have accomplished had he put his mind to it.

He'd settled too easily. He'd not expected much of himself. He should have pushed himself to accomplish more, to achieve more. It was not enough simply to have one goal. A man must have a series of them in order to keep himself moving forward through life with enthusiasm.

Margaret understood that. She viewed each painting as a challenge. Each successive portrait was an opportunity to be better, to learn more, to achieve more, and to triumph over her last execution. It wasn't enough simply to look at one portrait and say: this is what I've done; ergo, this is what I am. She'd always known her talent was fluid and must be captured, trained, and used.

So, too, was his talent, such as it was: an ability to persuade, perhaps. The ability to see the broad scope of a problem, then narrow it down to its infinitesimal details. The ability to communicate outward to a stratum of people with fire and passion—one of the reasons he'd been one of the youngest Scottish nobles elected to the House of Lords.

No wonder, then, his life had become slightly rusty around the edges. No wonder he'd been vaguely dissatisfied and unknowing why. He'd not challenged himself, not set for himself another series of goals.

Have your ships arrived? She'd challenged him that day in the churchyard, and the knowledge was there every day. What would he do? What could he do?

He'd finally figured it out, and for this gift of insight, which she probably didn't know she'd given him, he'd procured a gift for Margaret. Quite an illicit gift, as it turned out. A man did not purchase articles of clothing for a woman not his wife. He'd taken his mother's dressmaker aside and whispered instructions to her, promising her a monetary reward if she could have this particular garment finished by the time he left Inverness.

The garment was done, but he was still in Inverness.

Let her dismiss it and him. Let her tilt her very aristocratic nose up in the air and level that intense green gaze on him. He'd just demonstrate another of his assets—his incredible tenacity. He'd just present his gift to her again.

In his mind's eye, he saw his home, a deep, shadowed glen scooped out of the earth in the shape of a giant's thumb. The sharp cliffs of Ben Mosub glinted silver and black against a mourning sky. The scent of a winter's day, the chill of the air so cold and pure that it almost hurt to breathe it, was laced through with the pleasant tang of smoke from Glengarrow's chimneys. The trees were laden with ice; snow covered the lane, and in the midst of his mental picture, standing defiant and resolute, was a woman in a red-woolen cape.

Miss Dalrousie. Margaret. Maggie. Difficult, arrogant, and too invested in vengeance for his peace of mind.

Somehow, he would have to find a way to sway her from her task. Somehow, he must turn her face to the future, a future that seemed a great deal more promising than it had a month ago.

There was not a woman in Inverness who equaled her, and that knowledge should have disturbed him. Instead, he felt a curious sense of satisfaction, as if he was proud of her independence, her arrogance, and all those character traits that still had the ability to fascinate even as they annoyed him.

It was time for him to go back to Glengarrow. It was time to see Margaret again. What happened after that was something he didn't need to contemplate at the moment. It was enough he returned home.

He left the parlor, signaled for a maid, and gave the footman instructions.

In less than an hour, he was packed, ready and waiting at the front door for his horse to be brought from the stable. The wind was blowing from the north, and any hint of spring had abruptly vanished in the resultant chill. Riding home was going to be miserable, payment perhaps for his impatience.

He strode back and forth across the tiled floor of the foyer, no doubt making the footman at the door a little nervous. Robert didn't give a whit about the young man, and only noticed him when he turned and began to retrace his steps.

"Are they reshoeing the bloody horse?" he finally asked, stopping in front of the footman. They were the same height, another irritation since he was more familiar with towering over people.

But then, footmen were selected for their height, were they not? And no doubt their physical appearance. Every young man in his mother's home was tall and physically attractive.

"Don't badger the man, Robert," his mother said, coming into the foyer. "He hasn't done anything to you, and you're intimidating him." She flicked her fingers to the left, and the young footman melted away as all good servants do.

He turned to face his mother. "I was simply questioning the time it took to bring my horse around," he said.

"And what would he have to do with it? Address your complaints to the stable master. Are you in such a hurry to return to Glengarrow, then?"

He walked to where his mother stood and surprised her by hugging her quickly.

"Yes, by God, I am," he said, and found himself smiling.

Ten minutes later Margaret stood, making her way to the kitchen, brushing her hands over her face and hoping her eyes didn't reveal too much. If anyone asked, she would claim she'd been walking so quickly, the wind had stung her eyes. Never mind the day was truly a temperate one, and there was only a gentle breeze.

There was no one in the kitchen necessitating she lie. She made her way up the back stairs to the second floor and to the Winter Parlor. No one had disturbed the painting. The drape was placed just as she had left it.

Carefully, she removed it from the easel and left the room. At the doorway, she turned and, placing the painting against the wall outside the room, retraced her steps. Turning right, she opened the connecting door leading to the suite Amelia had shared with McDermott.

Here, the sun did not shine so brightly, and the atmosphere was somber, as if gray netting had been placed across the air itself. Amelia's perfume was strong here, as if the woman had just sprayed the scent.

The last time Margaret had been in this room, she'd been first shamed by her actions, then terrified when McDermott had discovered her. Now, she felt a curious sadness, as she said farewell to both Amelia and Glengarrow.

Margaret walked to the center of the room and turned slowly, viewing the bed and the twin armoires standing side by side. Amelia's vanity as well as the two chairs beside the window were draped in shadow.

"Are you angry, Amelia? Are you angry you are dead and he is not? Are you determined, somehow, to keep him with you, to keep your memory alive, always in his mind?"

She walked to the vanity, stood looking in the mirror. The shadows were so deep, the light in the room so dim, that she appeared no more substantial than a ghost herself.

"Let him go," she said softly. "Let him live again. Let him find love and happiness. Let him smile. Let him laugh. He has such a beautiful laugh, Amelia, and it is so rare."

She turned in a slow circle, her hands pressed against her chest, feeling like weeping again.

"Let him find love, Amelia. If it isn't with me, then let it be someone who deserves him. Someone who can bring him happiness. I know you loved him, and I know only too well how much he loved you. But you cannot keep him. Let him go. Please."

Amelia was silent.

But then, Amelia had never been there.

She turned and left the room, gathering up the painting and her supplies and making her way back to Blackthorne Cottage.

Once back home, she put the painting in the room beside her bedroom, propping it up against a trunk she'd not bothered to open. Tomorrow she would gather up the easel and the rest of her belongings. And her heart? Where was it scattered? Another foolish question, another silly thought.

Closing the door to the trunk room, she descended the stairs, wandering into the kitchen to prepare her lunch. Something propped up on the table captured her attention, and she reached for it.

She had rarely received any letters, and only from her solicitor. She recognized his distinctive handwriting long before she crossed the room and picked it up from the table.

For the longest time she simply held it in her hands and wondered what news it could bring. Her parents? Her mother didn't know where she was living, and she doubted if any of her siblings actually cared. They were busy with their own lives, and the actions of a sister who'd left home a long time ago could not possibly interest them.

Her solicitor had discovered the name of her benefactor. He had information about the coat of arms.

The best thing for her to do was to open the letter.

She sat at the table and arranged herself very primly on the chair. She slid the envelope across the table surface with one finger and stared at it for a moment before gathering up her courage and slitting it open with a fingernail.

Dear Miss Dalrousie,

I have been successful in the second task you gave me—that of identifying the crest. The coat of arms is that of an ancient and distinguished family, the Blanhelms, the family name for the Dukes of Harridge.

The words simply sat there, slowly registering in some far-off part of her mind. The Duke of Harridge. The name wasn't familiar.

There was another sentence or two, self-congratulatory words, as if the solicitor was determined to applaud himself and his actions. She should write him to tell him she appreciated his efforts on her behalf, and the fact she'd evidently obtained good value for her money. She wasn't going to write him, however. She wasn't going to acknowledge the letter in any way.

"Miss Margaret?"

She turned to find that Janet had returned from Glengarrow. The older woman's face was wreathed in concern; there was a look in her eyes that was far warmer than that of a mere servant.

When had Janet become a friend, an almost-mother? When she'd delivered a posset and insisted that Margaret drink it? When she'd fussed at her for walking each day, yet fussed even more when she didn't? Or when they all sat in the parlor at night, and sometimes Margaret would look up from her book or her needlework. Janet would look over at that moment and together they would share a smile at the sight of Tom with his head back, mouth open, snoring.

"What is it, Miss Margaret? What's wrong?"

There was no point in lying. Instead, Margaret folded her hands in front of her and faced Janet resolutely.

"I need to go to London," she said. "Can you ask if Tom will take me to North Linten?"

"Is it bad news, Miss Margaret?" Janet asked, coming forward.

"No. Yes. It's news I've wanted to hear." She turned and looked out the window to the back of the cottage where the bales of hay stood, testament to her growing precision with her pistol.

Janet stood just a few feet away. Vengeance vying with friendship—what a strange and discordant thought. Could she banish one in favor of the other? A troubling question and one for which she didn't have a ready answer.

"Janet," she began, and unexpectedly found herself unable to speak. She stared down at the floor, gathered her composure, and continued. "I've given you the cottage," she said. "If something happens to me, I want you and Tom to have it."

"Miss Margaret, you can tell me what's troubling you. I'll never breathe a word of it."

Margaret smiled. "I know that only too well. And whatever you do learn, Janet, you'll not divulge."

Janet looked away, then nodded.

"You know, for example, that the earl and I . . ."

Janet glanced back at her. There was no dissembling in the other woman's gaze, but neither was there any condemnation.

"Have sought comfort from each other?" Janet suggested.

Margaret nodded.

"Tell him good-bye for me. Tell him . . ." She hesitated again, and this time, her composure was not regained so readily. When she finally could speak again, all she could say was, "Just tell him good-bye."

Janet didn't say a word as Margaret left the room.

What, after all, could she say?

Robert didn't ride into the stables at Glengarrow, but turned left and made for Blackthorne Cottage, instead. Once he'd dismounted, and tied the reins of his horse to a branch of nearby pine, he unfastened the box from the back of his saddle and strode to the front door.

Janet answered his knock with a gasp of surprise and quick, bobbing curtsy.

"I've come to speak to Miss Dalrousie," he said.

"Your Lordship, she's not here. She's gone to London. Tom took her to North Linten not a few hours ago."

"London?" he said, congratulating himself on the fact he'd been able to utter that one word.

She turned and retreated into the cottage. He slowly followed, stooping to avoid hitting his head on the low lintel. He'd only been in the cottage twice in his life, and both times had been with Margaret. He hadn't paid much attention to the structure or its furnishings, but he looked around now as he followed Janet.

The front parlor was small but cozy enough, and warm.

He nodded to Tom, seated in one of the overstuffed chairs. The older man moved to stand, but Robert waved him back into place as he followed Janet into the kitchen, a room he remembered only too well.

"Why London?" he asked as Janet turned and handed him a letter.

By the churning feeling in his stomach as he began to read the letter, he knew. Even before his brain made sense of the words, he knew what she had done.

Maggie had gone after justice, and in doing so she had condemned herself to death.

Every single loss he'd suffered had happened

without warning. He'd simply been left to deal with it. On this occasion, however, he had some foreboding, some warning. He was being given a chance to prevent a tragedy, and he was damn well going to try.

Without a word to Janet, he turned and retraced his steps, stopping at the door of the parlor. This time, when Tom tried to stand, he didn't wave him back into place.

"Can you take me to London?" he said.

"London, Your Lordship? Me?" The older man looked stunned at his request.

"You're still a coachman, are you not?"

"Aye, sir, I am. And I keep all the carriages in fine shape."

"My horse is too tired, and I've not the patience to bargain for mounts along the way. Can you ready a coach?"

"You would trust me, then, Your Lordship?"

The two men studied each other for a long moment. Robert finally understood the older man's hesitation.

"I never faulted you, Tom. Not once. It was an accident. It could have happened at any time, to anyone. It was not because of your driving."

"You never said, sir." Tom looked down at his shoes.

"Something else to lay at my doorstep, then, Tom, that I never thought to do so."

"You were injured, sir. I understood."

"I should have told you later, at least. I should have eased your mind."

Tom looked up at him, his features softening.

"You have now, sir, and I'll have the coach and horses readied in the hour."

Robert turned to leave, glancing at Janet standing in the hall, unabashedly weeping and making no effort to conceal it.

Words weren't important or even necessary at that moment. Robert did something he'd never done in all the years Janet had faithfully and tirelessly worked for his family. He enfolded her in his arms, and let her cry against his chest.

Sometime later, she pulled free, blotting at her tears with her apron.

"There's something you should see, Your Lordship," she said, turning and glancing over her shoulder at him. He had no choice but to follow her again, even as an invisible clock began ticking in his mind.

At the head of the stairs, she turned to the left and opened a door. He had to bend over to enter the room, and when he did, he saw Margaret's painting.

"I looked, sir. I shouldn't have, but I did."

"I'm prohibited, Janet, from removing that drape."

She nodded and strode past him, pulling the cloth free and exposing the portrait. He hadn't seen it after that first day, and now he could only stare at the unfinished work.

"I think it explains some, don't you, Your Lordship?"

He didn't have a response as he turned and left the room.

"Your Lordship?"

He hesitated, glancing over his shoulder.

"She wanted for me to tell you good-bye, sir. But I've never heard anyone sound as sad."

He didn't have any words for Janet as he descended the stairs, intent on London and saving Margaret.

Chapter 26

Her homeland was occasionally barbaric, but never so much as in matters of travel. Tom had taken her to North Linten Village, where Margaret took a small coach to Inverness. From there, she had a choice of traveling overland to Aberdeen and taking a ship to Edinburgh or simply traveling south to Glasgow by coach to connect with the Caledonian express train to London. Granted, by taking the train she'd cut twelve hours from her trip, but she'd spent twice that much time—not to mention the expenditure—in getting to Glasgow.

Margaret hadn't the funds for a first-class ticket, so she and a hundred or so other poor souls shared the third-class compartment, each of them no doubt pretending not to notice the cacophony, the smoke, and the sheer awfulness of the accommodations.

The train reminded her too much of her childhood, the grimy faces, the noise, and the sheer effort to keep clean. Margaret never thought of her mother without a rag in her hand and a chiding look on her face, the caution, "Mind you, child," on her lips.

Her mother had still been a young woman when
Margaret was born, but by the time Margaret left
for Italy, her mother had grown old.

A little girl with wide brown eyes peered over
the seat in front of her, reminding Margaret of her
oldest sister, Elizabeth. How old would Elizabeth
be now? Ten years older. A matron, if she'd married. How many children did she have?

Ten years. In one way, it was so very long, and in
another, such a short span of time. How innocent
she'd been, and how utterly brave.

Courage was a commodity of the very young
and the very naive.

She'd sent money home, half the proceeds of
her first commission. She'd been so proud of that
painting, the portrait of a wealthy child. The little
girl wouldn't sit still, and Margaret had finally allowed her to play on the floor with her puppy. It
had only been a natural progression to paint the
girl in that pose. The parents had been ecstatic, her
mentor had been furious, and she'd learned a very
valuable lesson.

She should listen to her own intuition above any
other voice.

Her mother had never made mention of the
money, and Margaret had continued to send money
when she could. There was never a thank-you,
never a word written between them. She wasn't
certain the money had ever actually reached her
family. The only clue was a badly scrawled letter
from her oldest brother saying he appreciated how
she helped when she could.

Why was her family so much on her mind?

The little girl grinned at her, showing a gap-toothed smile. Margaret had no choice but to smile back. If she'd had a sweet, she would have given it to the child, but all she had was a pistol in her reticule.

Had Penelope been as charming? No doubt she had been, and McDermott felt her loss each and every day.

Was that why she was thinking of families? Was McDermott in her mind even now?

Next you'll be telling me you're only human. If that's the case, why are you playing at being God?

Go away, McDermott, and thankfully, he did, leaving her to the somberness of her thoughts.

Did she really want to die for the sake of vengeance? If she wasn't caught, if she somehow escaped the consequence of her actions, did she want to live knowing she was a murderess?

Did she want to destroy her future for the sake of the past?

The questions were intrusive, a conscience given voice. Where had it been resting all this time?

The truth was, at one point, she'd wanted to die.

In Edinburgh, when she had been destitute and alone, when her talent had left her, and she'd nothing and no one else, she'd known complete and utter hopelessness. Death seemed like a culmination in the book of her life, a final page simply needing to be written.

But then she'd come to Blackthorne Cottage and learned that life was not made up solely of pigments and brushes, and the play of light on silk or the lustrous nature of pearls. Her life had become long walks, the sound of foxes, and the wind through the trees. Her life had become Glengarrow, Janet's smile, and still, cold winter nights.

And passion.

Her life had always been measured by her paintings. Point to a portrait, and she could recite the year, the place it was painted, and how much she'd charged for the commission. She could relate, in excruciating detail, each brush she'd used, the techniques she'd employed, and what pigments she'd mixed and when.

But she could not recall if she'd been sick or well, if she'd learned anything about her subject, if the days had been mild and fair or stormy. Life had simply stopped for her in those months, and she'd no memories to recall—only the finished portrait of a stranger.

Each successive painting reflected the essence of her life, the whole of it. In the last year, however, she'd no talent, no commissions. She'd had to rely on herself for meaning each day, and somehow she had found it. The initial grief at losing her way had been supplanted by a strong and determined instinct for survival.

Somehow, in the midst of simply surviving, Margaret Dalrousie had become more important than her painting. Happiness, simply living well and completely from day to day had become a goal more reasonable, realistic, and exciting than the completion of another portrait.

She'd returned to herself in an odd way, one she hadn't expected. She'd learned, in these last months, that she didn't like cabbage or lamb, that she enjoyed strong tea throughout the day. She disliked poetry but loved novels. The sunrise here in the Highlands touched her heart, as did the small, brave yellow flowers growing along the lane in the summer. Despite the fact she'd only initially barely endured her daily walks, she'd come to enjoy them.

She was no longer simply Margaret Dalrousie, painter. She was Margaret Dalrousie, woman, friend, neighbor, and lover. Not everything was pressed down and moved aside to make room for her painting. Her art, her talent, her ability to capture the essence of a human being and place it on a flat linen surface was no longer the whole of her. Surprisingly, startlingly, shockingly, it was only a part of who she'd become.

Did she want to die now?

Unbidden, McDermott came to mind: his striking face, his arresting eyes, and a look of sadness deep enough to melt the coldest heart. His voice, low and resonant. His quick temper, and his scalding wit. His physique, a beauty so natural it pained her to look at him sometimes, knowing she didn't have the skill to paint him the way she wanted.

Being with him had been an interlude, nothing more. Being with him had been like a sweet on a crowded train, an unexpected delight in the midst of misery.

Why, then, did she have the sudden feeling that what she was doing was morally corrupt and elementally wrong? Worse, this act of vengeance was capable of destroying hope, and hope was an emotion she'd not felt in a very long time.

*   *   *

In less than an hour, Robert was away from Glengarrow, heading toward London.

Let him be in time, and the entreaty was made to a God he'd not solicited for a great many years. Ever since Amelia died, he'd felt as if God himself had turned His back on him. Now, divine intervention seemed not only wise but necessary.

He knew Harridge by reputation. The man was an idiot. He'd come to his title barely a teenager, and ever since then had spent a great deal of time and effort attempting to squander his fortune. Robert wished he'd kept up with society in the three years he'd been gone. But it didn't surprise him one whit that Harridge might have been among the group of men who'd attacked Margaret. The man's reputation had been deplorable before Robert left for France. He doubted if the intervening years had improved it.

He wasn't crossing Scotland for the sake of the dissolute Duke of Harridge, however, but for an impossibly stubborn woman with fire in her green eyes. A woman who'd forced him to stop looking over his shoulder at the past and directed his attention to her, instead.

He would not lose another woman he loved.

Margaret felt as if she'd been traveling for weeks instead of just days. Grime clung to her, and her clothing was streaked with soot from the train.

She loved London, wasn't that odd? The city was like a giant beast into which she'd crawled. London never slept, but thrummed with activity, its heart beating with the call of its inhabitants.

The city smelled like sulfur sometimes, the fog almost yellow in the fall. But this was almost spring, and she could swear she smelled flowers.

Although her solicitor had not provided her with the Duke of Harridge's address, Margaret found it wasn't all that difficult to discover it. Evidently, men like the duke did not make a secret of where they lived.

She paid the carriage driver and turned and looked up at the town house occupying most of the fashionable square. The steps were wide and lined on either side with a metal railing. The door was painted black, with a gleaming brass knocker.

She knocked on the door, and it was opened immediately by an imposing man with white hair and a stocky frame. He frowned at her, but bowed, nonetheless.

"I should like to see the Duke of Harridge, please."

"I do not believe His Grace is at home to callers, madam."

She clutched her reticule tightly and forced a pleasant smile to her face.

"Are you entirely certain?"

"I am especially certain, madam."

"I have come a very long way," she said. "I'm a friend from Russia."

He regarded her stonily for a moment, then relented, opening the door only barely enough that she could enter. Thank heavens she'd not thought to wear her full hoops. She would never have made it through the door.

"If you will wait here, madam."

When had she become a madam and not a miss? Had the last year become visible on her face? Her age had never been a touchy subject with her, which was just as well now.

The footman stood beside her in the foyer, no doubt a guard in case she decided to make off with the phenomenally ugly, and therefore no doubt valuable, vase standing beside the bench. Two Japanese plates were arranged on the sideboard, as well as a bronze lamp in the shape of a horse. Was the rest of the Duke of Harridge's home filled with such abysmally ugly objects?

Before she had a chance to mull on the fact that being a peer didn't necessarily mean being born with any type of good taste, the majordomo returned. This time, his frown was slightly deeper, and the smirk on his face indicated the Duke of Harridge was indeed home but chose not to meet with her.

Her face heated, pinpricks of feeling that seemed to go through her skin to the bones beneath. Her heart began to pound loudly, and her breath grew tight. Her eyes filled with tears, making her even more enraged. Why was it every time she became angry she wanted to cry?

She forced her fists to unclench, all the while forcing herself to breathe deeply. She needed to have her emotions under control. Her composure restored, she pulled the pistol from her reticule.

"I am very sorry," she said at the look of astonishment on the majordomo's face, "but I truly must see the duke."

The footman didn't appear the least concerned she was leveling a pistol on them. He followed the majordomo down the hall, with Margaret in the rear.

The duke's taste did not become appreciably better the farther they traveled. Brightly hued flowers edged the crimson carpet in the corridor, clashing with the beige-and-brown-checkered silk pattern of the wall coverings. The duke evidently had a passion for all things bronze. The sconces mounted on the wall were twisted stems resembling vines gone amok, ending in flowers made of blown glass tinted a pale pink.

Altogether, it was a rather hideous scheme.

The majordomo hesitated before a heavily carved door and looked back at her. Margaret remembered the gun in her hand and leveled it at him.

"Go ahead," she said, nodding toward the door.

The majordomo knocked, and when a masculine voice answered, opened the door slightly.

"Your Grace, forgive my intrusion, but the young lady is most insistent."

The majordomo had a gift of understatement. Margaret nearly rolled her eyes.

He pushed the door open wider, stepped aside for Margaret to precede him, and then glanced at the gun again. A lifetime of decorum was not easily pushed aside, it seemed. With a sigh, he entered the room, followed by the nonchalant footman.

Margaret followed, finding herself in what was no doubt the duke's library. The room was masculine and comfortable, and one of the few places unmarked by the duke's atrocious taste. Walls of gilt-decorated books darkened the room, but two large windows on either side of the fireplace let

in the sunlight. Two hunter green chairs were arranged in front of the fire, while a massive mahogany desk sat in front of the far wall.

Turning, she waved the muzzle of the pistol at
the majordomo.

"You may wait outside," she said.

He looked as if he wanted to protest, but one
last look at the pistol changed his mind. The two
men left the room, and she slowly closed the door
behind them before facing the Duke of Harridge.

At first she couldn't see him. But then, she caught
sight of a figure on the far side of the room, standing in front of the crimson draperies. A man in
shadow.

Before she could address him, the painting over
the fireplace caught her attention. Slowly, she
walked toward it, each footstep soliciting a corre-
sponding beat of her booming heart. The closer she
got to the painting, the harder it was to breathe.

The top edge of the frame hung only three inches
from the ceiling, but then the portrait was nearly
life-sized and required a great deal of space.

She'd labored on this painting for three solid
months. The Duke of Harridge, taking his grand
tour and a little more.

She hadn't remembered his name, but she remembered the young man only too well. He was
the product of an upbringing characterized by
benevolent indifference, his arrival feted as befitted a male heir; his rearing left to nannies and an
occasional brave tutor. His companions were not
unlike himself, bored young men who all shared
a dislike of their parents' injunctions and society's
restrictions.

They did not, however, attempt to gain more worthwhile employment for their hours. They were, after all, nobility, young men whose sole purpose was to marry well, wager less heavily than their fathers, and maintain a slightly indifferent air toward their inferiors in order to impress upon those poor souls they were in the company of their betters.

Their preeminent occupation was waiting for their fathers or uncles or guardians to die so they could assume a position of power. The Duke of Harridge had already come into his title and because of that, he was one of their leaders.

The attack on Margaret had been a diversion, nothing more, a night's occupation to relate with laughter at a later date.

Maidservants and footmen alike were loath to interrupt this particular group of young men once the sun had set. Even their peers avoided them. Margaret, however, imbued with her own arrogance, had thought herself protected. What an utter fool she'd been.

The duke had chosen to be painted in a French-style drawing room, the brilliant blue of the curtain echoed in his embroidered waistcoat and stockings. He'd been posed standing, his face and eyes intense and directed toward the artist. One hand had been at his side, the other arm with elbow bent, his palm flat against his waistcoat.

Memory flooded into her mind. He'd been the most obnoxious young man, refusing to obey her dictate of silence, always trying to charm her into allowing his friends into the sitting, attempting to shock her with non sequiturs and double entendres.

She'd not been amused, only grateful when the sittings were finally done. He'd paid her more than her commission, an insult in itself. She'd returned the extra money in a note.

Was that why he'd singled her out to be attacked? Because she'd dared to refuse him? Because she hadn't considered herself fortunate to have garnered his attention?

And now, she faced him across the room.

Slowly and carefully, well aware her hands were shaking, she slid the gun into her reticule and looked back at the Duke of Harridge.

"I've been practicing to kill you," she said. "I've been planning on it for many months. Nearly a year. And then I realized you simply weren't worth the effort. You weren't worth the anguish I'd suffer. You weren't worth the guilt I'd feel. Not because *you* died, but because I was the instrument of your death. I will not harm another person the way you harmed me."

"Could you tell me what I've done to incur your wrath?"

The Duke of Harridge stepped out of the shadows slowly. His gait was not due to caution but age. His hair was no longer blond, but white, and although his eyes were the same green as the young man in the portrait, they were marked by lines radiating outward from the corners. This man was an older version of the young man she'd painted. Time had been kind to him; there was no doubt of the family resemblance.

"Who are you?" she asked.

"The question is, I'm afraid, who are you?"

"Margaret Dalrousie," she said.

"Oh yes, the painter. I noticed your name on the corner of the painting of my nephew."

"Nephew?"

"My late, and very much unlamented, nephew, I'm afraid. The fourth Duke of Harridge."

"You're the fifth, I take it," Margaret said, walking to one of the chairs in front of the fireplace. She really did have to sit down before her legs failed her.

"I take it by your words that my nephew has damaged you in some way? Forgive me if I wished to avoid another tale of his exploits. I've spent the last six months being regaled with tales of his deplorable character."

"What happened to him?"

"The young fool went to France. He was killed by the husband of a Frenchwoman. A woman he'd claimed as a prize in some idiotic game."

Now she did sit down.

"For whatever he did, I am most apologetic. Is there anything I can do?"

Another man, offering to solve a problem that couldn't be solved. What had McDermott said? Doing so eased a man's feeling of being powerless. And a woman? How did she cope?

How strange she wasn't entirely certain at the moment.

Tom was very conservative in his driving, despite Robert's expressed need for haste. The roads of Scotland were nothing like the treacherous roads of Amelia's homeland, but he understood well enough Tom's caution. The second day, after a short stay at an inn, long enough to obtain a meal and some fresh horses, they were on their way again, and he was grateful to see their speed increased.

They reached London midmorning, and found the Duke of Harridge's home without too much difficulty.

When Tom pulled the carriage to a stop in front of the town house, Robert ran up the steps, knocked on the door, and was startled to find it immediately opened by a wild-haired and frantic majordomo. Before he had a chance to speak, the man grabbed his lapels and pulled him inside the house.

"Thank God, sir. I must prevail upon you to help him. She is a madwoman, and she threatened my life, sir. Now she is in with the duke. His Grace is in great peril."

He followed the man down the corridor, and when the majordomo stopped in front of a door and simply pointed at it, Robert grabbed the handle and entered the room. The scene that met his eyes was not what he'd feared.

Margaret was seated on a chair before the fire. Sitting beside her in a matching chair was a white-haired gentleman. The two of them looked as if they were amicably conversing, two friends of different generations sharing snippets of gossip, a knowledge of the financial world, a question about politics.

The majordomo was so close behind him that Robert could nearly feel the man's breath on his back.

"Margaret?"

She turned her head and surveyed him calmly.

Spots of color on either cheek, however, revealed she wasn't as composed as she appeared on the surface.

"I haven't killed him, McDermott."

"So I see."

The elderly man seated in a chair regarded him with a great deal of interest. "You're the Earl of Linnet, aren't you? I heard a speech you gave once."

He nodded assent as Margaret addressed him.

"Why are you here, McDermott?"

Robert ignored the question, choosing, instead, to view the portrait dominating the room.

The young man pictured there had the haughty stare of those who believed in *noblesse oblige*. A slight sneer curved his lips, ennui filled his eyes. The sunlight glinted on his blond hair and detailed each single fiber of his blue-wool jacket and embroidered vest. Behind him on one side was a mirror, revealing the back of his jacket adorned with ornate braiding. On the side was a small portrait of two children with their parrot, and even this was so perfectly rendered Robert could see each separate feather on the bird. The tassels on the curtains were so perfectly painted he could see each individually twisted braid.

The Duke of Harridge almost walked out of the portrait, so real did he appear. Even the hound at his feet looked ready to bark any second.

Over the months of knowing her, Robert had become accustomed to Margaret's braggadocio. He'd excused her for it, never once wondering at the depth of her ability. But this, this, was beyond anything he could have imagined. The portrait with its shadows and light, the colors, so rich, and true to life, awed him.

He'd never seen anything so masterfully done, so beautifully rendered, unless it was the half-finished portrait in her cottage.

Her talent struck him speechless.

"The duke did not give me Blackthorne Cottage," Margaret said from behind him.

"No," he said almost absently, turning to face her. "My mother did."

She appeared surprised, but it was the day for it, wasn't it?

"Did you come here to prevent murder?" she asked calmly.

Should he give her the truth? She would have to cope with it, sooner or later.

"No," he said. "I came to protect you, regardless of what you chose to do."

He liked the sight of Margaret confused. He liked that look of uncertainty in her eyes, the tremulous curve of her lips that wasn't a smile but was very nearly there. Once in a while, it would be a good thing to confuse her.

Wait until she discovered what he planned next.

He had that look on his face again, an expression that warned her he was up to something. At this moment, however, she could have forgiven him anything.

I came to protect you, regardless of what you chose to do.

As a declaration of affection, it lacked a good deal, but she'd never before had anyone offer to protect her. There were times when she didn't want to be the indomitable Margaret Dalrousie. Let someone else be strong for a little while. Let someone else be capable. She would be weak and revel in it—at least for a few hours.

"Are you ready to return to Glengarrow?" he asked.

Even the sound of home was lovely.

"On your horse?" she asked.

He smiled, and it was a crooked, almost boyish expression, one she'd never thought to associate with McDermott. "Tom is outside. I've brought a carriage."

Their gaze met, and she wanted to kiss him for what he'd done. It could not have been easy for him to ride in a carriage, but he didn't brag of it.

"Yes," she said, smiling at him. "I'm ready to return to Glengarrow."

She turned away from McDermott, making her way to the door. The outraged majordomo still stood there, visibly shaken about the day's events. Not any more than she.

McDermott followed her, placing his hand on her shoulder. She glanced up at him and wished she didn't have the absurd desire to cry. She especially never cried before such an interested audience.

They said their farewells, McDermott preceding her out the door. At the threshold she stopped, turned, and sending an apologetic look to the elderly duke, withdrew her pistol from her reticule.

Extending her arm, she shut her left eye, and with the aim she'd perfected over the last year, shot the fourth Duke of Harridge right in the middle of his forehead.

"You shot your own painting," McDermott said.

"Yes," Margaret said, lowering the pistol. The stench of gunpowder was thick in the room. "I gave that portrait life," she said, holding the smoking gun away from her with two fingers. "I can take it away." She glanced up at him. "*That*, McDermott, is playing God."

Chapter 27

They descended the steps in silence, McDermott's hand on the small of her back. She could feel the warmth of it there through her cape.

When they reached the carriage, he called up to Tom, who nodded and greeted her with a smile.

"See Miss Dalrousie home to Blackthorne Cottage," he said, then stepped back, dropping his hand.

"Where are you going?" she asked, pushing back the incredible surge of disappointment. So, she wasn't to share the journey with McDermott. It was just as well, anyway. They might have become overwhelmed with passion, she in her soot-stained clothes and McDermott looking as sartorially perfect as usual. How did he do it? She must ask him sometime.

Not now, however. Not with that smile playing around his lips, and his gaze on the spires of the Palace of Westminster.

The sense of abandonment was so sharp she could feel the talons of it shredding her skin. Especially today. Most especially today, when her nerves were raw, and she was too close to weeping.

She stood tall, breathing as deeply as her tightly laced corset would allow.

"First I must compensate the duke for the loss of his painting," he said, his gaze revealing only amusement. "Then I have some business to attend to. Tom will keep you safe. Not to mention your skill with a pistol will serve you in good stead."

She looked down at the gun still in her hand and slipped it into her reticule.

"I don't require the services of a nursemaid, Mc-Dermott," she said. "Go about your business. Take care on the journey home."

With that, she turned and mounted the steps into the carriage, deliberately not looking in his direction as Tom drew away.

A week later McDermott had returned, but Margaret hadn't seen him. He had not called upon her. Nor had she seen him on her walks. And he had certainly not been waiting in the woods at nightfall.

He was very distracted, Janet said, with all manner and sorts of activity happening at Glengarrow.

Janet was the one who alerted her to the first visitor four days ago, knocking on the door of the trunk room and peering inside.

"There's a man come to Glengarrow, Miss Margaret. He says he's an architect, here from Edinburgh. He says he's going to change Glengarrow."

"Is he? Perhaps the earl is bringing a new countess home," Margaret said, feigning concentration on cleaning her brush.

Janet's eyes narrowed. "And who would he bring home?"

"Someone he met in Inverness, perhaps?" Margaret said. "He stayed there long enough. Someone he's always known? A marriage of convenience?" Frankly, she didn't know and didn't care. Let McDermott wed whomever he pleased.

Janet looked as if she would say something further, but she just pursed her lips in silence and closed the door, leaving Margaret to frown at the painting in irritation.

She thought he was causing this chaos in his life in order to make room for a new countess. Margaret had always been quick-witted. How like her to figure it all out so soon. And how like her to muddle it up just as fast.

Robert stood atop Glengarrow's roof. He hadn't come here to stir the cistern or check the water supply. His only reason for being here, buffeted by the spring-scented wind, was Margaret Dalrousie, lately turned hermit in her snug little cottage.

Janet reported that she refused to take her daily walks. Nor had she discussed anything that had transpired in London. Instead, she holed herself up in the trunk room, working night and day on the portrait he'd commissioned.

Robert smiled. She couldn't help but think of him. Was she annoyed? Hurt? A touch of both, if Janet was to be believed.

What a complicated woman Margaret was and how fascinating it was proving to learn about her.

Amelia had loved without reservation; Margaret had reservations about loving. Margaret was restrained, so private that the world never knew the degree of her pain. Amelia had lived her life with unbounded enthusiasm, carrying a buoyancy into each day. Would she have been able to recover if she'd had to face the same circumstances Margaret had? Unfair perhaps, to ask those questions, since they were two different people, two unique women.

Very well, today was the day. The messenger had come from his solicitor, and Janet knew her part.

Everything was in place.

The portrait was done, and normally that was a cause for celebration. Not this time, however. This time, Margaret wanted to crawl into her bed and spend days weeping simply because the work had taken so much from her.

Each painting was draining in its way, drawing from her reserves of emotion. This commission, however, had been the most difficult of her entire career. She'd infused this painting with all the confusion, desire, grief, and rage she'd felt over the last three months. The toll it had taken on her was enormous, but then, it might well be her best work.

How very sad, since no one would ever see it.

She would keep it for herself alone, and whenever she was tempted to think fondly of Glengarrow, she would look at it and force herself to see the truth. She would not remember the sight of McDermott angry, with his tortured eyes and his face ruddy from the cold, or the wind tossing his hair over his brow. Nor would she recall the sight of him in moonlight, his body not perfect but still endearingly beautiful.

Her stomach clenched, and she pressed her fists against her midriff. Blinking rapidly, she stared out at Glengarrow. Spring was nearly here, the trees budding. In a month, she'd be unable to see the house.

Glancing back at the portrait, Margaret wished she might have known Amelia. But then, if she had, she might have envied her as well. She might have coveted the relationship between her and McDermott, or even coveted McDermott.

She would probably have embarrassed herself by parading her accomplishments before Amelia in an attempt to make the other woman appear less talented, less important. She knew herself only too well, and when challenged or feeling inept, she had a tendency to do foolish things, stupid things.

Amelia, no doubt, would have simply smiled at her gently, forgiveness in her eyes, her sweet nature excusing all of Margaret's faults and frailties.

That was the problem with ghosts. They were perfect. They never changed. Nor could you argue with them or best them in any way.

She slowly draped the covering over the painting, wondering if she would ever have the courage to look at it again. Perhaps it would be better simply to destroy it.

A knock on the door interrupted her thoughts, and she walked to the door to find Janet standing there, her usually placid expression replaced by a look of confusion.

"I've been meaning to take this back to the earl, Miss Margaret. But I looked in the box a minute ago, and I think it's for you."

"What is it?"

"A lovely coat, with the softest collar and a hood. In the prettiest blue wool."

She opened the top of the box to show Margaret.

"He left it here, Miss Margaret, the day he went to London after you. I'm thinking it's a gift."

Margaret reached out her hand and touched the fabric. Janet was right, it was the prettiest blue wool, and soft as well. Even in spring she might be able to wear it. If she accepted it.

Who was McDermott to give her presents?

She'd always returned those items sent by wealthy admirers lest they believe she was the type of woman easily seduced. The Earl of Linnet would receive the same treatment, but this time, she would not simply have a messenger return the offending gift. No, this time, she would take it back to him herself.

She donned her serviceable cape and made one last check of her hair in the small mirror beside the door. Her cheeks were flushed and her eyes sparkling. Anyone looking at her would think she was excited about the coming confrontation.

How absurd.

She left the cottage, began to walk toward Glengarrow.

A squirrel chattered at her from the side of the lane. She stopped for a moment and watched him, completely and utterly charmed, and grateful for the respite from this task.

"Are you lecturing me, Mr. Squirrel?" she asked.

He stood on his hind legs, holding up both paws. His scolding did not cease, and she found herself amused to be chastised so fervently.

"I shall remember my decorum around him. On that, you can be assured."

He turned and, in a flash of bushy tail, disappeared up a tree, leaving Margaret alone again.

She looked to the left, where Glengarrow was visible through the trees, perched in front of Ben Mosub, then to the right, where the lane led to the main road.

The day was beautiful, the afternoon bright and, although chilly, the foretaste of spring was in the air. She wouldn't have been surprised to see the first of the spring flowers poking their heads up from beneath the snow. One brave bird perched on the fence post as she walked by and sang to her for a scant moment before flying away.

The snow in the lane had melted, leaving muddy puddles of gravel and water. She avoided the larger ones with ease, but by halfway along the lane, her shoes were damp and streaked with mud.

Perhaps one day McDermott would go back to France, and Glengarrow would once again be a silent, almost watchful, structure. Not the home of an arrogant earl who summoned up passion as easily as anyone else might call for a servant.

If he left, she'd use the path around Glengarrow once again. At least it was paved with gravel. If he left, she would occupy her days with painting again, but she doubted she'd have the heart for portraits. Instead, she'd paint birds and squirrels and perhaps Glengarrow itself.

If he left, what would she do?

She pushed the thought away, finding it surprisingly painful. She was simply feeling a little sad today, that was all. How suddenly it had come upon her. In a blink of an eye, a spark, the time it took a snowflake to melt, she had become almost bereft.

Another sign, perhaps, of how mindless she'd become about the Earl of Linnet.

Two wagons were trundling up the lane, one filled with sacks of what looked to be sand, the other holding huge panes of glass between layers of batting.

What was he doing? It was none of her concern. McDermott could set Glengarrow on fire, and it would be none of her concern. Was he bringing a wife home? A new countess?

She couldn't bear this; she really couldn't.

Stopping between the gates, she bid both hello and farewell to the lions. Clasping her hands around the box, she resolutely walked to the front of the house, circling the fountain, and taking the steps slowly, all the while daring herself to do this. She had done so many difficult things in her life; this was just one more task.

At the top of the steps, the door opened, and he was there, almost as if he'd been waiting for her arrival.

"I knew you wouldn't be able to refuse the opportunity to give me my comeuppance," he said, smiling down at the box.

She frowned at him.

"You planned for me to return it?"

"I knew you would," he said. "You're a very prideful woman, Maggie."

"If you wanted to see me, you should have sent me a note."

"You would have ignored it."

"You could have sent word through Janet."

"You would have told her to tell me no."

He leaned back against the frame of the door and crossed his arms over his chest.

"I was forced to be a little devious," he said. "The condition of my leg makes it impossible to bodily carry you to Glengarrow, but I did give some thought to it."

"Janet conspired with you?" She couldn't help but feel a little hurt at the thought.

"In more than one way," he said obliquely.

He really shouldn't look that handsome. Not smiling the way he was, almost boyishly, as if he was thoroughly delighted with himself.

Foolish man, he was attired only in a white shirt and black trousers. Despite the fact spring was only weeks away, it was cold.

He held out his hand and she stared at it for a moment, then slowly gave him the box. He dropped it on the floor behind him and extended his hand again. This time, she placed her hand in his. His grip was firm, his touch warm.

Turning, he entered the house, pulling her after him. He was a force of nature, and she had no choice but to keep up with him.

He stopped abruptly, turned, and faced her.

"Do you know you have the unlikely ability to make me angrier than any human being I've ever known? I've been irritated before, but nothing comes close to the emotions I feel around you, Maggie."

"The feeling is mutual, McDermott. And are you going to insist upon calling me Maggie?"

He started walking again. "You can be Margaret Dalrousie to anyone in the world. But to me, you'll always be Maggie. It isn't a subject open for discussion."

"You're acting exceedingly uncivil today, McDermott."

He glanced at her over his shoulder. "That's another thing. Stop calling me by my surname."

"Stop calling me Maggie."

He began to smile. "I guess I can live with McDermott, then."

Once more, he turned and began leading her up the grand staircase and to the second floor. They walked down the corridor to the Winter Parlor in silence, but she doubted they would have been able to hear themselves talk if they had conversed. The room was swarming with workmen, men removing the windows, and knocking down walls. The door to the Winter Parlor wasn't there anymore. Nor was the suite McDermott had shared with Amelia. All the furniture was gone, and so were the doors. All that was left were the outer walls.

Janet hadn't said anything about this.

He held her hand tightly, but Margaret didn't try to pull away. Instead, she stood there in absolute astonishment.

"What have you done? What are you doing?"

He began to smile again.

"I'm making a life," he said. "Not the same one I had, but another one."

The dust in the air was making it difficult to breathe, and was probably the reason for her sudden wish to cry.

She pulled her hand free, finally, and wrapped her arms around her waist.

"I think if I went back to Inverness or to Edinburgh, I could find my share of polite, beautiful, accomplished women. Charming women, who would insist upon being personable."

"No doubt," she said. She frowned at him. "And no doubt their mouths would not be too big," she said.

"Oh, Maggie, your mouth was never too big. It's just right. It just needs kissing often."

She felt herself warm as several of the workers glanced at him curiously.

"I need your advice," he said. "On a building matter."

"I'm leaving for London," she said. "As quickly as I can pack my trunks."

He ignored that comment as he took her hand again, leading her down the hallway and to a smaller set of stairs to the third floor.

She'd never seen this part of Glengarrow, but it was not unlike the second floor—the plasterwork on the ceiling and the carvings on the wainscoting were just as beautiful.

At the end of the hall, directly above the Earl's suite on the second floor, there was more activity. Three men were removing a section of wall.

Another man was standing slightly aside, sketching on a large pad. He glanced at them, smiled at McDermott, and nodded politely to her.

"Show Miss Dalrousie your plan, Franklin."

Robert turned to her. "Franklin is an eminent architect, Maggie. I managed to convince him to oversee the changes at Glengarrow. If you like what he's done, we can always have him come to London to do the same with that house."

She glanced at him curiously but still didn't understand.

Franklin, a young man with sandy brown hair and an engaging grin, came to her side.

"May I say what a pleasure it is to meet you, Miss Dalrousie. I consider it an honor to work on this room for you."

She glanced at McDermott, who smiled.

"She's extraordinarily talented, Franklin. Probably the greatest artist of her age."

She really did not understand, but the hope, the excitement, the sheer terror of what she was thinking was bubbling up and vying with tears for dominance.

Franklin turned his sketch pad so she could see.

"You'll have both an east and west vista, which will give you a good play of light most of the day. Because the room faces south, it shouldn't be too warm or too cold, but we have plans to enlarge the fireplace just in case."

She stared at the drawing and looked over at McDermott.

"It's a studio," she said.

In the middle of the expanse, along the sides of the walls were places to store canvases in the process of being prepared. In the middle of the room, Franklin had sketched a small platform where a subject might sit in comfort. Beside the fireplace were two comfortable chairs, for when she grew weary or needed to sit.

The third floor was above the top of the trees, and sunlight would stream into the room, making it possible for her to work for hours.

"It's a studio," she repeated.

McDermott nodded to Franklin, and the other man folded his sketchbook and left them.

One more time, McDermott held out his hand, and this time when she placed hers in his larger one, her fingers trembled. She followed him without question, and he led her down the steps to the second floor once again, but instead of retracing their path, he led the way to the other wing, to a series of rooms she'd never seen.

"Am I to be your mistress?"

He stopped and turned, facing her. She'd evidently managed to surprise him.

"I've been proposing, haven't you noticed?"

When he would have pulled her along again, she refused to budge. She began to shake her head, too distraught to speak for a moment. Thankfully, words came to her aid soon enough.

"I was elected an honorary member of the Scottish Academy when I was twenty-five, one of the first women ever to receive that distinction. When I was twenty-seven, McDermott, I began participating in exhibitions of the Royal Academy and the Society of British Artists."

Dear God, she couldn't breathe, and all he did was smile.

"Shall I begin a litany of my accomplishments, then? I'm the Earl of Linnet, after all."

"Exactly." She threw up her hands. "I cannot marry you. Acres of differences stand between us: upbringing, parents, friends, and the past itself."

"Haven't you figured it out, Maggie?" he asked gently. "None of that matters, least of all the past. I've tried to show you, but if that's not enough, what will you have from me? The words? I love you, Margaret Dalrousie, for reasons that are not easily understood. I love you because you gave me back myself. I love you because I become a better person when I'm around you. I love you because I'm alive when I'm with you. I love your passion and your ambition, and the fact you're afraid most of the time and yet have the courage not to show it. Shall I go on?"

She couldn't speak again.

He took her in his arms. Both hands moved down her back, pressing her gently closer. She turned her head until her cheek was resting against his chest.

A moment later, he pulled away, strode to a door set midway into the corridor, and opened it. He stood aside, waiting for her to precede him. She did so, to find herself in a small sitting room darkened by deep emerald green draperies closed against the sun.

In the middle of the room, resting on her easel was the portrait she had just finished a few days earlier and left in the cottage less than an hour ago.

"Janet again?" she asked. She would have to

have a long talk with Janet, one in which Margaret attempted to express her thanks.

"I do not believe that any painting I have ever endeavored has traveled quite as much as this one."

She moved to stand in front of the portrait.

"I should scold you, you know. You promised not to look."

"I can't say I'm sorry," he said.

"I knew I couldn't paint Amelia," she said softly. "I don't care how beautifully you described her."

Instead, she'd painted him, sitting by the window, his bearing erect, his hands along the arms of the chair, his gaze fixed on something in the middle of the room. In his eyes was love, the pain of longing, grief itself. Yet the expression on his face was stoic and closed.

He spoke again, his voice low and earnest. "I don't want to be the man in that portrait, Maggie. Instead, I want to be alive, to live with passion and curiosity. I want to love you until Fate decrees we can't love anymore. I want you to love me with the same ferocity."

She clasped her hands in front of her. Had she laced her corset too tightly this morning? In the future, she should take care not to do so again, especially if McDermott was going to take her breath away with his words.

"What do you mean, Franklin can come to London?"

He smiled, as if he knew she couldn't address the subject of love right at this moment. She was trembling inside, and she wasn't entirely certain she was going to be able to continue this conversation without bursting into tears. She wasn't an overly emotional female, but she was coming close to the boundaries of her own restraint.

"I'm going to stand for MP again. I've been told there's a good chance I'll be elected. It's the one way I can help the plight of the Highlanders."

She turned and walked to the other side of the room and sat in a chair beside a small table. The room was dim, but the afternoon outside was sunny so the atmosphere was gray. Not entire darkness, only an illusion of it, almost like gloaming.

Margaret abruptly stood and opened the curtains, almost defiantly banishing the gloom. This view was of the lane, and the trees standing guard on either side.

She turned back to him, then the painting. Slowly, she approached the easel again, and reached to the side of it where a small table stood. On the table, until now shrouded in darkness, was a small drawstring green velvet bag. She picked it up, and heard the clink of coins.

"Gold sovereigns," he said. "I could have had it changed to notes, but I like the clink of the coins."

"For me?" she asked. "Another inducement to marry you?"

"It's your money from Russia. What was owed to you."

How much more was she supposed to endure without bursting into tears? She carefully replaced the bag back on the table.

"You've been busy," she said.

"I have."

He was standing there watching her. She could tell, because the blush was radiating up from her bosom to encompass her neck and her cheeks.

She looked at the painting rather than at him. In the corner of the canvas, barely seen, was a flounce of her skirt. A casual watcher might think it a part of the drapery or a backdrop of sorts. In her mind, however, she saw herself slightly off to the side, watching him intently and being unprepared to do anything else, captivated by his appearance, his sadness, and his character.

He came and stood behind her, his hands gripping her shoulders, pulling her back against him. His breath on her temple nearly weakened her resolve to remain strong.

"I cannot be the wife of a Member of the House of Lords. You cannot have a wife who's an artist. I cannot marry an earl. I can't be a countess." Despite her resolve to appear calm, her voice sounded panicked.

"You asked me once if I was only defined by my title. And I'm answering you. I'm Robert McDermott. Can you marry me?"

She glanced over her shoulder at him.

"That isn't fair, McDermott, using my own words as weapons."

He smiled. "I'll use any weapon at my disposal, Maggie. You aren't to be wooed with soft words but with cannon fire."

She shook her head. "I can't stop being who I am, not even for you. Painting is something that's part of me. It *is* me."

"Have I asked you to give up anything of yourself, Maggie? Have I asked you to stop being an artist?"

"No."

"All I ask is that you love me, that you share your life with me. More than that, I don't have the right to ask. Nor shall I."

She held herself tight, feeling as if she would shatter into a hundred pieces if she didn't.

"The woman I fell in love with is an artist. Why should I ask you to alter that which makes you unique? Why should I ask you to give up your talent as payment for love?"

"You need a wife who would be pleased to be nothing more than a wife," she said, pushing the words past lips that felt numb. "Someone who would want nothing more than to care for you."

Silence stretched between them. "I don't ask you to be Amelia, Maggie."

"Even if I insist on painting all night? Even if I grow sad, and you don't know why? Even if there are times when I need to be alone, with nothing else but my brushes and a blank canvas?"

"Only if you know there are times when I, too, need the same. When I need to be reading or just lost in my thoughts."

She could almost see it, the complicity of two people intent upon their individual desires. When the day was done or when one of them was bored or needed the other, they could come together to hold a hand, share a kiss or a thought.

What would her life be like if she were loved?

"Are you going to lie and say you don't feel the same for me as I do for you, Maggie?"

She shook her head.

"Then are you going to say something foolish like you don't deserve me?"

"It's probably closer to the truth that you don't deserve me," she said.

She felt, rather than heard, him chuckle.

He wrapped his arms around her and kissed her temple. "I want to feel alive, Maggie, for as long as I have life. I'm alive with you. For a very long time I didn't feel that way."

"Perhaps it took those years to say farewell," she said. "To say farewell to Amelia."

"Amelia's my past, Maggie," he said. "You're my future."

She turned and regarded him steadily.

"You do love me."

It was more a statement than a question, and one he responded to by folding his arms in front of him and smiling.

"Of course I do. And you love me."

"Of course I do," she said.

She'd come to Blackthorne Cottage wrapped in misery, seeking a reason to live, and a miracle. The miracle had happened, but it wasn't solely that she'd begun to paint again. She'd begun to feel again. She'd learned to laugh, to marvel at the seasons. Her curiosity had been aroused, and her heart touched. She'd gained two friends in Janet and Tom.

When she'd first come to this part of the Highlands, she'd been like an encased seed, buried beneath the frozen earth. She'd been enraged at the world, unable fully to understand what had happened to her, and singlemindedly protective of herself to the exclusion of all other emotions.

Somehow, spring had come to her soul. She'd put down roots and begun to sprout, tiny shoots appearing first before she began to flower. She'd allowed McDermott to touch her in passion and heat and felt only pleasure from it. She had held him in her arms and wanted to protect him, wanted to give something of herself that might aid in healing his wounds as ably as he'd healed hers.

She'd wanted to become better than she was, less selfish, less pragmatic, more giving. She'd been brought to tears by his pain and his loss, even as she envied him his capacity to love.

Once she hadn't known anything about love, other than what she'd heard from her maid, who fancied herself in love with a footman, or from the court females expounding on their bed sport. She wasn't certain what love was for anyone else, but she knew only too well what it meant for her.

Although she might be alone from time to time in the future, she would never be quite as lonely again. There would be a tiny bit of McDermott with her, a portion of his soul, perhaps, and most certainly the memory of his smile, and the sound of his voice. She would always feel cherished, and blessed, and as long as she drew breath, she'd ensure McDermott felt the same.

The house seemed to sigh around her, and in that instant, when the light faded toward gloaming, when the workmen gathered up their tools and began to leave Glengarrow, Margaret Louisa Dalrousie, lately and lovingly named Maggie, felt as if the house embraced her at last.

If there were ghosts here, they were sweet ones, a small delicate shade clutching primroses in a tiny palm, and a fair-haired beauty leading her by the hand. At the end of the lane, a wisp of light, a trick of the eye, made it seem as if the two stood there, looking back at Glengarrow.

Maggie felt a breath on her cheek, the lightest softest kiss of breeze. Then the breeze, too, vanished, accompanied by the faint sound of a child's laughter.

"What is it, Maggie?"

She turned to McDermott, tears flooding her eyes. "I think we've just been given a blessing," she said. Or perhaps a final farewell.

Reaching up, she wound her arms around his neck, smiling as he bent his head to kiss her.

Author's Note

Margaret Dalrousie's painting career is loosely based on that of another Scotswoman, Christina Robertson (1796–1854).

Christina was an artist who, instead of painting the stereotypical Victorian formal portrait, chose to reveal her subjects in poses emphasizing their beauty and accomplishments.

Little is known about how Christina learned her craft. Her personal life is shrouded in mystery as well. All that is certain is she married another artist, and they had eight children, four of whom lived.

Her reputation as a fashionable portrait painter began in England and Scotland. Eventually, she traveled to Russia, becoming the darling of the Imperial Court. St. Petersburg's Imperial Academy of Arts honored her with membership.

Some examples of her work, housed now at the Hermitage Museum in Russia, can be found online. She was a truly talented artist, especially in capturing light on fabric and in portraying details such as the intricate hairstyles of the day, lace, and the luster of pearls.

The description of pigments and paints used in the nineteenth century was as accurate as I could make it. There were no standard names for colors until the late nineteenth century. One artist's sapphire might be another's cerulean. It was true that a great many pigments were poisonous, and too many artists died from exposure to the arsenic found in them. Egyptian Brown really was also called Mummy, and was nothing more than ground-up mummies.

The period from 1846–1852 saw nearly 2 million people leaving Scotland because of the potato blight in the Highlands. The crofters of the Highlands had, for several decades, been forced closer and closer to the sea in favor of sheep. Potatoes could be farmed on small plots of land, and although true famine was a constant prospect, it wasn't until the fungal disease struck the potato crop that people began to starve.

Some landowners tried to help; some chose to ignore the situation, while others incurred the wrath of the rest of Scotland by giving their crofters a choice—starvation or emigration. They furnished ships to Canada and Australia and offered free passage to desperate people.

The poet quoted in the book was Robert Burns: *Address to the Devil.*

In 1853, only sixteen Scottish peers were elected to the House of Lords, their tenure in office lasting only for the duration of a session of Parliament.